PRAISE FOR

BOOKS BY ANDREA RANDALL

In The Stillness

Nocturne (with Charles Sheehan-Miles)

Something's Come Up (with Michelle Pace)

Bar Crawl

Jesus Freaks
Sins of the Father
The Prodigal
The Broken Ones

November Blue
Ten Days of Perfect
Reckless Abandon
Sweet Forty-Two
Marrying Ember
Bo & Ember

Non-Fiction

Become a Full-Time Author (with
Charles Sheehan-Miles)

JESUS FREAKS

THE
BROKEN
ONES

ANDREA RANDALL

www.andrearandall.com

Published by Cincinnatus Press
PO Box 814
South Hadley, Massachusetts
United States of America

ISBN: 9781632021441

V03312016

DEDICATION

This book is dedicated to the readers who never left my side. Who never stopped believing in me, or this book, during the fourteen months it took to get it here.

ACKNOWLEDGEMENTS

F IRST and foremost, I want to thank my unwavering beta readers for their support and encouragement over the last fourteen months. They read a third of the book before I trashed it and started over from scratch, then read the whole thing again with me—some of them twice. Laura, Krystle, Dimitra, Liz, Sally, Nicole, and Megan, thank you, from the bottom of my stormy heart.

Charles. It's quite the life, living with another writer. Because we both know. But over the last year, you've held my hand through some pretty awful things, and you never once let me give up on this book, or myself. It got dicey there for a while, and you stood firm in your resolve for me and for my work. The only way to repay you is to keep doing what we both love: writing. I can't wait to be your wife. I love you.

Finally, my Safe House girls. You know who you are. I love you

.

CHAPTER ONE
DUCK AND COVER

Kennedy.

REATHE...

Resonant tones from Tibetan singing bowls floating through the halls trigger an automatic response in me. It's noon, and time for pre-meal prayer and meditation. I stretch out on my bed, setting down the C.S. Lewis book from Roland's mom. She gave it to me during Christmas break. Before everything went to hell.

Pushing those thoughts out of my head for a moment, I roll onto my stomach and rest my forehead on my folded arms, taking another deep breath before I begin my meditation. Meditating first helps me organize what I need to be praying for. After I've prayed, I'll meditate again and listen to anything that might come from God.

It's funny, really, that since being here I've heard from God more directly than in my entire first year at Carter University. *Here* being a Buddhist temple wedged deeply in the nooks and crannies of thick green vines and masterfully overgrown bushes of a New York City block, where I've been for the last three and a half months. In hiding.

The mid-May day is uncharacteristically muggy, but a resuscitating breeze flows through the window of my single-occupancy room, accompanied by a gentle sunlight that warms the back of my neck.

An emotional chill whisks across my shoulders as I recall a similar heat that flooded my body when the Today Show aired photos that had been sent to them, anonymously of course, almost the second my live interview with Greg Mauer ended. An interview in which I discussed coming to terms with myself as a child of God and loving the people around me. One where I stood on my own two feet, not only as a student at CU, but as the daughter of internationally-beloved pastor Roland Abbot.

The pictures, the heat on the back of my neck reminds me, were various angles of the same scene: Roland, Matt, and Matt's dad, Buck Wells, exiting The Pink Pony—a strip club in Georgia near Matt's home. It was pitch black, well after midnight, when the pictures were shot, but the faces were as clear as if it were noon. Even clearer were the people in the foreground of the picture: yours truly, and Jonah Cross. My good friend, and a *good* guy, caught in the crossfire. Coming back to the focus of my meditation, I run my hands through my hair, tightening them as I squeeze my eyes against the once-again flowing tears.

Breathe...

Tears that come unbidden and at the most inconvenient times.

Breathe...

Tears that remind me of all I've lost. *Who* I've lost.

Breathe...

Stopping the panic of that moment in Georgia from over-taking my body is sometimes a minute-by-minute exercise. I let it wash over me now as my stomach twists in knots.

Sometimes the tears have to come. I've learned that each droplet contains a salve for my soul that I've been unable to cultivate from any tangible means: trashy TV, comfort food, throwing things... Nothing works like tears do. And I hate that.

Jonah and I had driven to Georgia with Roland just after Christmas and stayed at the Wells family home the night before some national conference on *family friggen values*. The night before the conference, Matt went missing. Only Jonah and I knew, since it was after midnight. We tracked him down in the skeezy plaza that contained at least two pawn shops, a bail bond establishment and the bright yellow glow of a Waffle House sign.

Step right up, get your girls and waffles...

After several failed attempts to get Matt to leave on his own accord, Jonah and I called my dad. It was a last resort, and I can't say I was surprised when he showed up with Buck. I mean, Matt *is* his child after all—regardless of whatever strained relationship they're dealing with.

I thought that night was as bad as things would get.

I wish.

Matt stopped talking to me. Altogether. Stopped looking at me. Made quick work of living as if I wasn't. As if I didn't exist and hadn't ever existed. On a dime. I'd caught him in an act he deems as unforgivable, given he hasn't forgiven his father for the same transgressions. At least he hadn't at the time. I wouldn't know now; I haven't spoken to anyone from Carter University since a few days after those pictures surfaced.

Allowing a long exhale to bring me to a sitting position, I pull my knees into my chest and allow the tears to fall. Continuous. I tuck my earbuds into my ears and turn the music almost as loud as it will go. Sometimes the silence is too much. Sometimes Pitbull is the only thing that crowds out the music I can still hear from inside The Pink Pony. It's safe to say I'll never listen to Britney Spears again, though I never really made it a habit to begin with.

You promised you'd take care of her, my mother had sneered at Roland the night she picked me up to bring me back to Connecticut. Plucked me from school without an attempt to listen to any protestations from me, though I didn't have any. There was nothing I could possibly conjure up to convince her why, after everything that went on over the past several months, I should stay there.

Maybe it wouldn't have been so bad if half of the student body hadn't turned on me as well, as if they were following Matt's silent lead. The attention I'd received after I was revealed as Roland's daughter was nothing compared to the vile uproar of those labeling me as the heathen who'd poisoned two of their "golden boys."

Lead me...

I clench my jaw, rolling to my side, wrenching with what I'm sure are loud sobs if I bothered to let myself hear them. I turn the music up as loud as it will go. What had happened with Matt was supposed to stay between the five of us there that night, and the members of the counseling staff Buck and Roland had spoken with. I can't help but replay the look in Matt's eyes the night he and his father arrived at Roland's house for what would be my second media-induced mini-seclusion in my entire life. Never mind that it was only months after the first one. Venom poured from his eyes. Acid, boring holes in my heart as he stared at me until I had to be the one to look away.

That was the very last time he looked me in the eyes.

The song ends and I bring my pillow to my face, letting out a guttural, cleansing scream into my pillow. A knock on the door has me worried that I've disturbed the Zen—or whatever—of the guests, but my fears are quelled when the smiling face of Rao, the monk and retreat leader at the monastery, greets me.

"Are you sure you won't join everyone for lunch today, Miss Sawyer?" His smile is accented by the gold sash draped artistically around his deep maroon robe. "It would be good to see you eat."

He has the grace to look past my surely red and swollen face. He doesn't ask me why I've been crying. He hasn't ever. I'm sure he knows, but I appreciate the space.

What I want is a burger.

I don't say that out loud. Not even as a joke. Ironically, the regulations around here are tighter than they ever were at CU. There's no meat here at all. No fish, no chicken, nothing that was once living with eyes is allowed here. I already had the modest dress requirement down pat before my arrival, so there was no adjustment period there, but I'll be damned if I haven't absentmindedly plotted how to sneak in a pepperoni pizza or some chicken lo mein.

It's not that I've *never* dined with the retreaters, as I call them. I just like to avoid excessive attention right now. I doubt most of the people here have heard of Carter University, let alone the scandal that befell the school when the strip club pictures erupted. Because they didn't just surface. They splattered their lava all over us. I know I'm a special case here, and I hate that. Even though it's allowed me the privacy and anonymity I craved. Even though that's likely what I'll be for a while, if not forever—a special case.

But here at this particular monastery that has a name I can *never* pronounce, the staff is well aware I'm the daughter of Roland Abbot. It was an act of grace, maybe, that months prior to this debacle Roland became a leading member of an Interfaith initiative that had him making a few trips to NYC a month. Visiting various temples, monasteries, mosques, whatever.

So, here I am.

"Kennedy?" Rao's voice turns on an edge of slight concern as he's caught me staring into space yet again.

I nod and swallow hard. "I'll come. I'll be right down."

With a pleasant nod, Rao turns on his heels. But before he takes his first step down the hallway, he turns back to me.

"Miss Sawyer, if I may?" He asks permission to speak, stopping my closing of the door.

"Of course," I answer quietly.

"Your worst enemy cannot harm you as much as your own unguarded thoughts." The young monk quotes Buddha as his soft thumb wipes a tear away from my cheek before he glides silently away.

Ha, I think, checking myself in the mirror before heading to lunch. *Clearly he's never met anyone from my side of the religious tracks.*

I throw my hair into a loose and messy bun as I make the corner for the dining room. It's more of an atrium, really: fully lit by the sun through a glass ceiling and matching glass walls on three sides. Tables aren't pressed against the windows— planter boxes are. Filled with wide-leafed greens, flowers of every color of the rainbow, and trickling water features. Tables abut these rich, narrow and fragrant gardens. Walking in here always makes me feel like I'm happening upon a secret garden rather than a cafeteria.

While I do have a mini-fridge in my room stocked with hummus, cheese, and Brie, I'm hopeful there is something with a little more depth prepared for lunch today. The few times Roland's visited me here, we've snuck off to a nearby burger joint. I can still feel the grease on my lips, but I push those very literal carnal thoughts out of my head as I wander toward the selection area.

Hardboiled eggs. That, I can do. I scoop three of them on top of a bed of lettuce, add a few spoonfuls of walnuts, slivered almonds, and dried cranberries, and drizzle it with an admittedly gluttonous portion of blueberry vinaigrette. The ceremonious preparation of my lunch is almost in vain when I nearly drop my tray at the site of Asher sitting in the corner of the dining room with a bright and mischievous look on his face.

I make a noise that sounds a little like "eep," trying not to disturb the rather peaceful lunch experience, and scoot over toward him as quickly and gracefully as I can. His face melts into a wide grin, and when he rises, his broad shoulders expand even more as he holds out his arms to welcome me into a hug. After I set down my tray, I squeeze the living daylights out of him. I can't help from bouncing up and down a little.

Asher holds me at arms length for a second, taking me in before releasing me and taking his seat, gesturing for me to do the same.

"No," I say, my response bright. "Stand back up and give me another hug."

He complies and finally speaks. "If you insist," he says quietly, covering me with another warm embrace. He smells like freshly ground coffee and whatever cologne he wears. It's almost a little fruity, but it works in conjunction with his razor's-edge exterior.

"What are you doing here?" I ask, finally sitting. "How'd you know I was here? Roland told you, didn't he? Still, *what* are you doing here?" I'm vibrating. Alive with the excitement of seeing someone from my old new life for the first time in months. It makes me miss everyone else almost twice as much as I did this morning. I swallow back the tears, demanding they stay at bay for at least a few moments more.

Asher's eyebrows form a comical arch above his blue-grey speckled eyes. "You okay?" he asks sarcastically. "I'm just here to see you. It's been a lonely few months at Word," he says of the coffee shop he owns, and where I work. Or worked. His vagueness isn't anything new, but still swirls some discomfort through my stomach.

I laugh. "I'm sure Chelsea is excitement enough." I say of my "alternative" coworker. Covered in tattoos and sour language. I love her dearly. Under normal circumstances I probably wouldn't have much of an appetite, but I shove half an egg in my mouth and chew while I wait for him to continue.

Asher leans back, crosses his arms in front of his chest and offers a non-committal shrug. We've had enough conversations in the past for me to recognize his signal that he's going to make me do most of the work in this conversation. "What happened?" he asks innocently.

"Broad question," I counter, taking a swig of water. "I could be asking the same thing of you, right?"

Asher leans forward, looking more like my boss than a friend for a fraction of a second. "I'm serious."

I don't answer. I try a poker face.

Then, he speaks again. Ruining everything. "K. Sawyer..." he pleads softly.

As if thrown into a dream, the floor feels like it drops from beneath me and I'm falling down, up, and sideways at the same time. I grip the edge of the table as a wave of dizziness crashes through me.

K. Sawyer.

"I thought it might have something to do with that football player," he says, correctly assessing my reaction to the nickname that *only* Matt called me. Because he gave it to me. It's his.

I bite the inside of my cheek, trying to get ahold of myself. "Don't be a jerk," I whisper. "You did that on purpose."

Until winter break, Matt had spent almost every shift of mine at Word, "hogging counter space" Asher liked to tease me. Until I reminded him that Matt's money was as good as anyone else's. Still, he liked to give me crap.

Asher doesn't flinch at my emotional response, and I can't decide if I'm angry. Clearing my throat, I attempt to redirect the conversation. "What *happened* is I make an easy scapegoat."

In the early aftermath of Photogate 2.0, allies were few and far between. No one seemed to know what to make of pastors and CU kids "hanging out" at a strip club the night before a major, national conference on family values. Despite initial intentions to keep the whole thing private, Matt's night of infinite rule violations was fully exposed.

"Explain," Asher demands without offering an apology for the jerk move of using Matt's nickname for me.

I tilt my head to the side, and begin. Monotone. "The Office of Academic Affairs took mercy on me and let me finish out my freshman year via independent study. I'm on summer break." I don't really care for my own tone, but it's clear he's not here for a simple friendly visit.

His left eyebrow twitches, unamused. "Irrelevant."

I sigh, pursing my lips before I speak. I let it out all at once. "Half the student body is convinced that it was Matt's close relationship with me that led him to believe such a *lewd* form of entertainment is, in fact, entertainment. The other half seems to want to be on my side, or did. You know, the side of truth. But some of them are scared to admit it, and others have flat out told me their parents have told them to stay far, far away from me, or risk losing their college funding. In fact," I pause for a brief sigh, "before my mom dragged me off campus, Bridgette was packing her bags because her parents *demanded* she be removed from my room. So," I shrug, "here I sit. Orphaned by my life."

"Orphaned?" Asher questions through narrowed eyes. "Your mom? Dad? Stepdad? Friends?"

"Mollie, my best friend from before my swan dive into Jesusville, hangs out with me here as much as possible. My stepdad, Dan, does the same. Especially if he has work in the city. Roland's been here a few times, too. Business," I answer all matter-of-factly.

"And your mom?" he presses.

"We've, uh," I clear my throat, "have always had a complicated relationship. This hasn't helped."

He waves his hand, instructing me to continue and, despite my annoyance, I comply without hesitation.

"She blamed Roland for getting me *involved* in such nonsense. She was furious there were no plans to tell her about the incident at all. I think she truly enjoyed watching all the finger pointing at him and Carter that was going on in the first couple of weeks thanks to the Court of Public Opinion." I grind my back teeth in anger.

Asher chuckles. "I don't buy it. I watched the news, too. She wasn't absolved."

Of course there was talk over the conservative media about my mother's choice to raise me without Roland. How she encouraged him to sign over his parental rights. Encouraged being their word. How she raised me in a liberal state, a liberal town, a liberal church, and, you guessed it, a liberal home. In the short couple of weeks the story was even a story, my mom's and Roland's relationship trajectory played out over and over again across the media.

"Maybe," I finally offer. "But she was all too excited to have an excuse to take me out of there early. She's been sending me transfer info and contact information for Cornell and Yale ever since my school year officially ended. So, you see," I turn up my sarcasm, "there is nothing in there about *the football player* that you didn't already know. We were friends, he made mistakes, so did I, he hates me, the end." I've practiced that list in my head many times. Our own trajectory.

Asher chuckles. "Okay. So, you know that the media coverage surrounding the whole Pink Pony business has died down and now everyone's focused on why you've disappeared?"

"I've hardly disappeared."

"Just no phone or social media presence," he counters, looking pleased with himself.

I shrug. "Social media is lame," I answer. I tired of it well before this incident, given what happened with the original Photogate, when my classmate, Joy, assumed Roland and I were sleeping together. This just sealed the deal. I closed all of my accounts the day The Pink Pony story broke and I haven't looked back.

I've never felt so alone in my entire life.

Asher looks around. "So you live here now?"

I pull my eyebrows in. "No. I'm just... staying here."

"How'd your dad agree to this place?

"Interfaith initiative. And he was worried I'd be hounded at his. And at my mom's too. My mom agreed this place was far enough away from CU in more ways than just distance." I sigh, recalling the resigned look on Roland's face when he realized my mom was right—I'd have to go away for a while. Until things died down.

"Why didn't you come back when the media lost interest in the story?" Asher questions, seeming to read my thoughts.

I set down my fork. "That was a week after spring break. I may have been able to catch up in my classes, but socially? That would have been nearly impossible."

Eden and Jonah kept texting me for a while, until I got an apologetic response from each of them a couple of days apart. Jonah's simply said, *I can't talk with you right now. Soon, I hope.* Eden's was clearer. Angrier. She said her parents were stupid and couldn't see facts in front of them. That Matt had struggled long before I'd showed up and I wasn't even *with* him when he chose to go to the strip club. I told both of them I understood. Every once in a while Eden still emails me from a random account she only accesses from a public library downtown, whenever she can get there. I don't tell Asher that, though. I know I should, but I don't trust anyone right now.

"I don't buy it," is all he says.

"I'm not selling anything," I spit back, pushing my plate away from me.

"Cut the shit, Kennedy," Asher says. It startles me to hear him cuss.

"Excuse me?" I reply, rather indignantly.

He offers an unamused squint of his eyes.

"What is it you're really hiding from?"

CHAPTER TWO
THE HURT AND THE HEALER

Kennedy.

THE *football player.*

I want to say it. To tell Asher that he's right. That the weight of everything that went down between me and Matt over the last year is too much for me to bear, so I'm hiding. From Matt, even if it means from everything else I'd set out to do at Carter.

"I didn't expect everyone at CU to be perfect," I start with a shaky voice. "I just expected them to try a little harder to fake it, I guess."

Liar. You wanted them to be perfect and you wanted them to fail. At least until you fell in love with all of them.

I think about Joy and her very early betrayal. About the tension between Jonah and his father, and the red rage Matt felt toward his. The way Matt fell apart in front of me again and again and demanded he was no good for me. Even as a friend. How my RA Maggie, who I thought I'd be close with, didn't really seem to know how to handle me, even though she'd once lauded me for my "potential." I even look back at Jonah and Eden and how obviously perfect they were for each other, and how they didn't pretend when it was over. Even if it meant an awkward car ride with me and Roland.

"You make it easy for people to be themselves around you, Kennedy," Asher says, looking a little vulnerable for him. "Seems to me like you made some actual friends. Ones who didn't feel like they *had* to pretend around you. You told me you wanted to come to CU to learn about Roland and about his life, and maybe a little about yourself. But, you can't deny to me for even a second that you didn't think you could swoop in and teach these *simple-hearted-Jesus-freaks* a thing or two about the *real world*."

I pull my head back, my mouth gaping open. "Well, what a refreshing taste of judgment." I push back my chair and stand, discarding my trash before exiting to an outdoor path. I know he's going to follow me, so I choose somewhere that will give us some privacy.

"Tell me I'm wrong," he commands in a normal tone, but one that sounds so loud in this sacred space. He catches up to me on an uneven stone path and puts a hand on my shoulder, stopping me. I face him and his eyes are electrified. "Tell me I'm wrong and I'll apologize. It wasn't a *judgment*, Kennedy. It was an observation. Those are two different things. I think you can understand that," he tests me. He's been watching me all year. He knows how I watch people, filing away their interactions for later review. I've even told him as much in conversation.

I cross my arms in front of me. "So what if that's what I thought. That's not what I think now. I just wanted some friends. Some semblance of people to tether me to the earth while my family life was shaken apart. And my best friend, *the football player*, couldn't be bothered."

"Did you ever stop to think," Asher starts in a sagely mellow voice, "that it's not about you? Didn't that become clear to you the night you found him carelessly drunk in a strip club? Did it ever occur to you that he might need you more than you need him?"

I hold out my arms. "I tried to help him, Asher!" I nearly shout. The little yellow birds nearby flutter away in startled displeasure. "I tried to get him to talk to me, but he wouldn't even look at me, let alone listen to anything I had to say. And I did a good job of blowing any trust he had in me when I called my dad. Or when I followed him there in the first place, I guess. I don't know..." I trail off into tears, grabbing the edge of the bench behind me and sitting on its cool stone.

Asher sits next to me with a heavy sigh. "I was afraid of that."

"Of what?" I sniff.

"That *you* were trying to help him."

I stare at him, gape-mouthed once again.

He takes mercy on me. "*You*," he repeats. "Not *Him*." Asher points to the shocking deep blue sky definitively.

"Matt doesn't want *Him*," I state. "He's so angry."

"Doesn't mean he doesn't need Him. Hey, what has Roland said about all this?"

"Nothing," I answer honestly. "He comes to the city, we hang out, we eat, he goes back to Asheville." It's been so refreshing spending time with Roland *away* from everything. It's just been nice to be away.

Asher grins and gives a slight nod. "I like his style."

"You're weird," I say. "And that doesn't help explain how I'm supposed to use—" I cut myself off because there's a question more pressing than the one I was about to ask. One I haven't even brought myself to ask Eden.

"What?" Asher nudges me.

"How is he?" I force out in a tiny whisper, lowering my eyes to the tiny sprigs of grass poking through cracks in the hard stone of the path

"The football player?"

I nod. "Matt," I confirm. It stings to say his name out loud.

Asher wraps his arm around my shoulders, giving them a light squeeze, but not answering.

"It's not even that I liked him like *that*," I start. "Even when he turned me down, we were still friends. Best friends. I felt like we'd be those decades-long friends no matter what, if anything, happened... romantically."

"Maybe you will."

I chuckle. "That would take a miracle."

Asher takes his arm back. "Maybe. Maybe it'll also take time."

"You haven't answered my question. How is he?"

Asher twists his lips around like he's working out an appropriate answer. "Angry," he says in a deep breath.

"Self destructing?"

He shakes his head. "Doesn't seem to be. He actually looks better than the last time I saw him before... everything. His hair is cut, face shaved. He's working out a lot, getting in killer shape for what's promising to be a heck of a football season. He's their star," Asher says with a wistful smile.

"But you say he's angry. Have you talked to him?" Asher gives me a long look. "Come on, Asher. Throw me a bone," I press.

"He still comes into the shop all the time. Even since the year ended. He's taking a few classes this summer, I guess. To catch up on the nosedive his grades took." Asher wipes his hands on his jeans. An anxious move I haven't seen him exhibit before.

I look between Asher's eyes and his hands. "What?"

"Consider coming to volunteer for my prison ministry this summer. I could help you arrange on-campus housing, or you could always just live with your dad," he throws me a wink that doesn't match the nervous hand-wiping habit. "I think it would be good for you, and it would help fill community service hours."

"For students of CU," I state flatly.

Asher pales slightly, his Adam's apple bobbing once against a hard swallow. "You're considering not coming back?"

"I thought that was just kind of a foregone conclusion," I admit, without admitting I have no backup plan. Yet.

He shakes his head. "No one is a foregone conclusion, Kennedy. No one." He says this with the intensity of someone saving a life. Maybe literally.

He stands and walks down a winding garden path. The monastery takes up almost a full city block, but it seems even bigger given the extra architectural design. The way the paths are sculpted into the landscape allows you to walk for far more than one block's length. Confused, I follow him through the rich greens, trees cloaked with knotted vines, and past wrought-iron gates that lead to nowhere, covered in aggressive ivy.

"What am I supposed to do?" I ask, rather gruffly. "Just go back and face all the naysayers *again*?"

Asher stops and turns abruptly on his heels. "Kennedy, do you want to follow Jesus?"

"Yes," I answer quickly. Without thinking.

Interesting development...

"I mean *really* follow him. Like walk away from all the crap, all the expectations, and into a life with *Him*?" He's moving his arms around to illustrate all the throwing out of old things.

I swallow hard. "I don't know," I answer honestly this time. "I don't know what it means," I admit.

Asher's shoulders sink, but not in defeat. He looks relieved as he puts his hands on my shoulders. "Then take the time to figure it out. Let me help you. Let Roland help you. Jesus never said following him would be easy. Just that it would be worth it."

I sigh, resuming our walk forward. "What *did* he say about it? The church I grew up in did a great job of painting a picture of Christianity as a magic eraser for our trials."

He chuckles, giving me a light squeeze which causes our bodies to bump into each other as we cross a small bridge over some bright white and orange koi swirling through the pond. Frogs dart past them and leap onto real, live lily pads.

"I have said these things to you," Asher starts, "that in me you may have peace. In the world you will have tribulation. But take heart; I have overcome the world."

"Bible quote, I assume?" I hardly feel bad about asking this question around Asher. I'm not fluent in scripture.

He nods. "John sixteen, thirty-three." He stops, pausing to look around, realizing we've walked in a large loop. He gestures to the door to the atrium dining area.

"That hardly seems reassuring. It also doesn't give an answer."

He grins broadly. "It gives *the* answer, Kennedy. I'll text you tomorrow and we can talk about the volunteer stuff, okay?"

"Okay. Hey, tell me you didn't come all the way to NYC just to talk to me. I have a phone."

He winks, shrugging. "Not the same. It's good to see you, Kid. Think about it, okay?"

There were lots of "its" we discussed this afternoon, but I nod anyway. He means all of them.

I watch Asher turn on his heels and cross toward the parking lot in a few long strides. "Hey," I call after him.

He turns around and shouts back. "Yeah?"

"How old are you? For real."

Asher laughs. "Why?"

I shrug. "You seem wise. I need to know how much time I have for all the catching up I need to do to get on your level."

"Wisdom and age aren't the same thing. You've got plenty of wisdom, Kennedy. Right on track, I'd say."

"Come on," I plead.

"Twenty-three," he answers without a fight.

I jog to catch up to him "So you've only been out of CU for a year?"

"Something like that," he says with a weird look in his eyes.

"And you've opened the coffee shop and started the ministry in that time?"

"Took over the coffee shop, actually. And, yeah about the ministry."

I shake my head and back slowly off the sidewalk. "You're wrong," I say. "I've got *lots* of catching up to do, spiritually and missionarily speaking."

"Missionarily?" He calls me out on my made up word. "This isn't a contest, you know."

I laugh. "I'm from the greater Manhattan area. *Everything* is a contest."

"You're like forty-five minutes away from Manhattan."

I stick out my tongue. "Not at the moment." I gesture to our surroundings. "Asher?" I ask before he leaves.

"Yeah?"

"I think I might need them more than they need me," I say of my friends at CU.

He shrugs. "Maybe you all just need each other. You'll never know if you keep hiding." He treks toward his car without a word, while I turn and make my way to my room with some sort of electrifying energy inside me.

Could I really go back to Carter University?

✝

"I'm happy you're all here," I say, taking a long breath. Staring at the faces of my mom, Dan, and Roland, I know I just have to dive in. "Thank you for taking the time to come see me here. It seemed like the most neutral place."

A mom, a stepdad, and a preacher walk into a temple...

"Of course, honey," Dan says. "Anything for you, you know that."

I know he means it, but I don't know if I've ever heard him say anything like that before and can't help but wonder if Roland's presence affects Dan's feelings of paternity with me. The facts are there: he's been more of a father to me than Roland has, but none of us live in denial as far as I know, so I don't think we need any reminders.

"I want to thank you guys for giving me the space... and finances... to spend the last couple of months decompressing. It's given me a lot of time to think about things." I cast a glance around my dorm-style room. It's always felt spacious. Lots of natural light, muted walls decorated with intricate wall hangings in languages I can't read. Spacious before I crowded it with three parents. I should be grateful that I have three whole people who want the best for me in this life. I am.

"What's up, Kennedy?" Mom says with an air of irritation in her voice. She's more a forgive and forget kind of person, and all the blowups we had over the phone in the past several weeks are as good as swept under the rug with her. I'm sure this waiting is making her uncomfortable.

"You love seeing Roland and my friends under fire, don't you?" I'd accused of her on the drive to the temple. *"Even if it means I'm shit on, too."*

"Nice language," was all she'd replied.

"Christians swear, too, you know."

"Yes, and they also apparently throw money at naked women."

I didn't even let her up into my room the day we got here, and she hasn't visited me since. I told her not to and I actually meant it. I'm thankful for the space she gave me for once. Maybe she needed some, too.

"Asher came to see me last week," I start. "My boss from Word," I remind my mom and Dan, who look confused. They nod, slowly. "He's got a prison ministry he runs just outside of Asheville, and he thought it might be a good experience for me to volunteer there this summer..." I trail off with the arch of Mom's eyebrow.

No one is saying anything. Not even Roland, who's been disturbingly quiet since this quaint gathering began.

"I know I could stay on campus if I wanted to, but I was—"

"Nope, not campus," Mom cuts me off. "Absolutely not."

"Buuuut," I accentuate my irritation that she's being all jumpy-to-conclusions, "*if* I do it, I was thinking it might be a better idea to stay at Roland's." I eye Roland, who looks up from his hands.

He's being weird.

"I would be one-hundred-percent okay with that. You know that," he says as if he'd prepared the sentence over a couple of days. He gives me a warm smile and I calm down a little.

"Have you checked your email?" Mom asks. I shake my head, and she hands me a few pieces of mail. "Here."

My stomach sinks. In a moment of frantic emotions in the three weeks I was at home before heading to the temple, I'd written Cornell and Yale, explaining my "circumstances," and asking if they'd consider my previous acceptances should I want to transfer for the fall.

"Open them," she says.

"Wendy..." Dan seems to caution, as if they'd "been over this" already.

I don't need to open them. It's obvious by her calm expression that they are letters telling me my acceptances from over a year ago are as good as new.

"If you do the volunteer thing over the summer, you'll want to make sure you leave time to visit those campuses again, and meet with—"

"I'm not going to either of them," I blurt out, really grabbing everyone's attention this time.

My mom sighs, as if I've exasperated her. "What's your plan? A year off? I'm not sure if the schools will grant you another year deferment. Unless you spend the next year curing cancer or something."

Ignoring her elitist comment, I take a deep breath. "I'm going to weigh *all* of my options," I state, eyeing Roland to make her understand.

"Are you kidding me?" Mom shouts, standing with her hands on her hips, pacing the floor." Her knee-length charcoal grey, cotton skirt sways as her Keene sandals scuff across the floor. When she turns, her pale blue tank top reveals a dark spot of sweat between her shoulder blades. It's always warm in here, but today seems especially so.

"Wendy," Roland and Dan say at the same time.

"After all they've done to you..." she trails off in fury.

"The *them* you're blaming is the media," I try to remind her.

"And all the picture takers. You don't even *know* who took the photos at the strip club." She eyes Roland for a second as she says it.

I have a choice. I can stand and get into a point-counter-point confrontation with her, or I can peacefully explain my case. I really, *really* want to yell. I take a deep breath and say a prayer instead. But still, I stand.

"The last year has been one of the hardest of my life, and one of the most rewarding. But a good friend told me something recently..."

Mom's quiet as Dan asks, "What's that?"

"I have said these things to you, that in me you may have peace. In the world you will have tribulation. But take heart; I have overcome the world." I've said the words over and over in my head since Asher left that day. "If Jesus can overcome the world, and death, and all of that... I can probably take some time to make a decision that will affect the rest of my life."

Mom looks at Roland and points to me. "Is this your influence? You weren't supposed to talk to her about going back there."

He holds up his hands in defense. "I didn't..."

"Excuse me?" I interrupt, annoyed about their evidently private conversations regarding me. "You know what, Mom? Enough is enough. He's an adult and, for that matter, so am I. You can stop punishing him for *leaving us* now. There were two adults who helped make that choice." My words sting her; evident as she pulls her head back and runs a hand through her frizzy curls.

"Well," she says, shakily. "Looks like you've thought this through."

"Why do I get the feeling you'd support me more if I dropped out of school completely?" Out of the corner of my eye, I see Roland and Dan gesture to each other.

"We're going to wait out here," Dan says before kissing me on the head.

The room feels a lot smaller without them here, I realize when the door closes.

"You're so angry with me," Mom says, sitting on the edge of my bed.

I'm confused, but answer her. "And you're so angry with me. You think if I do choose CU, it will be to somehow punish you."

"Won't it?" she asks in all seriousness.

My eyes widen. "Mom, this isn't *about you*. You raised me, for God's sake, can't you trust that I'm capable to make thought-out decisions."

She smiles. Small, but present. "Yes, but I also know that you're capable of making emotional decisions, too."

I shake my head. "Not entirely. You've taught me well. Making decisions with emotion behind them is different than making emotional decisions. And, even if this *were* an emotional decision—which it isn't—I'm nineteen now. I get to make those."

She wipes under her eye. Maybe a tear, maybe a tear she wants me to believe is there. It's a gesture of surrender either way.

I put my hand over hers. "You don't have to worry that I'll turn into Roland," I say. "And, even if I did, would it be the worst thing in the world to become a pastor that traveled around the world making a difference?" I chuckle internally at the very thought.

She takes my face in her hands and looks as serious as she ever has. "It scares me, Kennedy, because I believe you'd be absolutely perfect at exactly that. And, you'd have to face much harder times than what CU has offered you so far."

"I'm not going to be a pastor. Chill out," I try to reassure her.

She laughs. "You say that, but you've been ministering to me the whole time you've been there. Your grandfather made me see that one night. Your patience. Love. Perseverance. I like the woman you're becoming, Kennedy. I just don't want you to get hurt in the process."

I look down, my stomach dropping at the commitment I've just made. "I think I might have to get a little hurt, Mom."

CHAPTER THREE

LIGHTS, CAMERA ...

Roland.

PACKING her up took only a few minutes, but I held my breath every second.

She's coming to live with me.

My palms are sweaty against the steering wheel while I wait for her to say her goodbyes to Wendy and Dan. I have *no* idea what went on in her room when Dan and I excused ourselves, but it must have been just this side of a miracle because, to be honest, I didn't think there was any human way Wendy would condone Kennedy living with me under anything but the most extreme circumstances.

You promised you'd take care of her.

Wendy's chilling words have rarely left the foreground of my mind in the months since the pictures of Kennedy in front of the strip club were thrown all over the place. Sure, there were lots of us in the picture, but people focused on *her*, and the things they've said about her make my skin crawl. It almost came to a fistfight about keeping her enrolled in CU until I pointed out to the ancient Admissions Committee that there were *three* students, and two pastors/parents in that picture, and if the school was going to take a stance on one, they'd better be prepared to answer for all of them.

And a partridge in a pear tree...

They realized their judgment and held prayer sessions for all parties involved. I still don't trust Hershel Baker, though. I can't put my finger on it besides the obvious—he hates me and intends to rope Kennedy in with whatever his long-term plan is to see me fail. I'll be damned if I'll *ever* let that happen. Whatever issues he has with me will live and die with me, and I'll go to hell and back to make sure they never touch her.

Kennedy shuts her things into the trunk, then plops into the front seat of my Prius with a tired-sounding huff.

"Ready?" I ask, grinning despite my nerves inside.

She nods. "But you're not." She chuckles, pointing to the window, where I turn to find Wendy beckoning me out of the car with a wave of her hand.

Breathe.

I start to roll down the window, but opt to get out instead. My stomach still flips and sinks when I'm around her. There's so much heavy history and unspeakable hurt that I caused her. I still feel the good times, too. Like when Wendy took me ice skating for the first time in college. It was on a frozen pond and I was scared out of my mind, but I wasn't about to show her that. I fell more than I stood, and our cheeks hurt more from laughing than the frozen wind.

"I will, I promise." I hold up my hands in faint defense against her unspoken words. "I'd die for her, Wendy. I have no way to prove that to you, and I know I can't ask you to take me on my word, but—"

"Shut it," she says with a wry grin on her face. "I do trust you. With her at least. But those other people..." Trailing off, she shakes her head, looking into the distance.

"The world is full of *other people*, Wendy. Weren't we each other people once?" My throat tightens as I say the words. I'd meant to keep them to myself.

Her fierce eyes grow wide. She licks her lips and clears her throat. "I suppose you're right. Have her call me when you get back to Asheville," she says quietly before peering over my shoulder and blowing a kiss to Kennedy. I can't move my eyes from her, so I don't know if Kennedy returns the gesture, but the smile on Wendy's face gives me all the answer I need.

"I will. Drive safe." Ducking back into my car, I watch for a moment as Wendy wraps her arms around herself and climbs into the passenger side of Dan's Volvo. He shuts the door for her and offers me a polite wave before driving away.

"Uh... ready?" Kennedy asks. I whip my head toward her, my shoulders jumping slightly. "Jumpy much?"

I take a cleansing breath. "Sorry. It's been a long, weird couple of days."

Kennedy nods, a grin mimicking her mother's forming on her lips. "That it has. Hey," she says, sounding hesitant.

"Yeah?"

"Sorry I didn't run the whole living with you thing by you before I, like, announced it."

Warmth fills my chest and spreads to my face. "I'm happy to have you, Kennedy."

And I am. I answered so quickly up in her room because I was afraid if I didn't, she might change her mind, or take my hesitation as a *no*, and there would go the only chance I'd have.

"I wonder if Bridgette will keep rooming with Eden after all."

I take a deep breath. "I heard about that..." I put the car in drive and set out down the driveway of the temple at ten miles per hour, as instructed by the sign.

I've learned that parents of CU students involve a lot of people in decisions regarding their children. Preemptively, I'd received an email from Bridgette's father asking that I not take offense to their decision to have Bridgette switch rooms. And that they "knew" I had little to do with Kennedy's upbringing, so they weren't blaming me for her "actions." Little did they know, that offended me more than anything. Not the rubbing in that I wasn't there for her as a child—I don't believe that's what they were doing. But, they backhandedly implicated Kennedy in the messes she'd been in as if they were of her own creating. And, somehow, it was negatively affecting their daughter.

Of course, because I have an interest in both forgiveness and keeping my job, I told him not to worry about it and I would be praying for the best outcome in their daughter's living situation.

"Anyway," Kennedy waves her hand in the air and stares through the windshield, "we'll have the summer to figure out, like, if this works, or whatever. Then we can plan if I'll just keep living with you when the school year starts."

Kennedy and I jerk forward as I slam on the breaks.

"God! What?" she shrieks, annoyed despite the slow speed we'd been traveling.

"Sorry." I clear my throat. "When the school year starts? I thought you were going to visit with Cornell and—"

Kennedy's face twists almost comically as she arches an eyebrow and twists her lips. "Please," she giggles, "we all know I'm returning to CU."

I look around me, for clues, maybe. "We do? But your mother... was this what you were talking about when you two were alone?"

She tilts her head side to side. "Sort of. Let's just put it this way, Mom *knows* I'm going back to CU, and I don't even have to say it. But, I gotta say, you could stand to look a little more excited."

Dread attacks my equilibrium as I resume driving, turn onto the next street, and pull into a fifteen-minute-only parking space. "It's not... It's not that, Kennedy. I just... Ugh, I don't know if returning to CU will be the best course of action for you." The words are actually painful to say.

Kennedy looks heartbroken. Her lips part and I have to look away from her deep, wide, *how-dare-you* eyes. "Why? Did my mom say something to you? Give you an ultimatum, or something?"

"It's not that." I shake my head, speaking as emphatically as I can. I reach for her but she pulls her hand back.

"Then what is it?" she spits out with more hurt and anger than I ever want to hear from her. "Have you had enough of me and all the torches and pitchforks that follow me around?"

She uses her sarcasm in so many ways. Paints words with it, sculpts with it, murders with it. It's no doubt a skill she obtained from her mother. It's a great way to avoid being hurt. Something I guess I indirectly passed on to Kennedy through her mom. *Avoid getting hurt.*

Leaning back against my seat, I let out a small growl as I run my hand over my head and rest it on the back of my sweaty neck. "It might be for your own good," I try, hoping not to have to tell her all the details now.

"You've lost your mind," she finally answers after staring at me like I'd turned into a jigsaw puzzle. "I don't think CU has anything left to throw at me that I can't handle."

"True," I concede. "But the media might."

She shrugs. "They'll lose interest quickly."

Lord, she has no idea.

I decide to just blurt it out.

Help me...

"The university, Kennedy, has signed a deal with NBC to produce a reality show-documentary thing. At Carter. The deal is for fall semester only, but everyone at NBC and Carter knows it'll be picked up after the first episode to run all school year." Her face pales and she lets out a deep exhale, but I continue. "This hasn't been made public, but will be very, *very* soon, because the network will be interviewing students and faculty to find out who is willing to be followed and who they want to follow. Myself included."

Her eyes shoot to me. "Have you agreed to this? To let them follow you?"

I shake my head. "Not my personal life. Not my home. But as far as church services go, that's kind of fair game. CU's had a lot of attention in the last year, and a lot of the viewing audience of NBC wants to know what goes on behind the walls of the school and in the lives of the students. They're curious."

Kennedy faces forward again, resting her elbow on the edge of the window. She rakes her fingers through her hair as she puffs out her cheeks with a breath. Her body is still while her eyes dart around the scenery. I can almost read her next question across her eyes.

"Kennedy," I prompt.

She faces me again, not looking quite so ghostly. "Is there *any* possible way that I can avoid being part of this?"

I sigh. She's far wiser than I was at nineteen. "I think, without them saying it, the network is hitching their hopes on you returning. You're still technically enrolled..."

Her head falls against the headrest. "I can refuse to be filmed, can't I?"

I nod. "Yes."

She eyes me sideways. "You're worried that might make things worse, however impossible that may seem."

My mind slips back to an unfortunate conversation I had with school higher-ups last week.

"Is Kennedy continuing her schooling with CU?" One uptight suit asked.

"Suddenly interested?" I shot back. *"A few months ago you couldn't wait to get her out of your hair."*

Dean Baker snickered. *"Circumstances have changed. Carter University stands to bring in a fair bit of money if this deal goes through."*

"So you want to use my daughter as bait. To keep people tuning in until you can get your agenda situated and do with her whatever the audience wants?"

The blank stares I was met with said enough.

"Forget it." I stood and walked toward the exit. *"You're not using my daughter for your gain. And if you think that after all that's gone on she'll even want to be part of something so public, then you've been out drinking."*

I left right then, noting the blushing faces of more than one closet drinker in the pretentious crowd. Not my finest moment by far.

"Roland," Kennedy grabs my attention. "They've already talked to you about me, haven't they? Is that why you were so quick to let me stay with you this summer?"

"What? Kennedy, no. I assumed you wouldn't be coming back at all, let alone for the summer." At her core, Kennedy can't fully trust me yet. It's a fact, a consequence of the decisions I've made in my life. I start driving again. I think better while driving, even through the clogged arteries of Manhattan.

She's silent for several minutes. I watch her clench and relax her fists several times. I do that. I suppress a grin.

"I'll do it," she says out of nowhere. "On my terms."

I swallow down the nausea brewing in my stomach. "Kennedy, you don't have to do anything. And I'm not sure that you can really control what they film, or whatever. I haven't done enough research there yet, because I was hoping it wouldn't come to this."

She snorts in that sarcastic laughter she definitely got from her mom. "Oh, they'll let me. Do you know nothing about the entertainment business?"

"Some," I admit. "But New Life produces my sermons. We have our own production crew. So what's handed to the networks has already been edited. By us."

Stopped at a red light, I can see she seems surprised by my answer. "There's a reason for that. I went to high school with plenty of... those types." She winks at me as she says, "*those types*," since she hates so much when her mother refers to CU students as, "*those people*," I assume. I crack a smile. "Anyway, network exec's always come in guns blazing, but they know their ratings, and jobs for that matter, are contingent on a series of yes's from the people around them. *No* is a dangerous word for their Porsche-driving lifestyle. I've seen a lot of people get taken advantage of, so I know what to do to avoid that. Oh, God, Mom's going to lose her mind. Let's not tell her yet." Her speech speeds up the longer she talks.

"Kennedy, take a breath," I encourage. "We can make sure they don't take advantage of anyone."

She laughs, a little like a crazy person. "They'll exploit anyone they can get their hands on. That's kind of the nature of reality shows. It starts out sounding like a good idea..." Her gaze floats somewhere out the window as I start forward again, anxious to get out of New York and be back in Asheville.

"What is it?" I ask gently.

Kennedy leans forward, placing her elbows on her knees as she cradles her head in her hands for a moment. Sitting up, she takes another breath and flatly says, "I'll do it," again. "They'll meet me on my terms and I'll do my best to make sure they don't damage the people I love. They can crack their whips against my back if they must, but they're not touching my friends. Those are good people."

"You're a good person, too, Kennedy." I rest my hand on her shoulder for a moment and she doesn't flinch away. I leave it there a second longer.

"I know," she answers.

"But you just spent months locked away from any form of media. You have no social accounts left and now you're saying you're going to willingly participate in a national *reality show*." I know teenagers don't have fully-formed brains, but this seems borderline psychotic.

"Sometimes God asks us to do things that we wouldn't do if left up to our own devices," she says as plainly as she would talk about the weather.

I'm thankful for yet another red light that allows me to slam on my breaks. "God asked you to be on TV?" I ask, admittedly with some skepticism.

"Not like that, weirdo." She scrunches her forehead as her eyebrows draw inward. She sucks in her lip ring for a split second. As much as I hate lip rings on principle, it suits her. She looks like she's missing something without it. "He asked me to take a risk for my friends. On my terms. To not just be a reactive spectator anymore. I feel like the more I hide the more they'll push. I know I said they'd lose interest in me, but that was wishful thinking. I mean, they'll lose interest eventually, but bringing camera crews to the school does not seem like a step in that particular direction."

Once again, we're driving forward and finally winding out of the bounds of New York City, the highway opening up in front of us.

"Do you... hear from God often?" I ask. "How?" I offer an immediate follow-up question.

Kennedy shrugs, plugging her earbuds into her iPhone, giving me a signal that this conversation is rapidly approaching its end. "It's hard to explain. I guess, like, how some people say they have a sixth sense or intuition? I've always assumed whenever I've had those sensations that it was God talking to me."

"Always?" I question. Knowing the theology of the church she grew up in, I wonder what they taught her about hearing from God.

"Well I didn't always know it was God, but a priest I met once before deciding to come to CU gave me a copy of a book by St. Teresa of Avila. I jived with her. St. Teresa, not the priest, though I jived with her, too. I'm taking a nap now." Within seconds, Kennedy's seat is reclined and I can hear the faint thump of music through her neon green earbuds.

So, she hears from God. While I can't say that I'm surprised, I *am* surprised she talked to me about it, however briefly.

"She's got a feisty spirit, son. Guard her," my dad said just a day after meeting her.

"Nurture her. She's meant for something big," my mom said just behind him.

I hadn't spent enough time with her at that point to know if they were right, or just trying to be encouraging. Even a note from Wendy's dad, "just checking in" wasn't enough to persuade me. All children need shepherding, that goes without saying. But there are some that require special handling, if you will. Because Satan can spot the spiritually gifted among us almost faster than we can, and will stop at nothing to take them down. Doubt in Christ as Savior is a favorite tool of his.

The thought sinks my stomach. Is that what's been happening to Kennedy for the last year? Has she been at the hands of Satan? How could the thought not have occurred to me sooner?

You're too close to the situation to see things right away. And that's okay.

Glancing to my right, I watch the peaceful face of my daughter as she lip-sings along to her music with her eyes closed. She wants this. She wants CU, and the reality show, her friends, and me. Maybe her tenacity goes deeper than simply being strong-willed.

"God, you have to help me with her. Please. Help me shepherd her through what will certainly be more trying times than some pictures on the Internet. Show me how to guide her, Lord," I carefully whisper my prayers, but need to say them out loud. I need to protect her from what she needs protecting from, and let her fight where she needs to fight.

"Huh?" Kennedy props herself on an elbow, pulling out one of her earbuds. "Did you say something?"

I shake my head. "Just singing."

"It's off," she chuckles, eyeing the powered-off stereo system. "But, good for you?" she jokes.

"I know songs," I tease her.

"You're weird. Oh!" she says, cutting herself off excitedly. I love when she does that. "What's the name of the show?"

"What show?"

"Duh. The reality show. Does it have a name yet?"

I grumble. "You wouldn't believe it if I told you."

"Bet I will. Try me."

I can't help the ridiculous smile on my face as I say the words. *"Jesus Freaks."*

A sharp laugh from Kennedy's throat pierces through the silence of the car. "Oh," she sighs. "That's brilliant." She shakes her head without another word and puts her earbud back in, this time seeming to fall quickly asleep.

"Yeah," I mumble. "Just. Brilliant."

CHAPTER FOUR

ROOTS AND WINGS AND SCARY THINGS

Wendy, One year and two months ago...

"YOU know she got in."

"Yeah," I snort between sips of wine. "And she'll go if she got in."

"Not if," Dan says with an arched brow. He points to the large Carter University envelope sitting between us at the table. "And stop staring at that thing like it's a live grenade."

I take one more long sip of wine. "Isn't it?"

"You know," he says to me in the tone he uses when he's trying to make a point without making my head explode, "most of our friends are worried about if their kids will get in anywhere. And if their drug use will slow down or pick up when they're at college. Or if they'll get pregnant. And, you're worried about Kennedy... what is it you're worried about?"

I roll my eyes and point to the refrigerator, which holds the acceptance letters to two Ivy-League schools, among a few other private contenders that aren't too shabby. Purdue. Stanford. Amherst. All of them have accepted Kennedy. Many of them *want* her. Badly, judging by some of the scholarship offers. And here at the kitchen table is the thing that could ruin all of that.

"She has much more potential than this school can groom out of her and you know that. It's not even a top-rated school among small private schools."

Dan sighs. I'm clearly tugging at the threads of his patience. "If Kennedy has all the potential we both know she has, it won't matter *where* she goes to school."

I shoot him a look to match the derisive click of my tongue. "Don't patronize me. You work for top-tiered colleges and the NHL, for God's sake, and I've been in politics since before I even went to college. Where you go matters more for some jobs than who you are as a person."

He shrugs, grinning behind his scotch. "And what if she wants to be a pastor, huh? Go into the family business?"

"Politics," I snap, standing. "Politics is the family business. Roland is only her family because they share some pesky DNA."

"For now. Until she gets to know him, which she should. Kids should know where they come from. And, really, it won't be so bad. He's not the antichrist, you know."

I open the drawer where we stash the takeout menus and shove the CU envelope inside.

"And that, my love, is exactly why she doesn't need to know about this."

"You've finally lost it," Dan says. "What is it you're really worried about?"

I can't stop my eyes from stinging with tears of betrayal. "He didn't raise her," I squeak out. "He didn't stick around for the stomach bugs and the broken arm or the boys who broke her heart. Why does he get to have her now that she's a mature, awesome young woman? Why does he get to hang out with her and have coffee and dinner with her and talk God and politics with her and why do I have to stand by and watch it happen?"

"Oh, Honey," Dan says, wrapping me in his warm embrace. He kisses the top of my head before holding my face in his hands. "Because you're her mother. And it's your job to let her go now. This is part of the parenting deal."

"You're right," I say in a rare moment of clarity since Kennedy first announced she'd be applying to CU. "But I don't like it."

"And she won't like you if you hide this from her." He eyes the drawer like it's thumping with a telltale heart.

I move my eyes there, too, and give a heavy sigh. "Fine. I'll show it to her in a few days."

"Tomorrow," he commands, mostly serious, holding my chin between his thumb and forefinger.

I roll my eyes. "Tomorrow," I concede. "Why couldn't she have a tiny pill problem like that Tara friend of hers?"

Dan laughs and tickles my side. "Not our lot, Dear. Not our lot."

I wait two days before finally pulling it out of the drawer and sticking it back in the mailbox, so Kennedy can find it when she comes home from school. I spent the last two days studying her. Wanting to cast a spell to seal her wherever she went. Hermetically, like she has some autoimmune disease or something.

Those people won't understand her the way I do. They won't see the heart for God she has that scares the hell out of me. Because it will scare them, too.

And they'll tear her down.

CHAPTER FIVE

LET HER GO ...

Kennedy.

"**J**ESUS *Freaks*," I blurt out. "Isn't that just..."

Asher arches his eyebrow. "Insane? Degrading?"

I shoot him a scowl as I drop my application papers for the summer internship with his prison ministry on his desk at Word. "Degrading? Please. It's brilliant."

He tilts his head to the side, completely unamused, it seems. "Kennedy, the word *freak* is hardly ever a positive thing."

"You're looking at this the wrong way. Check out the Facebook and Instagram profiles of any student at CU. Twitter, even. I guarantee you at least seventy-five percent of them call themselves a Jesus Freak. Nearly a hundred percent of them use the hashtag Jesus Freak at one point or another. In fact, I know both Bridgette and Eden do."

Asher rubs his hand over his face. "It's different when it's among your own people. It's like how women call each other... certain things sometimes when they're with each other."

"Like what? What women?" I poke at him.

"I won't say it because I think it's unnecessary."

I huff. "Jesus Freaks is hardly on the same level as the slutty things women call each other in jest sometimes, Asher." He winces, but I continue. "It's provocative."

"No one will watch." He looks defeated.

"*Everyone* will watch. Ones who think we're all freaks, to see if they're right, and the ones who know we're not just to see if we're being portrayed accurately. And who cares, anyway? Jesus himself was a freak, wasn't he?"

"Yeah," Asher snickers. "And look where that got him."

Leaning forward, I put my hands on the edge of his desk. "Absolutely everything. Eternity? Oneness with God? I think you're looking at this freak thing the wrong way."

Asher grins standing and leaning in to match my position, his hands on the opposite side of his desk. "Pray you're right, Sawyer. Pray you're right. Editing is a magical tool, and I don't put it past a single secular network executive to edit the *freak* to their ratings advantage."

I playfully smack the side of his freshly buzzed head. "When will you get it? People will see what they want to see regardless of what's in front of them. Look, my mom's in policy, okay? She's a lobbyist. The scariest of lawyers according to some people. I know all about how sound bytes can be cut, copied, and pasted together. Everyone watching knows that, too. Sure, it had its heyday of believability a couple of decades ago, but not now. People don't *actually* view reality TV as reality anymore."

"Have you talked to all the people yet? Telling them you'll be back in the fall and that you're signing onto the show with a smile on your face?" Asher winks, picks up my yellow papers, and shoves all but one in his top desk drawer.

Ignoring his question I point to his desk. "What was that about? I worked hard on those essay questions!"

Asher's famous Cheshire-cat-like grin lights up the room. "I know. But you only *needed* to fill out this one. The rest are for my personal entertainment."

He laughs at me as my jaw hinges open.

"Jerk!" I shriek. "Those took me half of yesterday!"

"Calm down. Everyone has to fill them out. It helps me figure out where to put each person, though I already know where I'm putting you."

I cross my arms in front of me. "Where?"

"*Not* on TV." He arches an eyebrow.

I shake my head. "You haven't even asked me what my terms and conditions will be."

"Enlighten me," he jokes. There's a knock on his door, but Asher keeps his gaze on me as he moves to open it.

"First of all, I'm going to—"

Puke.

Asher's still not looking at the door, even when he pulls it slightly open to let the knocker in.

"Wh—oh..." Asher catches up to my sudden muteness as he assesses his guest.

Matt Wells.

Standing in Asher's doorway with a familiar looking packet of yellow paper. His eyes take a moment to focus on me, then they widen, which breaks my heart because it's the first time he's looked at me in months with anything but disdain. It's the first time he's looked at me in months, period.

Asher's right. Matt *does* look good. Healthy, clean, strong. As bright and cunning as the first day I spotted him in Word what feels like a lifetime ago. Thick brown hair just short enough to avoid an infraction, a strong jaw, unclenched for the first time in I can't remember how long, though it's tightening now. He looks so much like the boy who pleasantly ambushed me at the train station before Thanksgiving break.

The one who joked with me, protected me, and led me through the twisting social alleys of Carter University. There's barely a shadow of the broken kid from inside The Pink Pony left. Not a dark circle to be seen under his eyes so deeply brown they're almost black. Rich soil, I've always thought. He looks so much like my best friend that my chin quivers. I'm not inside the safe walls of the temple anymore—my tears have no business here. Not now. Not yet.

Matt clears his throat and turns his attention to Asher while I look at my feet. "Here's, uh, here's the papers you needed."

"For the prison ministry?" I blurt out, unbelieving that these are the first words I choose to say to him. I shift my gaze to Asher, so we can all pretend I was talking to him. Asher. Not Matt. Asher.

I've planned for months what I might say to Matt if he ever gave me a few seconds to say *anything* to him, and that sentence never came up.

Matt looks a little startled to hear my voice. He swallows hard. "Yeah." His voice is different. Softer, broken somehow.

Facing Asher, I try to saw him in half with a look of angry betrayal. He knew this whole time that Matt would be volunteering with him. And he asked me to join anyway. He knew this very situation would happen—*wanted* it to happen. I feel ambushed; Asher knows far more about how I'm feeling about Matt than almost anyone else in my life. And if Matt and I were going to come to any sort of terms with each other, I wanted it to happen organically. I wanted it to happen when each of us were in a place of forgiveness and trust—that he could trust me as a friend. I didn't want us thrown together by a meddling coffee shop owner.

"Well... I'll see myself out," I finally say, calmly, trying to mask my emotions. My sadness and Matt can't fit in this room together much longer. I'll cut Matt a break and go for a long walk before I start punching people.

Footsteps follow me toward the back door, but Matt's voice stops them.

"Let her go."

Let her go...
Fine.

Walking into a coffee shop two blocks away from Word, I'm comforted by the unfamiliarity. I hung out here a few times last semester, and I really like it as a non-work option. I love the atmosphere of Word, but who wants to hang out where they work all the time? Since it's still summer, the cafe is mostly empty with the exception of the soft glowing apples from the front of the MacBooks of a few grad-student-looking customers scattered throughout the large space. It's actually a coffee shop and a deli, which is perfect since I'm starving.

It's an industrial-looking space—polished cement floors, exposed wood and metal beams. A far cry from the cozy feeling of Word, but interesting in its own right.

I order a turkey, avocado, and bacon sandwich. After she takes my order, the girl at the counter stares at me like she knows me. This is an increasingly common occurrence, but I refuse to assume people *know* who I am, so I just smile awkwardly as she stares.

"You look familiar," she says, her eyes narrowing slightly. It's clear she's not a CU student based on her lack of knowledge of my face, and her "unconventional" hairstyle. It's shaved up the back and long in the front with a single blue streak. For a minute I think she looks familiar, too, but then I realize she just looks like my friend Tara from home.

I shrug. "I get that a lot. Sometimes people say I look like a young version of that actress... A—"

"You're Kennedy something-or-other. That pastor's kid," she cuts me off with accuracy.

"Yeah. That's me." I smile broader than usual because... I don't know why. I want people to like me? I feel like I'm on parade? Either way it's annoying, but I do it anyway. She stares a little longer as the guy to her right whips up my sandwich. "You don't remember me, do you?"

I squint a little, as if that will help, and I try to place her. Clearly my feeling of recognizing her was valid.

She leans forward, hooking her finger toward me to do the same thing. "Planned Parenthood," she whispers, one of her eyebrows slowly stretching into an enticing arch.

"Oh that's right!" I try to whisper, but it's a bit loud. "How are you?" I ask as if we're old friends. Her hair is slightly different, but she's most definitely the girl I talked to in front of Planned Parenthood at the end of my first semester. The girl Eden and Bridgette were throwing anti-abortion fliers at. She was with a couple of other girls, I think, but I remember her most.

"Not pregnant, thanks to my birth control pills," she says with just a hint of contempt in her voice.

I nod, slowly, praying for my sandwich to be done any second. "Good... I guess. What's your name, by the way?"

"Riley," she answers and, for some reason, it surprises me that she extends her hand to shake mine.

I take it and give her a warm smile. "It's nice to officially meet you, Riley."

"You too, Kennedy."

We stand in awkward silence for a few seconds, but my sandwich is ready before I know it.

"Thanks," I say before turning around and making a home in the booth furthest from the counter in the darkest, most-ignored corner of the cafe.

During my time at the temple, I researched a lot of different online Bible studies. I completed a few short ones that gave me a good overview of the gospels that I felt I was lacking, along with some of the smaller books in the Bible that I've found quite interesting. I don't have fully formed opinions on *why* I find certain things interesting... I just do. I pull out my journal and Bible to continue in the study I've been working on this week and take a deep breath. I don't know what's going to happen with Matt, or this reality show thing, or any of it. But for now I have a meditative focus on God's word, and I can handle that.

My respite in spiritual solitude is short-lived, however, when I spot Roland and Dean Hershel Baker, along with some other members of the faculty I only barely recognize, walk into the cafe. I shift my position slightly and slink down just far enough to hopefully remain being unseen while still being able to see them. I put in my earbuds, open my laptop to join the "apple orchard," and set my journal and Bible to the side. This way I can better conceal my staring. Hopefully.

Nobody seems to be smiling, which isn't out of character for Dean Baker, but is very much so for my dad. He looks overly professional even in his current choice of a casual suit. It's the coat, I think. Black, which he almost never wears. He never preaches with a suit coat on, and doesn't even teach class in one as far as I know, but he's in one right now. And a red silk tie against a shirt of the same color. I bet he's dying of discomfort. The group of four men and two women sit at a round table not too far from the right of me. They choose a table behind me, which I'm grateful for as I casually knock out one of my earbuds to better eavesdrop.

"Have you guys come up with the list of students you're going to ask to participate in this documentary?" Roland's sarcasm is quite evident as he says *documentary*. He's no fool. *Jesus Freaks* will either be a completely boring watered-down version of CU as curated by the university to help their PR image, or it will be an absolute freak show as curated by the network. The network almost always wins.

"We have," a soft-spoken woman answers. "But you know as well as we do that our suggestions are next to no good if we can't produce Kennedy."

Produce Kennedy? Like a dragon's head on the sword of a prince?

"I've told you over and over again that besides the many reasons for that not being a good idea in my opinion, I don't think you're going to get her to do it. She's kind of had enough media attention for one lifetime." Roland sounds bored, but my chest warms hearing him speak on my behalf. I bite my lower lip, enjoying the comfort of my lip ring—knowing in a few short weeks I'll have to part with it yet again.

Dean Baker slithers into the conversation. "That daughter of yours is going to have a lot more media attention than she ever bargained for, what with you as her father, and if she chooses to return to Carter. If Carter will have her back, that is."

I clench my teeth and roll my eyes at the same time. It's a complicated set of emotions I hold for this pile of a man. He's *so* icky it sends chills down my spine. And I don't even know the basis for having such a feeling despite his having that creepy vibe about him that would beg me to cross the street if I saw him walking in my direction and I didn't know him. Frankly, I'd probably do that anyway.

"She *is* returning, isn't she?" another gentleman asks. I don't recognize his voice.

"Folks," Roland starts, sounding diplomatic, "I don't know her definite plans. I do hope she chooses to finish what she started here at CU, but I also know her welcome at this university hasn't been a warm one. I wouldn't blame her if she chose to attend one of the several Ivy League schools vying for her attention." I grin as he slightly overstates my prospects.

"I think what Dean Baker is trying to say," someone else chimes in, "is that the whole deal is more likely to go our way if Kennedy *was* involved. Perhaps you could... persuade her of the benefits of her involvement."

"Which for *her* would be..." Roland challenges, and I have to sit on my hands for a second to prevent myself from fist bumping the air.

"An opportunity to present a unique side of Carter University," the soft-spoken woman answers.

Little does she know how right she could be, if editing weren't involved. I'd love to be able to show the Carter I see, but I'm sure no one would go for that—Jesus Freak or otherwise.

"Just please think it over, talk with Kennedy, and get back to us?" the other woman who I can't see pleads. I make a mental note that no one was able to give Roland a single benefit to *me* for agreeing to join the show.

Maybe it's already been discussed? Is Roland holding out on me?

The conversation shifts awkwardly to the nuts and bolts of logistics. Rules the school has, requirements NBC has based on wants and the needs surrounding the production of something of this nature. I'm perfectly still for several minutes, not wanting to miss a thing, and needing to remain hidden.

The sound of chairs scratching against the floor clues me into the meeting's abrupt end.

"I will," Roland concedes as everyone heads to the door. I can just make them out in my peripheral vision. Just before I'm about to turn around, though, I hear Roland continue his conversation with someone else. Someone who stuck around. "What are you after?" His tone is chillingly unlike him. Dark and commanding.

The slithering voice returns. "We both know you're going to have Kennedy on this show. It will benefit you *both* greatly."

"Baker, I don't know what it is you *think* you have on me, but there's nothing there. Not liking me isn't enough. Especially not now. And, *especially* not if this show gets on the air. In general I'm pretty well liked, which is more than I can say for you. I'd think carefully about my demands if I were you."

My jaw slacks open as I hear what I assume is Roland give a firm pat on Dean Baker's arm or shoulder before I watch him walk confidently out of the cafe with the dean following quite slowly behind. I crane my neck and see them take off in different directions. Roland in the direction of Word, and Dean Baker the exact opposite. I briefly wonder if Roland is trekking to Word to see if I'm still there talking with Asher, but I decide to just let all that I heard sink in. And I'm still kind of ticked at Asher anyway, so I won't be galloping gleefully into Word again today.

I'd think carefully about my demands if I were you...

I knew Roland didn't care for Dean Baker. Who does? But I'm oddly relieved to hear him speaking more like a human annoyed with something. I obviously never have had delusions of Roland being a white knight, all things considered, but I know and understand why he's well-liked and respected. He's real. And that's what I respect most of all.

Between Asher, Matt, and whatever that "think tank" meeting was, I shake my head and am determined to use the rest of my afternoon in quiet study time. Bible study. This is not something that ever interested me previous to my time at the Buddhist temple, but during the *very* long quiet hours there, I found solace in C.S. Lewis. From there, I began reading whatever I could get my hands on.

The library at the temple did have a variety of books on many different religious traditions, Christianity included. Not many, but enough that it kept me busy for a while. I decided I should turn to the Bible after I read a couple of books of opposing opinions. While I recognize that wars have been fought and countries created and destroyed over two people feeling they're a hundred percent correct in their interpretation of the Bible, I figure I can at least take a stab at it even for the sake of intellectual exercise.

I typically orient myself to face away from the door to avoid looking up each time the door opens, because I've always been insanely curious about people, which can be distracting. But I didn't move after Roland left, which means that as soon as Matt walks into the cafe and looks directly at me, I'm looking right back at him.

And there's nowhere to hide this time.

CHAPTER SIX

PLEASE

Matt.

S HE looks good. She seems a bit paler, and maybe a little thinner than usual, but she's still her. All of her. No matter what she's been through in the last couple of months, Kennedy's retained all of her feisty personality, and maybe even become a little more of herself. It's clear in her eyes and the way she flings her hair over her shoulder, looking down like she doesn't care to talk to me. She probably doesn't.

I can't go talk to her, what was I thinking? One swoop of my eyes from her long hair down her deep green sleeveless shirt and long, black skirt is enough to send my heart racing and my hands tingling.

She'll never talk to you. Not after all this time. Not after all you've done.

I decide to go with humor as I shakily approach a startled-looking Kennedy in the farthest booth in the room. "Bible, journal, *and* highlighters? You're really going for it, huh?"

My poor attempt to break the ice falls flat. She simply looks back to her writing. I force my trembling hand to gesture to the seat across from her. "May I?"

Kennedy's wide eyes shoot up to mine. I don't know what to expect, but she nods. So, I sit. She returns to whatever she's doing, not giving me a second look. The tops of her cheeks are a little red, but other than that, I see no sign that she's registered my presence. Or accepts it. All except for the silver ring on her lip that she sucks into her mouth. That's my open window. Her anxious quirk.

"Titus?" I remark, peering across the table into her Bible.

"Looks that way," she mumbles.

"Why?" I don't think I've ever been in such an awkward conversation in all my life, sexual counseling included. The back of my neck is on fire.

Kennedy sighs, sets down her pen, and lowers the top of her laptop slightly. "What do you want, Matt?" Her disinterest is obvious in the crossing of her arms. I still take the time to admire her eyes. They're always working on something. She quickly looks away, as if she's somehow onto me.

I shift in my seat and try to meet her gaze, but she's clearly more interested in pretending to study the cheap Americana art above my head.

Johnny's Diner. An American institution since 1952. Grab a Coke!

"I... I just want to talk to you."

At this, those eyes bore into me. "How does it feel?" she says just under her breath. I deserve it, but I'm not going to take total blame.

"You disappeared for months," I accuse, ignoring all the "I" statements my counselor tells me to use.

"Oh *please*," she spits back.

Her face screws up in that way I recognize from what feels like a lifetime ago in the dining hall. Usually when someone talks about politics or how to be a submissive girlfriend and wife. Her eyebrows are scrunched, lips pursed, and nostrils slightly flared.

"You knew *exactly* where I was," she continues. "And, even if you didn't, I'm sure Roland would have let you tag along in a second. Don't you dare come here and guilt *me* for *disappearing.* You disappeared from me long before either of us actually went anywhere."

I hate how smart she is sometimes. I do. And I don't mean book smart. I mean socially. Nothing gets past her. She's much more socially aware than I am, and that intimidates me. So, I decide to cut through all the bull she'd call me on eventually anyway.

Lowering my shoulders, I lean forward so she's the only one who can hear me. "Kennedy," I whisper. "I'm so sorry."

She gasps. "What? What did you just say?" she whispers back.

I've been instructed to forgive those I feel that have done wrong to me, and I'm working on that. But I feel it in my bones that if I'm ever going to have a second shot in this life, I need to get this girl to forgive *me.* I go all in, reaching across the table and taking her hand, noting that her palms are as sweaty as mine.

"Forgive me, two, three," I say, slowly, giving her hand a squeeze, hoping that our inside joke about CU-approved hugs from millions of months ago appeals to her heart.

I watch goosebumps crop up from her wrists to her shoulders and shoot across her chest. Moving my eyes to her face, I watch her chin quiver as her eyes fill with tears.

"Please," I beg, giving her hand another squeeze. "Please, I need you to forgive me, Kennedy. You're the only person who ever believed in me to begin with. *Please.*" I hardly feel emasculated begging for her forgiveness. I need a friend. No, it's so much more than that. I need *her.*

She swallows hard, lifting her eyes to the ceiling as a few tears roll down her cheeks. After a few agonizing seconds, she looks at me, no longer working to conceal the tears washing her face. She shakes her hand free of mine and slides out of the booth, sending my heart into my throat.

This is it, I fear. This is the absolute end of whatever we have. Forever.

Standing in front of me, Kennedy reaches for my hand and gives it a tug, forcing me to slide out of the booth and stand, too, facing her.

"Kennedy," I say once more, knowing I've probably already run out of time with her. "*Please.*"

Before I can say anything else, she wraps her arms around my neck, pressing her body tightly against mine as she rises onto her toes, and I feel her warm breath against my cheek.

"I forgive you, two, three..." she whispers.

And for the next few seconds, all is right in my world.

CHAPTER SEVEN

YOUR GRACE FINDS ME

Kennedy.

I DON'T know how grace works. I've been reading about it all summer—studying it, really—but there are no definitive answers. It's like asking someone to prove love. You just *feel* it. I feel it over Matt and me right now. He had the grace to forgive me enough to ask me to forgive him, and I accepted it. I don't think I need much grace to hold him against me and hug the crap out of him, but I'll take it anyway. I almost don't want this hug to end, because I'm afraid it just might be a dream. One from which I never want to wake. One where Matt and I can pick up right where we left off.

Alas, our hug is bordering on pornographic according to CU standards, and we both pull away after fifteen glorious seconds. The equivalent of five CU—approved hugs. We have a lot of catching up to do.

"Sit," I say, gesturing to the spot he stood from. "Just kidding." I stop him and yank on his hand once more, pulling him into another hug.

Two, three, four, five...

I could stay here all day. I almost say that out loud, but instead I let us just sit, like normal people.

"So," I start, followed by a horrendously nervous laugh. "Sorry. Is this real? I don't... what is this?" I ask, gesturing between us.

He tilts his head to the side and I search his eyes for something cold. Something like the Matt I last saw months ago. But it's not there. Sure, brokenness still flickers through, but I'm beginning to realize that it sits in all of us. The brokenness. None of us are completely whole, ever. And too many of us spend decades trying to fill those cracks and holes. Right now, I just see something like humility in his eyes. In the fertile soil of forgiveness that is their color.

"Matt?" I ask, beginning to wonder if he's going to disappear into a cloud of smoke like this has all been a dream.

"Sorry," he finally says, breaking into a grin. "It's real. Yes. I'm—"

"Still angry at me for involving your dad, right?" I wonder if I should have said it at all, and risk destroying this reconciliation. But we *have* to talk about it, right?

He bows his head for a second. "Kennedy..."

I reach my hand across the table and set it on his folded hands. "I need to know where I went wrong. I don't want to hurt you like this again, Matt."

"You can't think that you did anything wrong. Do you think that?" His eyebrows are furrowed as he studies my face.

I huff. "Of course I don't think I did anything wrong," I admit. "I was scared and you were just..."

"A mess."

I sit back and start waving my hands in a way that would make my high school public speaking teacher cringe. "Listen. I come from a society where we dissect and discuss and resolve our feelings. And if they're not resolved we talk, and talk, and talk some more. And if it's *still* not resolved, someone sends us to therapy."

He nods. "Prayer, prayer, prayer, counseling, God, and prayer over here," he says, pointing to himself.

I twist my lips. "Maybe we could be renegades and decide to just put this behind us and move forward?"

Relief washes over his face as his shoulders relax. "Nothing would make me happier."

"Okay," I say.

"But first," he says, reaching across the table and extending his hand. I quickly set mine in his. "I need you to know that you did *nothing* wrong. You did everything right. It's not your fault that I'm angry. It's not your fault that I have issues with my dad, Kennedy. You were trying to be helpful. You were being a friend." He gives my hand a squeeze and I wish we could sit like this forever, but he soon pulls back and folds his arms on the table in front of him.

My mouth, as I remind myself any time I can, tends to run away with me. I know this about myself and really need to focus on taming it. This is one of many tests I've faced in this area. I'm going to let the past go here, and truly focus on a future friendship with Matt.

"So," I redirect our conversation. "The prison ministry, huh?"

A slow grin forms on his face. "Don't blame Asher. Your dad suggested it. But I think that was before you came back. You *are* back, right?"

I tilt my head to the side. "Are you? You look back, but are you?"

He nods slowly. "I'm getting there."

"Counseling?"

"Yeah." He looks down for a split second.

"Is it as awful as the stories on the Internet? I've read blogs about Christian college counseling. Do they ask you *way* personal questions?" I read that they sometimes ask guys how often they're... pleasuring... themselves. I can't even imagine how that's possibly relevant.

"Yep," he confirms.

"Do you actually answer? Honestly?"

He lets out a loud laugh. One I haven't heard in a long time. "No. Just... no. Please don't ask me for more details."

I put my hands up. "Wasn't gonna." I take a sip of water, enjoying just being *with* him.

Matt leans forward a little, a playful rasp working its way through his voice like he's on a 1950s crime show. "Word on the street," he says, "is that the only reason you're coming back to CU is because of the show."

I chuckle with a mouthful of water, which causes me to cough and sputter for a couple of seconds. "What friggen street? What word? And who says I'm coming back?" I challenge.

"You *are* coming back, aren't you?" His eyes beg for an answer.

I look around, a new paranoia of seeing who might be eavesdropping. I nod. "But shh. I haven't told my mom yet. She knows I'm coming back, like, in her heart, but she doesn't know about the show yet. *Yet.* God help us all when she finds out."

"How has she *not* heard about it?" Matt looks genuinely surprised.

I shrug. "She ignores as much about CU as possible nowadays. Unless I tell her, she pretends none of it is happening. Besides, she's been oddly active in political campaigns this summer."

"Oddly?"

"Yeah. She's a lobbyist, so she's always kind of involved, but in the last couple of months she's spent more and more time volunteering for someone I think she's hoping will toss their hat into the ring for Democratic candidacy."

"Who?" Matt questions. "The Republican race is really heating up. There's something planned for the start of the school year."

I arch an eyebrow. "Here? Like what?"

"Some candidate that wants the young conservative vote, of course," Matt says with a grin.

"You don't know which one?"

He shakes his head. "It's all speculation."

"Give me a sec." I pull my phone out of my bag and dial my mom's number.

"Hey, Babycakes," she answers playfully. "How are you settling in?"

"Good. I'm sitting with Matt, and we're ta—"

"Wells?" she interrupts.

"Yes."

"That's new."

I nod. "Yep."

"Is it okay?" she asks, honestly.

I feel my cheeks turn red. "So far. I guess..." Matt looks at me curiously, but I wave my hand to dismiss speculation of my sudden blush.

"Want me to stop now?"

"Please." I chuckle and sigh in relief at the same time. "Anyway, Matt says that the *word on the street* is that some conservative potential presidential candidate might have some event or something here at Carter at the beginning of the semester." Matt sticks his tongue out at me for stealing his previous turn of phrase.

"Yeah..." Mom draws out. "Who?"

"Neither of us know, and nothing's been posted on the school's website. I was hoping you had some inside information on that."

She sighs for a long few second. "Well I *do* have some information, but probably not the kind you're looking for."

"Oh?" My voice rises at the end of the word, piquing Matt's interest. He leans forward, arms crossed on the table.

"Do you remember meeting Elizabeth Baldwin?"

Thankfully I'm sitting in front of my computer and can quickly Google her.

"Yes," I answer with confidence. "At the pro-choice rally in Boston a couple years ago, right?"

Matt looks fully confused now, so I turn my computer toward him and let him read Liz Baldwin's Wikipedia page while I talk to my mom. I study his face while he reads, watching as his teeth slowly work against the inside of his lip. I'm not sure if he's against what he's reading, for it, or simply uncomfortable. We agreed almost a year ago that we wouldn't talk politics and, technically, we're not. He's reading, and I'm talking to my mom.

"What about her?" I ask. "Is she actually running for president?"

Mom takes a deep breath. "You've not been following the news at all, have you?"

"There wasn't a single TV in the temple, Mom. I've been blissfully unaware."

"Or ignorant," she teases.

"Either way," I concede.

"Yes, she's running for president. Officially. The fall will be pre-primary campaigning ahead of the Iowa caucus in January."

"Hmm," I say. "That explains the rumor of a candidate hopping over here, I guess. Mom? You there?" She's uncharacteristically quiet.

She hesitates for a few seconds before speaking. "I'm going to be working on Liz's campaign full time," she blurts out. "She's asked me to manage her campaign."

"Really?" I yelp. "That's so exciting! It's something you've always wanted to do!" While my mom's always been active in local efforts for presidential campaigns, she's never been able to take on the full time requirements of campaign manager. She's spent a lot of time in Washington over the years, sure, but most of her lobbying efforts were centered on the state level so she could keep her family in Connecticut but do the job she loved.

"I'm thrilled you're excited," she finally says.

"You sound relieved."

"This is going to be very time consuming, Kennedy. Exciting and challenging, yes. What I've always wanted? Yes. But time consuming nonetheless. And public. Very. Public."

She says the words deliberately. Slowly. And, as they sink in, so does my stomach.

"Oh... right."

"What is it?" Matt whispers, looking half excited and half panicked.

I hold up my index finger as my mind races.

"Are you okay with this?" she asks, sounding sincere.

I swallow hard. "Of course, Mom. Don't be ridiculous. This is your, like, life dream."

"You're my life dream, Kennedy."

She's not normally this sentimental, and it makes me a little uncomfortable. Not in a bad way, just... we're not typically all out-in-the-open emotional. "I know," I say. "I just mean..."

"I know what you meant. I just want you to know that my priority always has been, and always will be *you*. I know you didn't get to choose Roland being in the spotlight. Or you being there."

Her words remind me that I need to tell her sooner than later about the reality show plans. "Mom..." I start, hesitantly.

"I don't know if I like the sounds of that *Mom*," she admits.

I decide to say it all in one breath, with Matt watching me closely. I whisper. "This is all top secret for now, and nothing definite. And I just found out a few days ago but I haven't seen or heard anything technically official..." *Besides Roland going a few rounds with CU admins about it.*

"Way to be vague and freak me out," Mom says with brewing urgency.

"NBC and CU are working on a deal for a reality docu-series about the lives of students in evangelical America."

As expected the other end is dead silent. I give her a few seconds.

"I haven't been asked to sign on, but I expect to be. Roland suspects so, too. Well, he's expected to sign on himself and he suspects that they'll ask me." I just let all the information hang out there, while Matt stares at me with wide, interested eyes.

"You're going to do it," she says as if it's a fact. "You've decided already, haven't you?"

I click my tongue against my teeth. "What are you even talking about?"

"You would have called me right away if you were for sure not going to do it. Outraged at such an idea. You might be growing and changing, Kennedy, but I *know* you. You haven't told me about it in the last few days because you've been mulling it over. And you sound calm."

"And you don't sound surprised at all that the unspoken thing in all of this is that I'm returning to CU for the fall."

Matt leans back against the booth and puffs out his cheeks as he exhales, feeling the tension in even half a conversation.

Mom's voice softens. "I think we both knew that."

"Yeah," I agree. "We did."

With Matt listening on, I take a few minutes to explain to my mom the reasons why I am, in fact, considering participation in the series. All the reasons I told Roland. Maybe I can be loud enough to encourage an honest look at some of the really amazing people here and keep attention away from the things I personally hate. Maybe I can just take the heat off of some of my friends. Maybe this just sounds like a ridiculously fun idea. It *is* TV, after all. What teenager wouldn't want to be on TV?

Me.

"Let's both just sleep on all of this," she says once I've finished. "We've given each other a *lot* of information today, and before we start slathering our opinions over one another, let's just... sleep on it."

I grin, feeling the tension in my shoulders release. "How PC of you."

"Well," she sighs wistfully, "I need the practice."

I laugh, realizing that despite the strong convictions it takes to run a political campaign, hotheadedness needs to take a backseat on the public stage. She's got a bit of work ahead of her there I think.

"Oh, Kennedy?" She asks just before I hang up. "Don't tell Roland any of this yet, okay? You, Jenny, and Dan are the only ones who know. And your grandfather of course."

"Uh... okay."

Absentmindedly, I realize it's been weeks and weeks since I've talked to my stepsister, Jenny. She's in medical school, and very busy, but I'd be lying if I said I hadn't avoided her calls once or twice. She can be a bit... much, sometimes. Even more so than my mother. The fact that she's Jewish and annoyingly hardheaded makes discussions about my choice of school a dead end street. She's liberal like I am, and she made it clear early on that my choosing to go to a school with extremists in my faith was negligent and borderline dangerous. She lumps all conservative Christians into the right-wing extremist category. In all honesty, I used to, too. This is one thing I'm hoping *Jesus Freaks* will at least attempt to accomplish—getting people to listen. But, I realize, that is likely a pipe dream.

Can't blame a girl for trying...

Mom's voice brings me back. "I just don't want to say anything until it's official."

I shrug. "No problem. Don't tell anyone about the show yet, okay? Until it's, you know, official."

She laughs. "Deal."

Setting the phone down, I take the last bite of my sandwich, long since gone cold, and look at Matt.

"How'd... all of that go?" he asks, lifting his eyebrows.

I sigh. "Matt, I have a feeling that things aren't going to get easier for me anytime soon."

He chuckles. "Just catching onto that, are you?"

I grin, thanking God by the second that things feel easy with him again.

"Wanna get out of here?" He asks. "Go for a walk and talk about it?"

"I'd love that," I answer with a rush of warmth surging through my chest.

Clearing my tray, I make eye contact with Riley, who is cleaning off a table to my right. I'm compelled to talk to her again.

"Bye, Riley," I say brightly.

She seems startled, but offers a smile and a wave. Peering over my shoulder, her eyes settle on Matt. "Hey you. I haven't seen you around in a while. Behaving yourself?"

Now it's Matt's turn to look startled. "Oh, hi. Yeah, you know, gotta get in shape for football."

"It's okay," I offer. "I'll eat his extra bacon next time."

As Matt and I escape into the hot summer air, I make sure the door is closed before I speak.

Hitching my thumb back to the deli/cafe, renamed "Butcher Block" since last semester, I whisper, "That's the girl Eden and Bridgette were talking to at Planned Parenthood last year. Did you know that? Or does she just know you from getting your feedbag on all summer?"

He shoves his hands in his pockets and shrugs. "Just from here, I guess. I'm sure she was wrapped up with the three of you on the sidewalk that day. If you remember correctly I tried to stay just slightly out of the line of fire."

I laugh. "Yes, and how chivalrous of you, indeed."

"Sorry," he mumbles, looking down.

"Shhh," I start to say the curse, but stop myself. "Shoot," I say louder, linking my arm through Matt's. "I'm sorry, Matt. I didn't mean to, like, bring anything up, like... I don't think you're less of a gentleman because of—"

He cuts me off. "No, no. It's not you. It's me. I've been working in counseling on some of the selfish behaviors I've been using as a... protective measure against getting hurt."

We didn't discuss where we were going to walk, but we both seemed to be heading to the trail we've walked on together many times before. The one that winds from downtown Asheville, up around the west side of CU, behind Roland's house, and disappears into the mountains.

"That's... honest of you," I admit.

"Yeah." He sighs. "I don't know how or why you bring that out of me." He shakes his arm free of mine and puts his hand back in his pocket.

"Oh... sorry," I say without really knowing what it is I'm sorry for, especially since I'm the one who feels suddenly abandoned without his thick arm around mine.

He shakes his head as we enter the trail. "It's not you," he tries to sound reassuring.

I don't say anything for a minute or two as we navigate the roots and loose rocks of the trail. Just ahead is the large boulder we've sat on before. Tucked just off the main trail, I nod in its direction and climb up, motioning for him to do the same.

"If it's not me, then what is it? I just want to know how to make things easier for you, Matt. If you're going to let me be your friend again—"

"*Let* you?" he cuts me off. "Geez, Kennedy. I'm so sorry I screwed us up so bad. I'm grateful you even let *me* talk to *you*."

I'm taken back and confused by his honestly, and I say so. "What? You were the one mad at me. I was never mad at you, Matt. God, you could have walked up to me a year from now and I'd have still let you sit with me. I'll always save you a seat, okay?"

"I was a jerk. Your forgiveness is incredible." He shrugs and looks at me out of the corner of his eye. "But, we shouldn't sit here for too long. Rules..." he says regarding alone time of mixed-gender couples in CU.

"It's summer," I remind him, sliding off the rock. He follows and falls in step with me.

He shrugs. "My rules though, too."

I stop. "What? What are you talking about?"

"Can we keep walking?" he asks. "It'll be easier for me to get through this if we're not staring at each other."

Without a word, I turn and continue north on the trail.

"I got into a really bad place over the last year," he starts. "I was so angry and resentful at my father, yet I found comfort in the same things that nearly broke up our entire family. I mean... it started out as just wanting to see what all the fuss was about—what was so great to risk your family for. But I just... loved it," he admits through a strained voice. "And I'm so ashamed about that."

"I get it, I think," I say. "It's like with Roland being a recovering alcoholic. I've always known that about him, even before I met him. My mom always cautioned me about alcohol because addiction is a disease and it can run in families..."

"Have you ever been drunk?" Matt asks.

I shake my head. "I've never had anything to drink," I admit. "At parties and stuff someone will hand me a cup and mostly I just walk around with it or pretend to drink from it. I just don't want to go down that road, I guess."

"How come you never told me that?" He stops and leans against a tree.

I shrug. "It's never come up. I mean, there aren't many parties around here where you'd have a chance to see me work my fake-drinking magic." I chuckle and so does he.

"How do you stay away from it?" He looks down and I sense the basis of his questioning.

Walking over to him, I speak softly. "From a very early age I had a healthy respect for what addiction could do to a person. It took my dad away before he had a chance to do the kind of damage your dad did. It's always been a part of my story. For you it came out of nowhere. And... you're a guy. Sexual experimentation is kind of part of the drill, isn't it? It's not like you knew if your dad was a sex addict or if you'd become one."

Matt's gaze shoots to mine. "I didn't call myself a sex addict," he snaps.

"Sorry," I say, taking a step forward to continue our walk. "I didn't mean—"

"No," he says, catching up with me. "I mean, you're right. But I didn't say that. How'd you know?"

"I know addiction," I reiterate.

He stops me in the middle of the trail and puts his hands on my shoulders. "Kennedy, I haven't had sex, though. It's just the general term. I guess I'm more of a porn addict, but the strip club stuff and the inappropriate fantasies..."

I honestly can't believe he's being so transparent with me. I'm grateful, and I don't want to say too much at the risk of clamming him up.

"It's okay," I whisper placing my hands over his. "We've all got... crap to deal with."

He starts walking again and I follow him this time. "I just want you to know I've never had sex is all."

"Okay." I shrug. "I believe you, you know. Though I don't know why you *need* me to know that."

"Because I need to hold onto a shred of integrity," he admits sheepishly. He's quiet for a few seconds—just my breathing and the birds filling the silence in my head—before he continues. "That's why I can't date anyone right now. Not for a long time. I'm too screwed up."

Not this again.

My stomach sinks a little at the speech he's heading into. My rational mind didn't even expect Matt to talk to me anytime soon, let alone date me. But I'd be lying if I didn't admit that falling into our old ways so easily with him at Butcher Block didn't ignite that old, hopeful feeling in my chest.

The one where Matt picks me.

"Matt," I start, but he cuts me off.

"Just listen, okay? I turned you down last semester because I told you that I wasn't good enough for you. I thought that because of all the behavior I was trying to hide from you. I didn't want you to find me out." He pauses to grin for a split second. "I guess I didn't know you as well as I thought I did. You're intuitive. What I'm trying to say is I'm *not* good enough for you. I'm not good enough for *anyone*. But, it's not because of all the crap that I'm ashamed of, it's because of the person I'm working to be and I'm not. Yet."

I stop because I need to take a breath. Not from physical exertion, but emotional. I can be Matt's friend. He's my best friend. I just hope this doesn't go down a road where he can't have any girls as friends period because I won't stand for it.

"What are you getting at?" I ask, looking down.

I almost fall apart as his index finger touches my chin and he lifts my face to meet his eyes. "I've got a lot of healing to do from all the junk I've seen and done in the last year, Kennedy. And stuff to work out with my dad. I need you to be my friend, but we need to be careful. I'm not good with boundaries here. I'll either push you away like I did last time, or I'll want too much from you, whether or not I actually want a relationship. I just need friends right now, okay?"

His finger hasn't moved from my face, and I feel like I haven't taken a breath in minutes. I nod slowly. "Okay."

Matt's eyes glisten for a split second. The sunny day reflects brighter in those deep, dark eyes of his. Quite the contrast. He's a contrast. I want to grab his face and kiss him and tell him everything will be fine and he's fine, but I can't. He still looks so vulnerable.

"I've pushed so many people away in the last year and I'm trying to rebuild those relationships." He takes a deep breath. "But right now my focus is on getting my heart and soul right before God. If I can't do that, I'm toast. I need friends, K. Sawyer. You'll still be my friend, right?"

I nod again, running low on oxygen and emotional energy. His face relaxes and he doesn't fight when I pull him into a hug.

"I promise," I whisper. "I'll always be your friend."

Two, three...

CHAPTER EIGHT

UNBELIEF

Kennedy.

"T HAT is some *heavy* stuff," Eden says, filling her mouth with a forkful of pancakes.

"I know," I agree, after filling her in on my conversation with Matt. "So is the fact that you're sitting here in Roland's house with me!"

A couple days after my walk in the woods with Matt, Eden showed up on Roland's doorstep, surprising me with news that she got wind of my joining Asher's prison ministry for the remainder of the summer and decided to sign up, too. She's staying in dorms designed for students doing local volunteer or missions work during the summer, which means she'll be spending most of her time with me at Roland's house because dorms aren't the most exciting place to be.

It's Sunday morning, and we're set to start work with Asher tomorrow. But first, church. I've slacked on church services in the last several months, and even since I've been back in Asheville—which is only one Sunday, but it still feels weird. So, today Eden is accompanying me to New Life's ten a.m. service.

During the school year, all my friends and I would always sit together anyway, but I have no concept of what the make-up of the church is when CU isn't in session. I'm glad Eden's here. I suppose I could have sat with Roland's assistant, Jahara, but I'm pretty sure she doesn't like me all that much. I'm sure I wouldn't like me if I was a part-time publicist, either, since I'm kind of a PR nightmare. But, that's not really my fault or problem right now.

"Stop trying to change the subject," Eden accuses, swallowing her last piece of bacon. "How are you *really* feeling about all this Matt stuff?"

I huff and set down my fork. "First of all, you have to *promise* me you're not going to tell anyone *any* of this."

She holds up her hand. "You know I promise."

I didn't use the term *sex addict* with Eden, because if my search through the Internet is accurate, that's a pretty divisive term. Incidentally, I've seen it used more frequently and honestly on faith-based sites than secular ones, but I refuse to assume I know which side Eden will fall on. I simply revealed the basics of his struggle and that he's not dating. She's my best friend. I have to talk about this with someone. Someone who will understand.

"I don't know how I'm feeling," I admit. "I did a lot of Internet research on all of this over the last few days and... is it really common for people not to date at all until they're looking to be married?"

Eden nods. "Don't you remember the conversation at the beginning of last year with Bridgette? People take courtship to mean different things, but there's a growing number of people who think it's best to wait as long as possible to date, if not until you're ready to be married then definitely as long as possible."

"I get it," I say, hesitantly. "I get that what's different here from the way I grew up is that where I come from people seem to get into relationships as a stepping stone in the way they get to learn about themselves. From what I've seen, it seems like evangelical kids are encouraged to know themselves, know God, learn how to be the best partner, *then* go look for one." Eden nods as Roland rounds the corner, fixing his tie.

"Or," Roland butts in with a smile, "people could just *not* date at all."

"Yeah?" I challenge. "Like what people?"

He shrugs, still grinning, and pours himself some coffee. "People who are under twenty, living in my house, and biological offspring."

Eden falls into a fit of giggles while I roll my eyes. "Is eavesdropping biblical?" I challenge, taking mine and Eden's plates to the sink.

Roland puts his hand on my shoulder. "I'm just teasing you," he says. "But, I think it might be." He winks.

"How much did you hear?" I ask, nervously. I can't pretend Roland doesn't know all about what's going on with Matt from conversations with Matt's dad, Buck, but I promised Matt I'd be private about this.

He gives my shoulder a slight squeeze. "Just enough to remind me that we have to have a dating rules conversation sometime soon."

"Ew," I respond, wrinkling my nose.

Roland laughs. "I know. So ew. Come on, ladies, we've gotta head over."

Roland's house is on New Life property. It belongs to the church. So by "head over" he means walk two minutes.

"You're so weird," I comment, closing the front door behind us. "I thought priests and pastors and stuff got to church early to pray and stuff before the sermon."

"I pray here," Roland says. "I get nervous if I spend too much time there before the service starts."

"Really?" Eden says. "I never thought you'd get nervous over anything." Her knee-length navy blue dress has a pleated, flowy skirt covered in tiny white daisies that seem to twirl as she walks.

"Me either," I admit, glancing at my own attire. I follow the dress code, but plainly. I'm thinking I need to have Eden take me shopping where she goes, so I can find feminine clothes and not monastic garb.

Roland chuckles as we march toward New Life's massive structure. Cars are already filling the lot and we've got a half hour before the service starts.

"I'm only human," is the only thing he says for the rest of the walk.

"Spending time in the Word isn't an optional exercise," Roland says with fierce reverence as he stands at the podium. "Psalm one-nineteen tells us that the Word of God is a *lamp* for our feet and a *light* for our path..." he trails off and surveys the crowd with intense eyes. In a low, somber voice, he asks, "How many of you are wandering in the dark?"

Goosebumps.

I haven't really *listened* to many of Roland's sermons because I've often been analyzing both him and the things he says through the filter of my background. But today, I seem to have let my guard down and I've been listening. Hearing.

"How many of you," he continues, moving to the front of the "stage" and pacing slowly, "are lost?"

A host of *yes's* and *amen's* are heard throughout the full house. During the school year, New Life adds an eight a.m. service in addition to its ten o'clock one to accommodate the overflow produced by the students. While both services are typically full, today's single service is almost standing-room only

"Isaiah forty tells us that even the grass withers, and the flowers fail. But do you know what endures forever? The Word of *God*. Friends, tomorrow there are a group of students from Carter that will be starting a four-week volunteer mission with Rays of Hope prison ministry. They need to have the Word before them and behind them in order to share their gifts and the heart of Jesus with all the people they'll be coming into contact with."

"Amen," a few people call out.

If we're going to be expected to evangelize, this is news to me. Asher said he was putting me to work with the prison's literacy program. Unless someone happens to be reading a Bible, I hadn't planned on discussing what little of scripture I know.

Roland picks up his pace across the floor. His smile widens, as do his eyes. He's always in the zone but he seems particularly passionate this morning. "Church, I'm going to ask you to pray for these kids. They've chosen to give up part of their summer to reach out to prisoners. Drug addicts, violent offenders, and prostitutes. Sounds like Jesus' kind of crowd doesn't it?" At this, the congregation hoots, hollers, and chuckles. And my stomach sinks. "What an opportunity they have!" he exclaims before walking back to the lectern.

"But," Roland continues with a heavy sigh. "While we must pray for these kids to be rooted in the Word. To have God go before them to light their path and to guard their backs, we must also think of those students who have backslidden, or are backsliding. It can happen throughout the year, of course, but we all well know that for the college population, summer is a time of freedom. For some it means complete freedom from the guidelines CU offers. Freedom from structure. Some students can handle that, having developed a strong relationship with God through their time on campus. For some... for some it means they've thrown themselves to the wolves."

My eyes widen as I look to Eden, but she seems thoroughly engrossed in Roland's message. I take a quick look around and realize there's a group of suits in the front right-hand portion of the sanctuary taking careful notes. Both men and women, ages thirty to fifty would be my guess.

"Hey," I whisper to Eden, despite being in the second row right in front of Roland. "Do you think those are network people?" I nod in their direction.

Eden and I have only spoken in rumor-speak regarding the show. It's true that no one really knows anything that's going on for sure, but we know they've got to solidify plans over the next couple of weeks if they hope to catch all the back-to-school splendor.

She shrugs and whispers back, "Maybe. I don't recognize them."

One of them makes eye contact with me and offers a polite smile. I'm not convinced of its sincerity.

Because you've become increasingly paranoid over the last year.

"Of course I have," I whisper.

"Huh?" Eden asks, facing me with a confused look.

I stare at her for a few seconds before realizing she hadn't said anything to me. No one had. No one human, anyway.

"Nothing," I mumble, returning my attention to Roland.

"Keep praying for the students of CU," Roland implores to the crowd. "They are the next generation of disciples that will go out and make disciples. When the school year starts," Roland's tone shifts from urgent to softer in a split second, "I will resume the best part of my on campus work at CU, which is teaching a New Testament course. I get to have direct contact with students every single day. To preach the gospel constantly, and use words only when necessary."

That statement couldn't be more accurate. I've heard it before, but it perfectly describes Roland. Unless we're in a scripture-specific discussion or I'm listening to one of his sermons, I don't hear him going around proselytizing to anyone. Yet week after week, more and more students and community members walk through the doors of New Life to hear what this unique pastor has to say about Jesus Christ. It's beyond charisma, I'm coming to realize. It might just be what everyone around me refers to as being "filled with the Holy Spirit," but I don't know enough about that phrase just yet to let it slide into my vocabulary. Still, there is something remarkably enticing about this whole Jesus thing when you've got a guy like Roland presenting it to you. He makes it real. And, for some reason, that scares me.

What if none of this is real?

Lord, help my unbelief.

I gasp as a line of scripture comes into my head. I remember it so clearly from prayer sessions throughout last semester. There was this boy that a father brought to Jesus. He had "evil spirits" in him and the father wanted help. Jesus told him that anything is possible for those who believe. The father, desperately seeking help for his ailing son proclaimed, *"I do believe; help me overcome my unbelief!"*

The man was so sure of his belief for Jesus, yet also so aware of his sinful, human nature that he knew there were parts of him that didn't believe, even if he couldn't feel them in his heart. He knew unbelief lingered and he asked Jesus to cast it out.

"I spent a lot of time in the temple praying for Matt," I admit to Eden when the New Life worship band finishes their closing song.

She looks around as if I've spoken out of nowhere. "I'm glad. I think a lot of us have been praying for him."

"I know in my head and even in my heart that God can help him. He's really the only one to help him at this point.

And as I prayed, I asked God to clean the unbelieving parts of my heart that bred skepticism that any of this would work for him," I say, gesturing to our surroundings inside the church.

Eden leans forward and hugs me in the quick, tight way she's perfected. "That's awesome," she says, smiling broadly as her deep green eyes twinkle. I swear to you, they twinkle

"Ugh," I roll my eyes, "you're so *stunning*. Could you not be? For like a second?"

She laughs, linking her arm through mine. "Me?" she questions. "You. *You're* stunning. And sophisticated."

"Eden," I say dryly. "You're talking to a preacher's daughter who spent half the summer hiding in a Buddhist temple. Not so much the high point of sophistication, if you ask me."

She gives my arm a tug. "I'm dying to know what it was like. I would have freaked out."

I remain planted in my spot. "Freaked out? Why? It was the most peaceful place I've been in a *long* time."

"It's based on a polytheistic religion," she starts. "Even if they deny a God, Buddha himself held Hindu beliefs. They don't believe that Jesus is the way to salvation, they believe in reincarnation, and all kinds of levels of heaven and hell." She catches herself panting a little and takes a deep breath.

"You've... given this a lot of thought," I say, looking around at all the chatting people around us.

Eden grabs my forearm and gives it a small squeeze. "I had to know what you were up against once I knew where you were. I prayed like crazy for you, Kennedy."

I'm taken back by the fervent pitch in her voice. "Oh," I reply for lack of anything else to say. "Thank you. But... who told you where I was?"

"Your mom," she answers plainly. "But don't worry. I didn't tell anyone. Except Jonah, and he doesn't gossip anyway."

"Jonah?" I ask, surprised.

She nods. "He was really worried about you after you disappeared. I didn't want him failing finals or anything." She winks. "I think he likes you, you know."

I raise my eyebrows. "I think you're insane." Scanning the room, a familiar all-American face catches my attention.

"I'm not crazy," Eden demands. "I know a crush when I see it. I had one on him for over half my life."

"Jonah?" I say, mostly under my breath.

"Yes. Jonah," she says slowly as if I've gone dumb.

I playfully smack her shoulder. "No, fool. Look!" I point behind her to the worship band area. "It's Jonah!"

Once she catches up, Eden shares in my excitement and we nearly skip over to the band.

"Ah!" I shriek as I'm greeted with his smiling face and hug him. He gives me a tight squeeze back before hugging Eden. "What are you *doing* here?" I exclaim, breathlessly despite myself. "Are you doing the prison ministry, too?"

Jonah picks up his guitar and slings the strap over his head, fiddling with the strings, still smiling. "No. The band is actually here for the next few weeks to work with the New Life worship band for a while. We're all going to a conference next weekend on leading worship. They're going to go over what it means to be a worship band, how to incite the Holy Spirit through our music, all that …"

"Oh, where is it?" Eden asks.

"Nashville," he answers with a broad grin. "I think if they reach a deal with the reality show thing, a crew will film us a bit there," he says matter-of-factly.

I look around. "So does everyone just kind of know about this?"

Jonah's eyes light up. "It's huge. My parents are unsure, but they're unsure about everything nowadays, and I'm nineteen anyhow, so..."

I nod in approval. "Good for you."

He bites his lip a little, and I can't stop staring at his snug blue T-shirt. He either bought smaller shirts, or he's grown into himself and needs new ones.

He doesn't need new ones, I catch myself thinking dreamily.

"Are you in?" he asks, setting his guitar down and focusing on the conversation.

Eden elbows me. "She'll totally be in. Promise."

My mouth drops open. "Assume much?"

She rolls her eyes. "You're going to do it even if it's just to make a point."

I shrug. "I don't know if I can take much more crafty editing of my life on the national level," I say half-heartedly.

"Oh!" Eden calls out. "I see Iris. I've gotta talk to her about something. I'll catch up with you back at your dad's for lunch, okay?" She gives me a quick hug and prances off.

"Who the heck is Iris?" Jonah questions.

"A prospective roommate, I guess. Bridgette's parents requested a dorm switch before I fled, and I think Eden is okay with that. Bridgette's moving to a quiet hall anyway, which isn't really Eden's style."

Jonah tilts his head to the side. "Why doesn't she room with you? You're coming back, right?"

I grin. "Yeah," I admit with finality. "But I'm not too sure what my living situation will be. Especially if I agree to this TV foolishness. I might ask Roland if I can stay with him or something. I don't know..."

"Well, wherever you live, I'm glad you're staying. You were missed when you took off." He picks up his guitar again, keeping his eyes on me the whole time.

He's kinda perfect, now that I get a real good look at him. Here in the middle of my dad's church. I get what Eden was so over-the-moon about with this kid. He's picture-book perfect.

Romance book even, but I don't know if she's ever read any of those.

"I'm sorry I took off so fast," I stammer. "I was just really—"

"Scared?"

I nod. "Exactly. And my mom was *so* angry."

"So was your dad—Roland," he corrects himself.

I wave my hand. "You can just call him my dad. It's all good. I'm not the first gal in America to have two dads."

He laughs. "I guess. But he was really mad at whoever sent the pictures. Do you guys know who it was?"

I shake my head. "And I haven't theorized with him, either. I've got some ideas, but I don't even want to say them out loud until I have a shred of evidence above my paranoia."

"Wise," he says. Then, out of the blue, he blurts out, "Would you consider singing with us?"

"Huh?" I look around for a second to make sure he's talking to me.

"We only had one girl in the band, and she graduated in May. We considered making it an all-guy band—"

"Progressive," I tease.

He twists his lips but doesn't look wounded. Perhaps he'll get used to my sarcasm yet. "But the sound is off. I've heard you sing in church before. You can not only match pitch, but you've got the sound we need."

"I mean... I sang in chorus in high school but... wait you were spying on my voice? Scouting me out without me knowing?" My voice is high and pitchy. Sure, Jonah and I sit next to, or near each other but I didn't know he was *listening* to me.

Jonah reaches out and puts his hand on my wrist, looking me straight in the eyes only the way guys from CU can. Perfect, respectful eye contact at all times. "You're excellent. Come rehearse with us. You can see if you like us, if we like you... all that."

"*Now?*" I blurt out ungracefully.

He laughs. "You strike me as kind of a fly-by-the-seat-of-your-pants sort of girl."

I twist my lips in a wicked grin. "I don't think you're supposed to have an opinion about my pants."

"Come on," he says again, blushing fiercely. "Just do it."

This feels like flirting. I think. Oh, Lord, I don't know...

I allow my lips to part slightly. "Jonah Cross, is this some bizarre form of peer pressure I'm detecting?"

"It's for *Jesus*," he whispers, his mouth morphing into a Disney-esque Prince Charming smile.

"Nice," I reply dryly. "Really nice. Bring *Him* into this. When do you guys usually practice during the semester?" I ask, because apparently I've lost my mind and am actively considering his absurd proposal.

"Saturday nights." I make a face and he looks nervous. "What?" he asks.

I shake my head. "Just... not the college weekends I had planned in my mind... but you know what? I think I'm okay with that."

I received about a dozen "hungover" text messages from Mollie last year. At first I was annoyed that I couldn't share the experience with her since I don't know what it's like to be hung over, but especially after researching statistics about what college life *can* be like with rape and overdoses and all, I'm thinking I'm okay with not being put in that position. Although, the thought of the group against Dean Baker I met with last semester comes to mind. Caitlyn's sister being raped while she was a student at CU is never far from my memory, and I need to get more information on the circumstances there...

"Sure," I blurt out to get out of my head. "Why not. I'm involved in *zero* groups. Wait... *wait*." The panic sets in.

"What?" Jonah lets go of my wrist but grins and bites his lip. I swear to you, he bites his lip.

"This is... like... a *big* deal. You guys are *the* worship band. I..."

"You've already said yes," Jonah teases. "Plus, I'll be here with you the whole time. There's nothing to worry about. Now, come in the back with me so I can introduce you to everyone and we can run through some simple vocal warm-ups before rehearsing."

Looking over my shoulder, I see that Eden's already left. I text her as I wind through the long hallways of New Life's *behind the scenes*.

Me: I'm joining Water on Fire. Apparently.

Eden: Yes! I told Jonah you would!

Me: You knew and didn't prepare me? I hate you.

Eden: Relax! You ARE good! I think you'll love it. You'll be famous... er. Famous-er.

Me: You relax with all the exclamation points. I don't want to be famous-er. Nice word, by the way.

Eden: You'll be famous one way or another. Control as much of it as possible. Wasn't it you who said that?

Me: I don't believe I asked you to feed my words back to me.

Eden: ;) Go. Rock it. Text me when you're done and I'll meet you for lunch.

Me: But I'm hungry NOW. Who rehearses for more things AFTER church?

Eden: It's for Jesus ;)

Me: I hate you and Jonah both.

Before walking into the small room Jonah's in front of, I spot Roland up ahead talking with the people I'd identified as network executives during church. They're looking as relaxed as they can as Roland appears to be giving them a tour.

"Give me a second," I say to Jonah before breaking toward Roland. He nods and leans against the wall, politely waiting for me.

"Hey," I say to Roland once I sense a lull in the conversation. "I'm going to hang out here for a while and practice with the band. Jonah asked me to. They need girls, or something..." I'm trying to sound as breezy as possible, but I'm insanely curious as to who these people are.

Roland smiles broadly. "Excellent! I look forward to hearing you guys," he says as if I'm a fully initiated member of the band. "Kennedy, I'd like you to meet a few people." He gestures to the group, but one woman with shoulder-length blond hair and a red blouse that's a little too tight across her chest steps forward. "This is Stephanie Williams. She's an executive producer with NBC who will be working on the docu-series."

"*Jesus Freaks?*" I ask with a grin, extending my hand.

"That's it," she says with a professional smile and a firm handshake. "We're hoping you'll join us for a brainstorming meeting tomorrow on campus."

I look to Roland, who has a bizarre mix of relaxation and stress on his face. He smiles, but there aren't any creases by his eyes like with almost all the smiles I've seen from him before. I briefly replay the conversation I heard between him and Dean Baker. They seemed to be holding things against each other. I also think back to the shady behavior other students have expressed to me about the dean. I call them "The Resistance," and I'm suddenly wishing I could meet with them right now to figure out how we could use this series to our advantage.

It's not an undercover sting operation.

You have to figure out what, if anything, is hiding in Dean Baker's closet, and who he has on his side.

There's something in his closet all right. Probably a few some-things. And they're big.

I drop my hand and give Stephanie Williams a confident smile. "I'll see you tomorrow after my volunteer shift is over."

I swear I hear Roland exhale in relief, but that could just be in my own head.

"See you at home later," I blurt out to Roland before turning back down the hall toward Jonah.

Did I just say home?

What in the name of...

"You okay?" Jonah asks when I reach him. "You look like you're going to be sick, or something."

I swallow hard and eye him seriously. "Nothing's going to be easy for me here, is it?"

Jonah cocks a sideways grin and puts a hand on my shoulder. "Nope. I don't think so. You ready?"

I shrug. "I hope so..."

CHAPTER NINE

SERVE

Kennedy.

"**Y**OU'VE had a busy day," Roland says as he cleans up our dinner dishes.

I nod. "It was good, though."

"It surprises me that you want to sing with the worship band," he says with raised eyebrows.

"Yeah? Why?" I ask, knowing most of the answer, but wanting to converse with him anyway.

He shrugs. "It's just a very public sort of activity."

"You and Mom are all about the word *public* these days," I say, clipping the end of my sentence as I catch my misstep.

"What's your mom saying about it?" he asks, furrowing his brow.

In a split second I have to either betray my mother's confidence or the school's. Easy choice. "I've told her about the reality show. Don't be mad."

He grins. "I'm surprised it took you this long. I suppose that means I can call her and she and I can walk through the ten thousand questions I'm sure she has?"

"Yeah," I chuckle. "That's all you. I've gotta go call Mollie anyway."

"That's your best friend from high school, right?"

I nod. The fact that Roland has to double check only highlights the growing crevasse between me and Mollie. I don't know how to stop it, or if it can be. I wander to my bedroom and shut the door behind me, my thumb hovering over Mollie's name.

"I was wondering when I'd friggen hear from you," is how she answers the phone once I finally press "call."

I laugh, relieved at her sardonic tone. "How much time do you have?" I ask.

"As much as you need."

"That's awesome that you guys are talking again," Mollie says of me and Matt. "But why do you still sound so sad about it?"

I stretch out on my bed and stare at the ceiling. "Because I don't know if he's still doing all that stuff. He wasn't at church, which is weird to me. None of us are *required* to go any particular place, but he wasn't at New Life, and he went there all last year, at least until... you know."

Admittedly, I'm still riding the high of my practice with Water on Fire this afternoon. It was a lot more fun than I thought it would be, and I never once felt pressured to raise my hands in praise during the set like the other lead singers did. Maybe it'll be different when I'm in front of actual people, but... I doubt it.

Concern for Matt always lingers in my mind. We've developed a relationship like so many of my mom's family members have: Loving the piss out of each other while moving like chess pieces around each other to avoid the really big issues. *Yes, Aunt Claire is morbidly obese, but it wouldn't be kind to talk with her about it.* Sure, *Uncle Paul might drink a little too much, but who are we to judge? Yes, Matt, I'm still your friend, so that means I won't ask if you're still slicing up your soul by staring at naked women day in and day out.*

I trust him when he says he's working on it, and he *looks* so much better than he did a couple of months ago, not to mention he has a resounding recommitment to the football team. But, my curiosity is nagging me to dig into his brain and his emotions. I really should just leave it up to his therapist.

"Like the strip clubs?" Mollie pulls me back into our conversation.

"That, and the porn he mentioned... all of it."

"So what's the big deal about him missing church?"

I sigh. "I don't know if he *missed* it, and it's a big deal because it's rules *and* it's something most of the kids here do, just like getting up and showering in the morning. I just can't ask him about it because then he'll think I'm, like, checking up on him and not in just a friend way either."

Mollie sounds frustrated. "What's the big deal about porn, again?"

Rolling onto my side, I situate myself into a lax fetal position. I shrug as if she'll see. "I don't know..."

I do know, but it's hard to translate to an outsider.

"Look," Mollie interrupts brightly, "if the poor boy can't have sex until he's married, there's nothing wrong with a little window shopping first, is there? To see what he likes, and stuff?"

"Mollie!" I sit up, settling on my elbows.

"What?" she huffs, sounding more impatient than ever.

"You don't get it," I mumble after preparing a huge monologue in my head about everything I've learned in the last year, and the last few months, that highlight exactly *why* it's not okay.

"So, *explain it, then.*"

I wince, feeling the strain of being stretched away from my best friend by more than distance. We haven't been talking as much, in part due to our schedules, but there's something more stuffing itself between us. What we talk about. I'm not talking about parties and hookups and abs. That's not all that Mollie talks about, either, but they are part of her conversation. I'm also certainly not talking about who I rubbed up against at a party and who I woke up next to. Mollie's only done that two or three times since she started at Yale, but...

Only?

"Sorry," she says before I can say anything. "It's just kind of hard to communicate lately, since you go to school on a different planet."

I chuckle. "Why am I the one on the different planet?"

"You know what I mean..."

"I do, but it still hurts my feelings a little. These kids aren't all that different from us and our friends, anyway. They're just not drinking or having sex... and if they are they're not telling anyone. But they want to. And they want to get married, and have jobs, and have kids and all that. Mollie?"

"Yeah?"

"What are the rape stats like on your campus?" I've already Googled this.

She pauses. "I don't know, it's probably like most other college campuses, I guess."

"It's higher than average, actually," I challenge.

"So why'd you ask?"

"Because I want you to be safe."

She clicks her tongue. "And I want guys to keep it in their pants. I am safe. Hardly ever alone on campus, and all that."

How much easier would it be if that were a rule for her?

I yawn. "You know rape isn't about sex, it's about power." My mom would be proud of me recalling that bit of women's studies information.

"Yeah? What about your campus?"

"There might be one rape reported every couple years," I admit, though I'm not sure.

"Reported." She catches the hole in my honest answer. "And, I bet they'd challenge your sex and power theory."

"It's not a theory, Moll. You know that."

"Yeah? Ask some of your friends, and see what they say. You're not the only one who has the Internet, Kennedy. I know all about *your* friends trying to keep men's intentions in check. Helping to keep them pure because they can't control themselves, especially not if women are flaunting themselves everywhere."

I run my hand over my face. "It's so much more complicated than that, Mollie."

"You're right," she says in a tone that tells me this conversation is on its last leg. "So, before you call me and accuse my school of being full of porn-riddled rapists, maybe you should check your side of the street? Didn't you say that one girl's sister was raped and the school did *nothing*?"

Caitlyn's sister. And no one did anything about it. More egregious than the rape itself must be the feeling that you're being told you're lying. Or wrong. Or to shut up.

"It wasn't the *school* who did nothing, Mollie. Christians aren't pro-rape, you know."

She huffs, and so do I.

"Things are weird," she finally says.

"They are. I feel like I need a sabbatical, or something."

"From what?" she asks.

Our friendship.

My life.

"I don't know," I say, craning my neck to peer out the top corner of my window. The sun is setting and, while I'm sure Mollie and I are staring at the same sun, it makes me wonder how differently we might feel about it.

Where we grew up, summer sunsets means long days in Hamptons' vacation homes turn into dazzling, fun nights. An earlier sunset means a rapid closure to the summer, where soon, caretakers will come sweep out the mini mansions in preparation for fall and winter.

In my prayer time with God lately, I've felt a pull to look for Him everywhere in my surroundings. Not church buildings or crosses, but in the flowers, the changing of seasons, and nature. The sun means hope, and I can only hope that Matt's darkness has been just a winter for his spirit. That the last days of summer will warm him, and he'll trust who he actually is, and not who he thinks he grew up around. I believe, deep down, that Buck Wells is a good guy who got screwed up, just like Roland did. The beauty of autumn will allow me to forgive the biting cold of the winter that soon follows, and I wonder—pray—that Matt will find the same peace with his father someday. If he doesn't, I fear he will never accept that he's worth the love he so deserves.

"Where'd you go?" Mollie asks. It gives me reason to smile for the first time in this conversation; that she knows I drifted away into my thoughts, even though we're not having this conversation in person.

"You really want to know?" I ask with the smile penetrating my voice.

"Hit me," she says like she's at a Black Jack table.

"Seasons, God, nature, and eternal love."

Mollie doesn't say anything for a second. Then, "I wish I could be there with you through this."

"Me, too," I say, only half believing either of us. "It's far more dramatic than I thought it would be. I mean, I thought I'd spend four years doing a get-to-know-you dance with Roland when, in fact, settling into a relationship with him has been the easiest thing I've had to deal with this year."

"Does that drive your mom crazy?"

I shrug again. "I don't think so. Our relationship is shifting, too. Still mother-daughter, but now that I'm becoming an adult... it's different."

Mollie chuckles. "Your mom is as emotional as you are, only she allows it to take over her more than you do. It's probably driving her crazy. She likes to feel all the feels, even if they might kill her."

I laugh. It feels good to have someone who really knows my mom. As the person. Not the scary liberal who wields a machete on Capitol Hill whenever she gets a chance. "As you can tell by the course of our conversation today, I'm starting to feel all the feels, too," I tease.

"It's good to see your stiff upper lip relax a little. But, hey, listen, I've gotta run. Burrito night with my friends downtown." Mollie's back at school early, too. Helping run orientation for incoming freshman. I've heard the cackle of said "friends" through our conversation in the background. Giggles, low-toned laughs from guys that shouldn't be in her room anyway, if you ask me.

Thank God no one asked, because that was probably the single-most conservative thought I've had in my entire life.

"Have fun. Talk to a stranger for me." I have to have a sense of humor for the CU rules sometimes, or I'll go crazy. They do make me grind my teeth on a daily basis, because I believe it's utterly ridiculous to impose such rules on adults. But, we're consenting adults—like those who sign up for the Army, I guess, and have to deal with insane drill sergeants.

You wanted this.

Mollie and I hang up, and while I don't feel hopeless about what the future of our friendship might bring, I've come to accept that we each have some searching and growing to do, maybe even away from each other.

Approaching the prison was far more nerve-wracking than I had expected it to be. I really hadn't given it much thought at all until we were driving through the first of many gates. The building itself in any other setting might look like a giant high school. It's a few stories tall, brick and cement—but on second glance, I notice the windows. They're different. Tiny and spaced evenly. Giving a troublingly small amount of natural light into what I assume are the cells. It gives me pause to think of something like looking out a window as a privilege rather than a right … or a given.

The perimeter of the green grounds is surrounded by a fence at least twenty feet high, topped with spiraled barbed wire. *To prevent escape.*

Suddenly, *I'm* the one who wants to escape.

"You okay?" Matt asks as Asher hands over paperwork through the car window to yet another guard.

I swallow hard. "This is … like … a *prison*."

He nods.

"Have you been to one before?" I ask.

"As a customer?" he teases.

"Come on."

Matt smiles. "Sure. I've done literacy stuff at different prisons for a couple years now, I guess. Summer stuff near my hometown.

"Oh," I say, my mouth dry as I look out the window.

Murderers. Prostitutes.

Soon I'll be face-to-face with humans dangerous enough that the courts deemed they should be locked away for a very long time. Crimes too heinous to allow these people to live amongst others.

Eden's in the front, as quiet as I am. I bite the inside of my cheek.

"You'll do fine, K. Sawyer," Matt encourages as Asher guides the car to a parking space.

"If you say so," I mumble as we exit the vehicle and march quietly inside.

I have to remember to breathe as we navigate through metal detectors and are lead past thick, boulder-like guards spaced throughout each hallway.

Asher nods to a petite woman who opens a door for us and looks comically out of place. Once inside the room, Asher sets a stack of paperwork inside manila folders in front of each of us.

"All right," he says, sounding motivated. "Let's get crackin'."

All I notice is Asher's smooth, collected demeanor through this whole process, though I'm thankful that at least for now he's not pointing out how nervous I seem. How nervous I *am*.

"Are you going to that network meeting thing once we get out of here?" Matt asks me and Eden while we fill out the paperwork.

"You know about that?" I ask, setting down my pencil.

Eden chimes in. "Yeah, we're all going to be there. The ones the network is hoping will join the series. Me, Matt, Jonah, Bridgette, Silas... a few people."

"All of our friends?" I say, my mouth wide open.

"You look horrified," Matt observes.

"It's like our own little Breakfast Club," I mumble. "The jock, the prom queen," I say, pointing to Matt and Eden respectively.

"Which one are you?" Matt teases with a wink.

I tilt my head and grin. "The one who smashes cereal into her sandwich and talks to herself in the corner."

They laugh, and I'm relieved we can share some pop culture.

"Wait," I continue. "Two things. One, why not follow upperclassmen? And two, are Bridgette and Silas' parents *actually* going to let them be *on* TV? They don't even *watch* TV."

Eden shrugs. "I think they're hoping for the same thing you are, just on the opposite end."

"And that is?" I question.

"Accurate representation," she answers.

Matt snorts. "Good luck."

"Speaking of which," I turn to Matt, "I'm shocked you're considering such a thing. A *reality* show."

He shrugs. "They need someone going through tough stuff. And they want an all-American athlete guy." He grins, pointing his thumbs at himself. "I'm your man."

"I'm just... startled that you're willing to be so... open."

Matt looks between me and Eden for a moment. "I need to be the best I can be. I'm hoping this will help keep me on track. I want people to be able to see that God can heal us from the inside out. And," his grin returns, "a little national coverage of our football team won't hurt anything."

"And the truth shall set you free!" I exclaim in laughter.

"Hey," he puts his hands up in mock defense, "I'm not saying I'd transfer if a D-1 or even a D-2 school scouted me. But I'm not *not* saying that, either."

I share in Eden's giggles of excitement, but the thought of Matt going *anywhere* but Carter sends my emotions into a shifty place. One I retreat from quickly.

"All right, guys," Asher says, entering the small room. "You're the last three of the day for the paperwork, I think. Want a tour?"

We stand and follow Asher through the small medium-security prison.

"Here's where the guys will be doing most of their work," Asher states, pointing to a room labeled as the prison's library. "Your literacy work will happen in here for a little over an hour each morning before lunch. You won't have lunch in the main cafeteria for all kinds of security reasons, but the men you'll be reading with will eat with you in a smaller dining hall. It's kind of a privilege thing for the inmates here."

It looks, well, like a prison in here. Sterile, white walls, lots of murmuring background noise, and cells that are behind a series of doors we won't be going down today but that I've examined online.

"Now, Ladies," Asher continues, "You'll be volunteering in the prison's community center next door. Your literacy activities will center around the wives, girlfriends, and children of the men incarcerated here."

Eden nods, seeming to take Asher's words in stride. I, however, trip over them.

"Um, what?" I ask, and the group of us stop in a small hallway between offices.

"Huh?" Asher asks.

I hold out my hands. "I signed up to work with the prison ministry. And I'm not working in the prison?"

"You are working with the prison," he highlights. "The ministry covers many aspects. Incarcerated members are one part, their family another, agency level things are another, and so on."

"But you didn't say that. I want to work with the prisoners." I stand firm, despite my rapid heartbeat. Eden and Matt shift uncomfortably.

Asher sighs. "This is a men's-only facility."

I'm grateful I still have my lip ring. I suck in my bottom lip and run my tongue across the cool metal. "You're kidding, right?" I ask, eyebrows raised. "There are women who *work* here, for God's sake."

"These are the rules, Kennedy," Asher states flatly. "And another one," he points to my lip, "is that has to come out when you volunteer here."

I shake my head. "Just when I think CU can't get any more—"

"It's not CU's rule," he cuts in, speaking in a stern, authoritative tone. "It's mine. If there were a women's facility nearby, I'd bus you ladies there. But there's not. So, you're going to be working with families torn apart by the incarceration. Are you going to make this a feminist-type issue, or are you going to look at this as a family and societal issue and serve where you're most needed?"

Matt and Eden are frozen on either side of me, and in my peripheral vision, I can see their eyes widen. Reprimand isn't new for me since setting foot on CU's campus, but I've never crossed a line with Asher, which is yet another thing I can cross off my list.

My face flushes and I lower my eyes, relaxing my shoulders—relaxing my war stance. "I'm sorry," I say. "I'll go where you need me."

Without another word, Asher turns and continues our tour around the campus of the prison, but I don't hear what he's saying. Instead, I'm wondering how much of my life and, admittedly, my mother's has been spent fighting the wrong uphill battle. All the rallies and protests. Sure, some were held for causes that I hold deep in my heart. But the others? Was I there to make noise? Was I wasting the precious time I have and ignoring a greater need?

Have I been serving where most needed, or have I been serving to make a point somewhere else?

Who, exactly, have I been serving?

CHAPTER TEN
UNSAVORY

Kennedy.

FOR the last hour, a group of us have been holed up in a spacious administrative university boardroom, listening to NBC executives talk about the show. Bridgette and Silas, along with their parents, are sitting across the long table from me, but we haven't had a chance to say hi to each other.

Jonah's here with his dad, Eden with both her parents, and a couple of other students. One I recognize as a senior and two more who I don't recognize at all.

"Who are they?" I whisper to Eden.

"Freshmen," she whispers back. "*Very* Conservative. The guy. The girl is from somewhere in Texas. Bridgette knows her from a homeschool conference or something."

"How do you know about the guy?"

Eden leans in closer. "Jonah met him this morning and says he's really intense."

"Yikes," I whisper back.

Jonah's one of the most socially neutral guys I've met here, and if he's highlighting someone as "intense," I should probably avoid them at all costs. Especially while cameras are rolling. I think he's called me that before, and he's right. If what he says is true, then the angry looking kid sitting down the table from me is the polar opposite of me.

"It's important that you all understand the distinction between what we're trying to do and a reality show," says Stephanie Williams, the executive producer I met after church yesterday.

She's in far more casual clothes today, but still put together in a pair of khaki capri pants and a long, fitted black T-shirt and red high heels. Her blond hair is up in a loose bun and she's sporting a pair of black-rimmed glasses that make her look like a hipster version of Cinderella.

"Our goal is to produce this as a ten-part docu-series. It's different from a straight documentary in that there will be a lot more footage of your everyday lives and interactions as opposed to interviews, and different from a reality show in that there will be more interviews than normal for a reality series. Production timelines are tight for this one in an effort to have the audience feel as *here* as possible, so filming to airing will be roughly a week to ten days." She pauses and I look to Roland with wide eyes.

The benefit of this is theoretically there will be less footage for them to cut and paste together as an editing gimmick. They'll have a week's worth at a time, rather than a couple of months. But it also means that should anything happen that the school needs to address, there's less time to do that before it airs. Like if a party is busted, or something. There's less time for word to get back to the school in order for them to do preemptive damage control. That could be good or bad. The fire in Stephanie's eyes tells me she thinks she's landed a real gold mine here.

"So," she continues, "all of you here have already signed the contracts presented to you and your families when we met one-on-one. Except for you, Kennedy. I've given your father the documents for you to look over this afternoon."

I stay silent, but don't have to work that hard, because Bridgette and Silas' dad pipes in. "Do we think it's wise to include Miss Sawyer in light of all the unsavory attention she's already brought to the university."

My eyes widen and Eden reaches over and squeezes my knee as Matt shoots me a nervous glance across the table. My jaw drops, but I have no intention of speaking. I couldn't if I wanted to. Bridgette and Silas look down, deliberately avoiding my glance.

Fine.

"I don't really think that's necessary language," Roland butts in. "Unsavory?"

A lump rises in my throat and I look up, preemptively stopping any tears that might form. Unsavory. A single word designed to make me feel like the piece of trash he clearly thinks I am, or he wouldn't have moved his daughter out of the dorm as quickly as he did when those *pictures* from The Pink Pony were leaked.

Mr. Nelson opens his mouth, maybe to defend himself but Stephanie cuts in. "I think we can agree that Kennedy's involvement with the university has brought all *kinds* of attention," she says as if she knows anything. "It's the main reason the network thinks a show like this could work. With her participation, of course. That and the rising popularity of Pastor Roland, who seems be bridging gaps between denominations of Christians that Christians themselves don't want to recognize are there." She shoots me an urgent glance.

I'd be lying if I said I hadn't wondered the same thing in the back of my mind. That the network was interested in the show because of me. Who the heck had ever heard of Carter unless they were involved in supporting it or criticizing it? Not many. I hadn't until I learned about Roland. My mom had, due to some of her lobbying work, but even then it was only a mention here or there. Now to have the most successful national network filming a show here, *and* during what will be the height of the presidential primary season?

God help us.

"I thought," Mr. Nelson continues, "that the school was interested in this project as a way to repair the damage that Kennedy's family has caused to the reputation of the school."

"Dad," Silas speaks over him. Silas. Silas of all people, while his sister looks meekly at her hands. "Please be kind," he whispers, but we can all hear.

Dean Baker, who I've been ignoring from the start of the meeting, stands. "We understand your concerns, Mr. Nelson."

"Please," he concedes, "call me Paul." I wrinkle my nose that the only person he's friendly with in this room is that slithering sloth.

Easy...

"Paul," Dean Baker corrects, "we're all aware of the... attention Miss Sawyer has brought to the university. But, it's not all bad." My heart nearly stops at this sentence, and I shoot Matt a suspicious glance. He shrugs, seeming to share in my confusion. "You see," Baker continues in his greasy drawl, "last spring, the university saw a ten percent increase in applications. A jump I've never seen before. And this summer we fielded more interest phone calls and gave more tours than in any year any of us in the administration can recall. We can't deny the draw that having a more... secular student who is so popular in the public eye has. This is an opportunity to, yes, correct some of the PR damage that's been done, but to also show the love of Christ in actually opening our doors to people in all walks of life."

"Dean," Paul Nelson says with a new softness to his voice, "you're right." He turns to face me. "Kennedy, please forgive my words. They were hurtful and unjust. It's just been a very... stressful time."

Suddenly, all eyes are on me, waiting for my pardon of Bridgette and Silas' dad.

"Okay," I mumble. "It's fine."

I leave my eyebrows furrowed as Dean Baker takes his seat and shuffles through some papers in front of him. As another executive rises to speak, Stephanie sits on the other side of Roland and is in my eye line. She gives me a wink and a friendly smile, as if the dean's words were genuine, but I maintain my scowl.

I don't trust him. Not one bit. There is no way Dean Baker wants more students like me running around this campus. He's already told me so much in calling me a threat.

He's lying.

And, if I'm lucky, he'll prove it in front of a few million trusted television watchers.

"You guys all set to start volunteering tomorrow?" Roland asks me, Eden, and Matt as we clean up from dinner. Roland barbecued some delicious meat and invited my friends over after the network meeting, since campus food is always subpar.

"Yes," Eden answers. "I can't wait to work with the little kids and read to them."

Matt nods. "It'll be interesting, I bet, but it sure beats sitting around all day waiting for football practice to start."

"When *does* training start?" Roland asks.

Matt stretches his arms far above his head and leans back slightly. "Two weeks, baby! But some of us who've been on campus have been at the gym every day." He takes a deep breath and my eyes trace down the gray fabric of his T-shirt to the small, holy sliver of sin that peeks out above his belt. It's the only view I need to see just how hard he's been working out this summer. There are definite lines carved into his skin. Not like the cover of a romance novel, but this is way better. Because it's real.

I swallow hard and clear my throat.

Give it a rest...

Roland leans against the counter. "So you'll have just about a week of overlap with volunteering and football."

Matt nods. "But we volunteer like seven to noon and practice starts every day at two, so it'll be fine."

"My door's always open," Roland says, seemingly out of nowhere.

"I know," Matt answers as if they've had this conversation before. Short but not rude.

"All right," I cut in, desperate to break the weird tension. "We're gonna go for a walk."

"Where?" Roland asks.

I shrug. "The trail? With just them. Not you. You're a grown up."

He laughs. "You're all over eighteen. You're grownups, too."

We all chuckle. "Right," I say, "but you're *more* of a grown-up. Like a real one."

"Going to downtown and back, or..."

I feign being wounded. "What ever happened to saying have fun and be back before dark? We'll walk north on the trail. How's that? I haven't been up that way much."

Eden chuckles and puts her plate in the sink. "You guys are funny. Thank you for dinner Pastor—er—Roland," Eden stumbles. "I know you told me to call you Roland, but that makes me uncomfortable."

Roland laughs. "It's fine, Eden. I just want you to know you *can*. Just know I'm far more than a pastor, okay? I'm more

Roland than pastor. They just needed something to print in the church bulletins.

She nods with another chuckle. "Roland it is then."

"Unless we're on campus," Matt teases.

"Right," Roland pipes in. "Then *pastor* me to death." He laughs some more at his own humor, then returns to the sink to load the dishwasher.

My heart warms at how easy this all feels. My friends. Roland. Life.

"Bye," I say as we exit the back door.

"Bye," Roland calls back. "Have fun. Be back before dark."

I stick my head back in the door and catch him grinning as he rinses off a plate. He, in turn, catches me staring at him.

"Oh," he says as if he knew I was there the whole time. His grin fades slightly. "Be careful. That's the most important thing."

I nod. "I will. Thank you," I say. "For... everything. And for not pushing me on this show *thing*. I know how much pressure you must be under to get me to commit to it."

Roland dries his hands and makes his way toward me. Placing his hand on my shoulder, he eyes me earnestly. "Kennedy, I couldn't care less if you signed those papers or set them on fire and put them down the sink. Carter University is not in the TV business, and neither is New Life, for that matter. I just want you to make a decision that's okay for *you*."

"Thank you," I whisper before turning for my friends, uncomfortable with the amount of emotion in his eyes.

"Always," he says, closing the door behind me.

"*What. Was. That?*" Eden says once we enter the trail. "With Bridgette and Silas' dad, I mean."

I roll my eyes. "I'm crap, didn't you gather that as he reviewed the evidence of all the *unsavory* attention I've brought the university?"

Eden clicks her tongue in disapproval as Matt speaks up. "You're not crap," he says angrily. "*He's* crap for making you feel that way, Kennedy. That was a... jerk move. In front of everyone like that?"

I shrug. "I'm less concerned about what he said than I am about what Dean Baker said."

Eden shudders. "Ugh, he's so creepy, isn't he? What *is it* about him?"

"I don't know, but I will tell you that little charitable arms-wide-open-and-welcoming ruse he's trying to pull off won't last that long. He does *not* like me, and I don't know what that was all about."

"He's trying to make sure you agree to do the show," Matt offers. "I mean, I agree that the university needs to be as welcoming as they claim to be, but that's fighting a stereotype of evangelicals that's decades old. That speech in front of the executives? That was to entice you and to placate them."

Eden furrows her brow. "No, that can't be it. Can it?"

I think for a moment. "He's probably right."

"I thought you *are* going to do the show," Eden says somewhat anxiously.

Matt shoots me a look that matches her tone, and I wave my hand. "Of course I'm going to," I answer. "But there's probably no harm in making them sweat it out a little. What did all of your contracts say? Like how many days and hours a day are they going to film and stuff? I haven't read through mine yet."

As we shuffle our way down the trail, Matt and Eden compare notes out loud about their contracts. It seemed to be a document presented by CU and NBC jointly. The network retains the right to film them a maximum of two weekdays during class, lunch, studying, etc. They also will choose either Friday or Saturday each week, but not both, and they'll allow filming before, during, and just after church on Sundays as allowed by each house of worship, but they'll comply with the school's request that all filming will cease by noon on Sundays. Further, cameras will be allowed in the dorms to film and interview during floor meetings/prayer sessions, but there are heavy restrictions surrounding in-room filming. It will only be allowed in very select circumstances, for limited amounts of time, and the RA must always be present. No exceptions.

"It sounds like someone at CU has a clue," I say as we round a bend near a small stream.

"I think your dad had a lot to do with the contract," Matt says, pausing to lean against a tree on the bank of the stream.

"Yeah," Eden says to him. "And that whole thing with the GoPro cameras and the student-like filming crew?"

I cock my head to the side. "The what?"

Eden faces me. "In order to have as little disruption as possible, the camera crew will be younger people from the network that can kind of blend in around here. They'll have a room in the dorm together and will sit in on some classes, eat lunch with us, all of that. And they'll have cameras recording while they go. Small ones. Not those big honkin' ones."

"That could be... interesting," I say slowly. I can't decide if this is a genius move on behalf of both the network and the school, or a disaster waiting to happen. "Will we know *who* the camera people are?" I ask, to help me decide.

Matt nods. "They have to have their badges visible at all times and all that. And the longer interviews will be conducted more formally in offices or classrooms. You're still in... right?"

Eden's eyes widen. "Yeah, you are. Right? You have to be. It'll be so much easier if you are."

"Why?" I chuckle. "So they follow me around more?"

She shakes her head. "No, not that. You're just... smarter about all of this stuff. My dad is worried I'll somehow get taken advantage of..." she trails off.

Your dad's smart.

"And you think I can help with that?" I ask, despite having thought the same thing when I first heard about the project.

"They're from your world. They think we're dumb little church-goers, and we're not, but it'll be hard to prove that if they're manipulating us or trying to catch us doing something, or whatever." She stares at her hands.

"I don't think you're dumb." I walk to her and put my arm around her shoulder. "I maybe had that thought about *some* of you. But not *you* specifically. I don't think that about anyone anymore though—not any more than the general population, anyway. I know too much." I chuckle nervously. "Of course I'm in. But, don't think I'm out of the danger zone. I'm willing to bet my CU career that someone either at the studio or in the school administration would love to see me fall flat on my face, morally speaking, while the cameras are rolling."

"Someone like Dean Baker." Matt chimes in without question.

"I'm betting on it," I answer.

Eden puts her hands on her hips. "You're right, Kennedy. He *is* creepy. What's his deal, anyway? Have you talked about all this with that group of kids, or whatever?"

Matt shoots me a betrayed look, but I hold my hand up in defense. "Chill, Matt. Eden's safe. And, it's not like this is an actual CIA mission or anything. But if it were, she'd still respect our confidentiality." I arch an eyebrow at him to accentuate my point. He relaxes his shoulders but holds question in his tight jaw.

"But," I turn to Eden, "I haven't yet. I'm not really sure if I should undertake a CU administrative shakedown, or let the cameras do the talking."

"Have you talked to Roland about it?" Matt asks out of nowhere.

I stare at him in confused horror. "No," I draw out. "I have *not.*"

"Why?" he asks, and I'm shocked by this line of questioning.

I shrug. "Because. Because... it's big. It's not just a vendetta Baker might have against me or Roland. This is like covering up *rapes,*" I whisper, because I believe the woods have ears. "It's breaking the law and participating second hand in sexual abuse and God knows what else. It's bad, and I want to be sure before I start pointing fingers."

They nod, and a noise in the distance startles our attention from the conversation back down the path that we just came from.

"Guys!" a male voice calls. "Guys?"

"Silas?" Matt mumbles, taking a few steps down the trail and peering around the bend. "It's Silas," he confirms, still whispering over his shoulder.

My first instinct is to run, which is foolish. There's no reason to. This is college, plain and simple, not a political thriller. The second is to mentally calculate how loud we've been, how far away Silas was, and how much he could have heard. My paranoia truly is fully intact, but given how far away his voice sounded when we first heard him, Silas was well out of hearing range. His dad sure seems buddy-buddy with Dean Baker, so any and all conspiracy theories must be carefully guarded around the Nelson siblings.

"Hey man," Matt says somewhat hesitantly as Silas comes into view. He's even taller than he was last year. So is Matt, for that matter. They're both easily over six feet. Matt's far broader and full of muscle, but Silas is lean like a long distance runner. All legs.

"Hey," Silas says, barely out of breath. His red hair is cropped around the back and slightly longer on top, held together with what seems like a fair bit of gel. Shiny and hard despite physical exertion.

Eden waves. "Hi Silas. Um... what's up?"

Silas walks directly toward me and places a firm hand on my shoulder. "Kennedy, I'm sorry for what happened earlier. With my dad and Dean Baker and all that. It was out of line."

My lips part and involuntarily my right eyebrow arches up. Silas and I haven't had much interpersonal interaction, but the little we've had has been bristly at best. It became clear very early on in our first semester that we were observing each other as if exhibits at a zoo.

I clear my throat. "I've gotta be honest with you, Silas. I thought you pretty much felt the same way..."

He drops his hands and his lips form a tight line as he clenches his jaw. "I know. I'm sorry. I haven't been that friendly with you. You... you scare me a little," he says. Out loud. With a shaky chuckle, but still. Out loud.

I nod, impressed with his candor. "I am quite scary. Just don't knock on my door around midnight on a full moon. I won't be held responsible for my actions." I turn and continue my trek on the trail. No matter how much I appreciate honesty, it doesn't mean I can't be offended.

"No!" Silas calls after me. "Kennedy, wait! Please?"

Something in his plea stops me and turns me around. Silas is a few steps behind me and I notice Eden and Matt hanging a few paces further back, both with confused looks on their faces.

"What?" I cross my arms, keeping my tone clipped.

"I'm not just sorry for what happened earlier," he says almost sheepishly. "I'm sorry for the way I've behaved around you up until now. I know you and Bridgette didn't always see eye-to-eye, and rather than get to know you myself, I just took her word on everything—"

"Everything?" I question, indignantly. "*Everything?* What is *everything?* Does she sit around gossiping about me?"

Silas shakes his head. "No. No. It's not that. She would just share conversations all of you had and I'd hear what I wanted to... look this isn't about Bridgette. It's about me. *I'm* sorry."

Freckles have always made people seem several years younger to me, and Silas is no exception. With his wide hazel eyes set in the middle of dozens of pale brown freckles, I can't help but see a shy, awkward ten year old walking to church ahead of several younger siblings.

"I forgive you," I say in an exhale.

This phrase, *I forgive you,* is not one I ever heard so commonly used before coming to CU. I'm used to people saying *don't worry about it* or *it's okay* in response to an apology. There's a different weight to *I forgive you.* I didn't say it to Silas' dad in the meeting, but I say it to Silas. And the weight lifts from Silas' face the second I say it.

"Thank you," he responds.

"So," I say as Eden and Matt move forward and stand next to us. "Does Bridgette hate me, or what? I mean, she moved right out of the dorm, doesn't talk to me..."

"My parents had her room switched," Silas clarifies. "And she wouldn't hate you."

I chuckle. "Well of course not. Love your enemies and all of that."

"It's a little more complicated than that," Silas admits.

"Enlighten me."

"You challenge her. And it scares her. Things with Bridge have always been so black and white. And, yeah, some things are. But grey exists. Except for her..."

I shoot Matt and Eden a thoroughly confused look. "Wait .. What? Except for *her*. Silas, I'm going to be honest again and tell you that I've always viewed you as *way* more intense than she is."

He grins. "In some ways, yeah that's true. When I have a belief I've thoroughly examined all sides of, prayed on, and lived out then, yeah, I'll go down fighting for it. But Bridge?" He pauses and shakes his head. "In an effort to try to keep things simple in her walk with God, she's actually made things way more complicated and alienated a lot of people. So many times she won't even *listen* to another opinion. That's no way to reach people."

"Or love people," Eden cuts in.

"Anyway," he says. "Just pray for her. She'll come around. She doesn't know I'm here actually, or she may have come with me. I don't know. I just needed to clear my side of the street with you. Are you doing the show? I think it'd be great if you did."

I roll my eyes as Matt and Eden chuckle. "Yes," I say for what feels like the tenth time in two days. "I'll do the damn show."

"You should watch your mouth," Silas says seriously. I shoot a shocked glance at him and he breaks into laughter. "Just kidding... sort of."

"Why do you think it'll be *great* for me to be on the show?" I question. Out of the corner of my eye I see Matt stare directly at Silas, as if he's more interested in Silas' response than I am.

Silas looks at an invisible spot between the air and the ground for a few seconds. "I don't know," he finally says. "I honestly don't know," he says again with a light laugh.

"Me either," I reply honestly.

I find myself staring at Silas as if I've never met him before. Something is different about him. How can one person look more relaxed and on fire all at the same time? I stand by my original observation of him that he's incredibly intense. There's a storm in those young eyes.

Silas is definitely fighting a battle or two inside that soul of his.

CHAPTER ELEVEN
OBVIOUS

Matt.

E ATING lunch in the smaller prison cafeteria with just the other volunteers feels a little weird. We're eating by ourselves today, instead of with the handful of inmates we've dined with this week, due to family visitation. The room is grey and sterile and I wonder how anyone who walks in here a sane person could possibly leave as one.

Maybe they don't come in here sane.

Maybe they never really leave...

The only volunteer here I know is Silas. The others are upperclassmen or non-CU students who seem to be regulars at this. We spent the morning reading with some of the guys here. At first I was more nervous than I've been in a long time. But, it was easy to settle in, actually. The guys are really cool and seem really happy to have someone new to talk to. Our first week has been a success on all accounts and has kept me out of my head for long chunks of the day, which is something I desperately need.

"So the other day," I say to Silas, who's sitting right next to me, "with Kennedy. That was... what was that?"

Silas turns to me. "What do you mean?"

I shrug. "You've never seemed to like her all that much. You lost your mind when she was going to take Bridgette to get her nose pierced last year..." I grin internally, remembering the excitement in Kennedy's eyes as we all stood outside the piercing shop in one of our first outings off of campus last fall.

"Give me a break." Silas grins. "That was like, what, the first week of school? I was still really paranoid."

"About?"

He shrugs. "That my parents were still watching, somehow."

Immediately my mind scrolls back to the meeting last week with NBC, where Silas' dad seemed very familiar with Dean Baker.

"What?" Silas asks, catching me staring into space.

"Watching you?"

"Yeah. Bridgette's their golden child. Follows every rule always without question. I was only allowed to come here because she agreed to."

My eyes widen. "Your parents told you that?"

He chuckles. "Not in so many words, but I know my family well enough to know. Where do you think that whole *rocks* business came from? That certainly wasn't my idea, man. I *want* to look at girls."

I think back to the first time I heard Bridgette say "rocks", and both she and Silas looked away. It didn't take long for me to realize that was their code word for lewd dress or behavior on another person, and that they were to avert their eyes.

"I hear you there, brother," I admit. "But... you know."

"Yeah," Silas says, resigned. "I *know*. Sorry."

I wave my hand. "Oh forget about it, dude. It's cool. I was just *really* stupid. I could honestly use a 'rocks accountability partner,' if I'm being honest. It's really hard to keep my eyes to myself sometimes."

"You don't want to look at any girls ever?" he questions, taking a bite of his prison-grade chicken-patty sandwich.

"Well not *ever*, geez. Just... not till things get settled. In here." I point to my chest just over my heart.

Silas extends his hand and places it on my shoulder. "I'll help you, man."

"Thanks," I mumble, reluctantly. I can't believe I just asked the most conservative kid I know to help me with lust.

Though, if what he says about his sister and his family is true, Silas might be just like the rest of us—a caged animal trying to break free and figure out just who the heck he is apart from his church and family.

"Are you going to date Kennedy?" he asks without missing a beat.

I shake my head. "Nah. I'm not going to date anyone right now. No looking. No dating. Just me and, you know, God." If I say the right words enough times they'll find their way to my heart and become my desires. "Why'd you ask about Kennedy specifically?" I question.

He shrugs. "You two seem kind of obvious," he says matter-of-factly. "But I think you're right on with waiting. You can always ask her out later, when you feel right *here*." He touches my chest with his index finger. "But you can't go back and do it again for the first time. It'll probably never be perfect, but it can always be better."

I nod slowly and stare at my tray. "What about you? Anyone got your attention?"

Silas flushes under his speckled skin. "Dude, no."

"What?" I ask, punching his arm. "You asked me all about Kennedy."

He laughs loudly. "Because it's *so* obvious. If you two wanted any privacy you'd stop looking at each other like that."

"Like what?" I ask, horrified.

"Well," he says softly. "I couldn't see you when I was talking with her on the trail the other day, but I saw her. And how her eyes hung on you each time she looked over my shoulder. It was borderline erotic."

I punch him again. "Shut up."

He feigns being hurt. "Uncle," he says, laughing. "I'm just kidding. Sort of. But seriously, aren't you worried she might be a little too liberal for you?"

I huff through my nose. "You don't know me very well, do you?"

He shakes his head. "Not really."

"Through no fault of mine," I point out. "You were the one who self-segregated all last year."

Silas nods, looking serious. "Total fail on my part."

"But to answer your question," I start. "I don't know. We don't really talk theology and politics."

"Well what *ever* else is there to talk about?" he says sarcastically.

"You know who her dad is. Even he doesn't preach on politics. And you respect him, right?"

Silas pauses for a moment. "I do. I don't know if I agree with him point for point on his theology, but he brings mad numbers in every Sunday. I see healing in that church."

I hold out my hands. "See? That's how my friendship is with Kennedy."

"But you don't want to date Roland." Silas brings reality in. "There are things we can handle in friendship relationships that won't work in marriage."

"Who said anything about marriage?"

Silas shrugs. "I'm just saying..."

"Okay," I say, frustrated. "Before we turn into girls, let's find something else to talk about."

"How's the football team looking this year," Silas switches gears immediately. "You and the other guys on campus this summer have logged some serious hours in the weight room."

I nod. "We're basically going to kill everyone."

Silas slaps my shoulder. "That's the spirit. Do it for Jesus!"

A couple of the older guys in earshot start laughing at Silas' remark, and ask me about the team. In no time we're wrapped up in a discussion of schedules, opponents, and plays.

It's not that I *don't* want a relationship with Kennedy. In fact, there are few things I want more in this world than to be the one that makes her face light up or to be the lucky jerk who gets to brush his lips against hers. But not now. Not yet. I'm going to keep trying though, to get better. For me and my family. And for Kennedy. Because when I do finally ask her on a proper date, I want to be someone she'll be proud to say "yes" to.

CHAPTER TWELVE
THE BOTTOM DROPS OUT

Kennedy.

RAP lightly on the thick metal door of Asher's office at Word. I spot his thick, rounded shoulders hunched in front of his ancient desktop. A desktop, no less, with a huge monitor that resembles a microwave.

"Hey," I say softly. "Can I come in?"

He looks up from his relic. "Of course," he says, sitting back and gesturing to the seat on the other side of the desk. "Take a seat. What's up?"

I sit, setting my messenger bag on the floor before crossing my legs and leaning back in the chair, taking a moment to study his face to see what kind of emotional space he might be in. He looks pretty relaxed, which bodes well for me. To be honest, Asher always seems pretty relaxed, but I got a taste of his stern side last week, which brings me to his office now.

"I'm sorry," I say, letting out a deep sigh. "About earlier this week. Being all... self righteous and, well, a brat," I admit.

It's hard to let my defaults hang out there like wet laundry, but I've heard my friends do it enough in prayer time, so I figure

I should give it a shot and *actually* tell it like it is. And not just about how I feel about other people, which is my M.O. But about me. About what's really going on inside.

Asher nods, his expression professional and unchanged. "I accept your apology."

"It's really hard to just... not get to do what I want, you know?" I start rambling. "Working certain hours, going off campus certain hours with certain groups of people, mandatory church attendance. After a year here I can't remember what I'd be doing anyway over what's been beaten into me with the *guidelines*." For the rest of my life I expect to say the word "guidelines" with a hint of dramatic sarcasm and accentuated hand quotes. "I just... I wanted to—"

"Be in control," Asher states, his eyes widening a bit.

"No," I answer quickly, before a thoughtful response can form.

He chuckles and retorts, "Yes."

"Explain yourself," I challenge.

He takes a deep breath. "Kennedy, how much prayer did you put into coming onboard this volunteer stint?"

I stare blankly at him.

"That's what I thought," he said. "It takes practice, but you need to know that the nightly prayer meetings, Bible groups, church attendance, all of that really *is* for your good. It's not for behavioral modification training... necessarily. It's spiritual modification training, if you will."

"Mmmhmm," I respond, unconvinced.

Asher stands, stretching his arms overhead before walking around his desk and sitting on the edge facing me so I'm now looking up at him. He folds his arms across his chest and it's a wonder his shirt doesn't rip. My mind wanders to all the bizarrely lean and fit guys at CU—disproportionately so, I think, than other universities. Perhaps the gym is a way to work out all *kinds* of frustrations. Before my mind travels toward sexualizing my boss and unlikely mentor, I refocus on what he's saying.

Pay attention, Kennedy...

"Regardless of what you think about the CU guidelines, what the goal is—or was at the university's inception—is to train students to seek God in prayer for *everything.* To practice listening and learn how God speaks to you. To make a habit of consulting Him for all matters. Big and small. To turn your life over *and* your will. Give it all to Him."

I stare at Asher with curiosity as words he says ring several bells.

Turn your life over and your will...

"What?" Asher asks. "What are you staring at me like that for?"

I look down, then back up again. "We never got together for lunch last year." The memory floods back. "We meant to, but then Winter Break happened and happened and *happened* and we never..."

Realization is apparent on his face as he takes a deep breath, but I continue.

"You told me you got arrested your junior year in college, but you never said why."

Asher runs a hand over his face, leaving it at his mouth for a moment before gripping the edge of the desk. "Okay," he says slowly. "Why are you bringing this up right now?"

"Something you said," I answer. "About me having to turn my life and my will over. I've heard that before. Read it, rather. It's one of the steps. The twelve steps. I've read through some of that blue book Roland has kicking around the house," I say of the Alcoholics Anonymous book. Roland tells me people just call it *The Big Book.*

Asher's jaw tightens, but he lets me finish.

"What'd you get arrested for, Asher?"

He takes another deep breath and stands, extending his hand to help me up from my seat. "Come, take a walk with me."

Without even a whisper of protestation I grab my bag and do as he asks, following him out the back door.

"You've been quiet," I observe after we've walked for about five whole minutes in silence, winding up the hill that separates CU from downtown Asheville. It's muggier than I'd like. I feel like I could part the air with a stroke of my hand.

"So have you," Asher says with a chuckle. "It's been nice, actually. That mouth of yours... running all the time..." For a second I think he's serious, but a tiny lopsided grin relieves my anxiety. And I punch him in the shoulder. "Violent to boot," he jokes before stuffing his hands in his pockets.

I keep silent for a few more seconds and try something. Taking a deep breath, I find a spot ahead of me to focus on. Meditate on.

God, help Asher. Whatever he's about to tell me can't be easy or he'd have done it already. If you don't want him to tell me, that's okay, too. Help keep me from nagging him. Chances are, it's none of my business anyway.

I take another deep breath when I'm finished with my mobile prayer and just wait in the still silence between the two of us. Not more than two seconds later, Asher begins.

"I assume since you've asked about my past you haven't looked it up?" he starts.

"What? Where?"

He grins. "The Internet?" he says as if talking to a small child.

"Oh," I say quickly, shaking my head. "No."

"Why?"

"It occurred to me the first time I knew you had... secrets." Asher winces a little but I continue. "But then I was spending so much time with school and online researching apologetics and all kinds of other crap that I honestly forgot. Then when I remembered again I just... well... I've had experience with people picking apart my life online and I decided to exercise restraint in that area. I don't even go on celebrity gossip sites anymore." I offer a playful pout and he chuckles. "Were you hoping I'd look you up?"

He hesitates for a moment. "Yes and no. I just... thought you might. It would have made it easier on me in some ways. Because I wouldn't have to sit down and tell you what happened. You could have just read about it." Asher sits on a bench about halfway up the hill between the coffee shop and campus. "Sit."

I comply, leaning my side against the back of the bench to face him. Pulling my knees into my chest, I wait for him to answer, recognizing that I'll likely hear a lot more if I talk far less.

"The first time I ever took a sip of alcohol was at a party my freshman year," he starts.

My jaw drops. "A party? I *knew* there were parties but, you were a freshman. I figured those were for upperclassmen or athletes or whatever?"

He grins. "Seriously?"

I put on my best comically indignant face. "Well *I've* never been to a party here... because I've never been invited."

"Consider yourself lucky."

"Pariah at most universities, but lucky here. Got it."

He arches his eyebrow the way he does when he's signaling to me at work that I need to get *back* to work.

"Sorry, go," I whisper.

"So," he takes a deep breath, "I loved it. There are no two ways around it. I loved the beer and the party atmosphere... all of it. It was so invigorating and so unlike anything I'd ever known growing up." My lips part again and he stops. "What? Something to say?"

"Ask."

"Shoot."

"It... it dawns on me I know nothing about your past. Your roots. Where are you from? It already strikes me odd that you're a, you know, one of them... us... whatever. But where do you come from that that was *foreign* to you as opposed to... frowned upon?"

He grins and shoots his gaze up to the sky for a minute. "You're perceptive, you know that?"

"It's a gift," I quip.

"Use it wisely," he retorts flatly. "Anyway, I'm from South Dakota."

"Weird, but, okay."

He laughs. "Why is that weird?"

I shrug. "It's just never occurred to me that people are actually *from* there." Now his jaw drops and I playfully hit his shoulder. "I'm just kidding. What'd you grow up in a seminary or something?"

"No." He huffs. "I'm from a Hutterite community," he says, looking down as if anticipating some unpleasant look from me that I don't have enough information to give.

"A... a what? Is that like... Mormon or something?"

"God, no," he says with a look on his face like he's smelled a burnt lemon. He quickly corrects his face though, shaking his head some. "No. Sorry. But no."

I sigh. "I have a feeling we'll need to come back to the whole Hutterite thing in some rich detail. But I won't let you use it as a diversion. For now, why don't you give me a clue. A generalization."

"Do you know about the Amish? And Mennonites?"

My eyes widen and I nod slowly, disbelieving where I think he's going.

"It's... sort of like that. In fact, Mennonites and Hutterites share a common ancestry, if you will."

I shrug. "I guess I'll have to until I learn more."

He waves his hand. "Basically it's a very conservative, secluded community, kind of like a co-op or a commune. You know what those are, right?"

"Yeah," I chuckle, "but I'm willing to bet that the communes I'm most familiar with involve a little more pot and a lot less clothing."

He laughs, thankfully. "Well, you get the idea. We had cars, and stuff like that, but we were a pretty self-sufficient community. Communal dinners, everyone working around the community on projects, farming, whatever. And, again, very conservative."

My eyes fall to his wrists and trace the intricate tattoo artistry up both arms. He seems to catch my stare, points to one of his arms and says, "All in the last two years."

"Interesting. I'm guessing whatever you got arrested for didn't bode well for your family especially."

"They didn't find out right away," he says with a long sigh. "They didn't know where I was."

"What?"

He eyes me seriously but with a far away look dancing across his face. "A few weeks before I turned eighteen, I ran away."

My jaw drops and my eyes bulge. "You... y... you—"

"I ran away, moved in with a friend of mine, who also used to live in the community, and I worked for him at his welding shop for several months. After some research we traveled to North Carolina, rented a tiny apartment, and set our sights on Carter. Our history proved persuasive with the administration. They offered us nearly full scholarships, which included a room and board stipend."

My mind is racing as every assumption I've had of Asher—good and bad—is dismantled in one fell swoop. I'm suddenly reminded of something Matt said last year that I'd completely forgotten— *Asher's the kind of guy that likes to challenge people's perceptions. Like he'll sit back and wait for you to have everything figured out then—Bam! He shows up with how it really is.* While the context of our conversation at the time was different, and about my attitudes toward other people, it leaves me wondering how much of Asher's story Matt knows. He knew about the prison ministry long before I did, after all.

"Kennedy." Asher snaps his fingers in front of my face, startling my attention back to him. "Have you had enough for today?" he says, almost like the family counselor my mom dragged me to for a year after I started actively seeking out more information about—and time with—Roland.

"We'll come back to this. I'm not kidding. But go on."

"Let's walk now." He stands and extends his hand to me. I take it, noting its sticky heat. Asher's nervous, and that makes me nervous.

Giving his hand a slight squeeze, I find his eyes as he looks toward me. "It's okay," I say softly. "Whatever it is, Asher."

He pulls his hand away from mine and shoves it in his pocket with a heavy sigh. "I don't talk about it much. Not to people out in the regular public anyway."

"You don't say." I chuckle, hoping some sarcasm will lighten the mood.

"I meant to do well... when I started at CU. I really did. I meant to comply with the guidelines and go to church and just keep my nose clean so I could graduate and get a job that would finally free me from a community I did *not* want to go back to." He's talking faster than usual, but instead of pointing that out, I let it go.

"Meant to? What happened?"

"People. Me. Excitement." Asher shrugs with each new word that passes his lips, as if he's watching the past flash before his eyes and he still can't believe it. "All those parties freshman year were so enticing."

I shake my head. "I thought those were just, like, the football team and stuff."

Asher grins the familiar cat-like grin I've come to find comfort in. "You mean to tell me you *really* haven't been to a single party here?"

I smirk. "Your obvious judgment aside, no. I stayed under the radar as much as possible the first several weeks here, and then after that... well... I guess my social pariah theory has finally been proven."

"Huh. I'd have thought people would intentionally invite the prodigal daughter out for some beers."

I shake my head. "I come from a wicked place." I arch an eyebrow. "Maybe they thought I'd cast a spell on them or something. Or tattle. Anyway," I lead Asher to continue, waving my hand.

He resumes his walk and I fall into stride next to him. We seem to be winding around the outskirts of campus. CU is in a pretty thickly wooded area of town, and I can say with some certainty that—guidelines aside—I'll never wander around out here alone after dark. I've never been able to trust the forest at night.

"I loved the parties," he admits. "I didn't even drink at them right away. I just loved being around so many people my age who seemed so relaxed in their language and clothing. The pretty girls didn't hurt, either."

"We never do," I cut in.

He laughs. "But of course I eventually took that first drink. I remember it like it was minutes ago," he says with a tone of dark nostalgia. Fear mixed with anger. "It was crazy. As soon as I drank that first beer I knew I'd made a fatal error."

"That's strong language," I say. "Sounds like something my dad would say, and he's an alcoholic."

"So am I," Asher blurts out. "Only, I didn't know it then. But, looking back, it's so obviously clear. Since there's no alcohol where I came from—at least none I was ever aware of—I don't know if anyone else in my family is. Maybe they know, but I doubt if I'll ever ask. And," he takes a deep breath before continuing, "if the physical reaction wasn't enough, the social assistance it provided me sealed the deal. Everyone liked me."

"Everyone likes you now," I point out.

"It was different then," he says, seeming impatient with himself. "It was so stereotypical of everything you've probably seen on TV or movies about kids in Amish or Mormon or some other community like that when they go into the '*real world*.'" He puts air quotes around the last words and I point to a bench that's dusted with fallen magenta petals from an enormous tree that promises to hug us with its shade.

"Let's sit."

He complies, and hangs his head for a minute, taking a long breath.

"Asher," I say, putting my hand in the center of his back. Even his shirt is hot. "I'm not going to judge you."

"You can't promise that," he says roughly, his head still down.

"I... okay you're right. I can't. But I don't *want* to. *That* I can promise. Did you, like, set an orphanage on fire or something?"

He lifts his head, a melancholy grin on his face. "No."

I hold out my hands. "Great, then we should be okay." I press my hand against his back again. "Please don't forget that I know exactly how it feels to be unfairly judged. I know too much about humans in general to judge them anymore anyway—as weird as that sounds."

Asher sits up, leans against the bench, and looks at me curiously. "How do you mean?"

"Everyone is so friggen broken, Asher. I think we better be grateful we *can't* eternally judge each other, or none of us would stand a chance."

He nods slowly, saying nothing.

I lean against his shoulder, resting my back against the bench as he is. "So," I whisper. "What brings you here?" I say in a gentle voice.

"Courtney Matthews," he says, much to my surprise.

"A girl," I observe.

He nods. "A sophomore girl who attended the same parties I did with the same regularity. We fell in crazy lust with each other. Fast."

I keep my mouth shut. I've heard enough of the girls around me talk for the last year, and thumbed through plenty of Eden's dating books and even some interesting reads on Roland's bookshelf to know that this is heavy. Serious. For society, for sure, but not everyone recognizes it. In Christian circles, though? Lust is a *big* deal. An emotional gateway drug.

"We kissed at every party, but as quick as it happened, soon enough we wanted more. *Needed* more, we thought. I'll spare you the play-by-play, but it very quickly became a game of seeing how far we could go without... going all the way."

I nod. "I've played that game, too," I whisper, speaking to no one in particular despite my present company.

"Then, it finally happened. It was inevitable, really, given how completely careless we'd been up to that point. But at one party during a long weekend, we'd both had far more to drink than usual, and we had sex."

Despite suspecting where he was headed with this story, Asher's honesty drops my jaw. It was only relatively recently that I discovered his core values, anyway, but given those, and the family he told me he grew up in, and just the kind of guy I know him to be, the thought of him having had sex before marriage makes me sad for him more than it shocks me.

"A lot at first, then we tried to stop. To space ourselves out. We tried to avoid going to the same parties because we knew the temptation was strong. We'd go weeks and months without seeing each other sometimes. Sometimes actively avoiding each other. It went on for almost two years. But... the temptation was stronger than my own resolve. And when she was a senior, and I was a junior... she got pregnant."

I fall forward a little, catching my elbows on my knees as I rake my fingers through my hair, giving it a little tug to make sure I'm awake. "Jesus," I whisper slowly. "Are you *serious?*"

He nods, clenching his jaw. "It gets worse."

Of course it does, I realize. Asher's never worn a wedding ring, has never mentioned a wife, child, or girlfriend. Of course it gets worse.

But, how much worse?

"I'm listening," I say, sitting up and taking his hand briefly, giving it a squeeze.

"We were both scared, ashamed, and devastated. It was a few days before Thanksgiving break that she found out and she was scared to go home and tell her family. I still wasn't talking to mine, and I'd been so far separated from any morals that I didn't know what to do. We talked about raising a child, putting it up for adoption, all of those things. But... we didn't have any counsel. We were scared. Fear is ugly," he says with a bite of anger. "We didn't even know if we *liked* each other, let alone love each other. We never courted, never dated. I barely ever saw her around campus. It was just parties and bedrooms..."

"Oh Asher, I'm so sorry."

He shakes his head. "Save your sympathy," he says coldly.

I swallow a boulder-sized lump in my throat. "What was a few days before Thanksgiving break?" I ask, holding onto that detail of the story.

"The last time I got drunk."

My heart skips a beat. I've heard Roland's story. About the last time he got drunk. According to my reading of his AA Big Book, every alcoholic has one. The *last* one. And they all seem to remember it with vivid clarity.

"What happened?" My voice shakes, unsure if I really want to know the answer.

"I crashed my car into a guardrail. Drunker than I'd ever been," he says flatly."

"No..." My stomach lurches, thinking of Courtney and the baby.

"I was the only one in the car," he says, seeming to sense my fear. Relief does wash over me... but it's brief.

I clear my throat. "What happened before that?"

"Courtney and I had kept partying even while trying to decide what to do about the baby," he admits. "I was *so* screwed up, Kennedy. We both were. We were so stupid. So irresponsible. Maybe somehow we were hoping it would all go away if we ignored it."

I can sympathize with this line of thinking. The few girls I've known who got pregnant in high school held onto that same magical thinking. I don't tell Asher this, though. It doesn't look like he's seeking camaraderie in this misery.

"What... happened?" I ask again, slowly. He looks like he's about to break in two.

His eyes lift to the sky, the reflection of a warm sun giving away the tears at the corners of his eyes. "A few days before Thanksgiving we arrived at a party separately. Courtney looked... off. Vacant instead of worried. Hollow. Resigned. I... I asked her what was wrong and she—" Asher's tears cut him off. Tears. He lowers his head and breaks into a sob right here on the bench. Shoulders trembling under his heaving breath.

"Oh my God. Asher," I say, swallowing my own unassigned tears. "Asher..." I take a deep breath, brushing my hand back and forth across his shoulders as he gathers his composure.

Through thick tears and a gravelly voice, Asher lets it out. "She got an abortion that morning, Kennedy!"

The world falls out from beneath me and I drop to my knees in front of Asher. His hands cradle his head as tears drop to the ground, some landing on his boots, some on my knees. Big, dark splashes of shame and regret. They'll never dry all the way. Placing my hands over his, I rest my forehead against his.

"It's..." I start softly, but he cuts me off.

"It's not okay!" he growls. "It's not."

I wasn't going to say that, I don't think, but I don't correct his outburst.

"She said she couldn't have a baby with where she was in her life, couldn't raise one with someone just like her—a drunk—and didn't know if she could go through with adoption. So she killed it. She killed our baby!" His words are vile but the tears tell another side of the story. "We killed it," he finally says.

"We?" I ask, our heads still pressed together.

"I wasn't there for her. I ran, emotionally. She couldn't trust me and I didn't ever say abortion wasn't an option. We hadn't discussed it at all."

I take a deep breath. "Asher... breathe."

Asher sits up and I can see his face. Red, swollen from the pressure of guilty tears. "The only death that day was that of my unborn child. I wanted to die, too, though. I can't remember. I blacked out long before I hit the guardrail. I was arrested on the spot and woke up handcuffed to a hospital bed."

I rock back slightly, sitting on my heels. "Holy... crap."

He finally makes eye contact with me, but it's still distant and filled with salty regret. "That's the first day I met your dad."

"Oh..."

"I hadn't been to his church more than two or three times. But in my drunken rant after the accident I told the officers and anyone who would listen that my non-girlfriend had aborted our baby and I would never stop drinking the pain away. All of this was relayed to a school counselor and my friend, who was listed as my emergency contact since I have no contact with my family. Courtney was removed from school and sent to counseling. They didn't kick her out though, which I was grateful for, but she left anyway. She couldn't stand the label of *murderer* that would have followed her around. That probably still does."

I huff. "So much for forgiveness."

Asher continues as if he didn't hear me. "I don't know what the school would have done with me had I just stayed at that party and out of my car that day. But the sexual misconduct, partying, drunk driving, the accident... not to mention my shaky grades. The school dismissed me almost immediately."

"Gracious..." I quip under my breath. I wonder how they would have handled him had he and Courtney gone forward with the pregnancy.

Asher sighs. "Roland caught wind of it all and was at my bedside when I regretfully regained consciousness."

I slowly move from the ground back to the bench. "You don't still wish you were dead... do you?"

He shrugs and lowers his head for a second. "Not every day. I can't say I'd be saying the same if your dad hadn't brought me to my first AA meeting that weekend."

All of Asher's little clues from earlier in his office fall beautifully into place. I assumed he was in a recovery program, but I couldn't have imagined the story that led him there.

"Is he your sponsor or something?" I ask.

Asher chuckles. Small, but it'll do. "No. And even if he was I wouldn't tell you. *Anonymous*," he reminds me. But before the conversation gets too light, Asher's face turns red and he buries it in his hands again, a sudden wave of sobs overtaking him. The remorse is sticky and palpable.

"No," I say firmly, once again kneeling in front of him. "Asher, it wasn't your fault. I don't even really think it was hers. It was just an awful situation."

"I never even gave that baby a chance," he growls. "Courtney knew she couldn't count on me. And I never told her *not* to get an abortion. Maybe somewhere in my soul I was hoping she would."

I shake my head. "Not possible. Not you."

"And she did it without talking to me about it. Like I had no say in the matter. Like... like she knew I'd tell her to do it or something." He folds forward and rests *his* head against mine now, and I'm speechless.

I've never thought the man did have much of a say in matters like this. But this horribly broken human in front of me has blown apart my theories and assumptions yet again. I want to help him, but I don't know how.

All those protests I've been to, and my mother's career has, from time to time, centered around this very thing. Not Asher crying on a bench, of course, but women being able to just up and walk into a clinic when all other options have dried out. I've never once seen this side. The invisible side. It's not just about moms and babies.

This is too much right now.
Do something.

Help him.

How?

"Asher," I whisper, shakily. "Can I pray with you?"

"Please," he begs, wrapping his hands around mine. "Please."

CHAPTER THIRTEEN

DAD

Roland.

THE knock on the door pulls my attention away from staring at the clock, wondering how long Kennedy will be with Asher talking about her attitude earlier in the week. Wondering if she made plans after that and didn't tell me. Because she's not technically required to. The second knock actually gets me to walk to the door, my mind loud with how terrifying teenagers are. I'm not scared *of* them, just *for* them. Especially when the *them* is my daughter.

"Asher," I say, slowly, opening the door. My heart sinks, and I pray he's not coming by to look for Kennedy. Either way, she's not where I thought she was. Refocusing my attention on Asher, I notice the swelling in his face. Tears. "What's going on?"

He shrugs under a black leather coat that must be a thousand degrees to wear. He wears it everyday regardless. "Is Kennedy back yet?" He drags the heel of his hand under his eyes, seeming to wipe away tears.

Yet.

I swallow hard, opening the door and stepping back so Asher can come in. "I haven't heard from her since she left to go meet you. She *did* meet you, right?"

I have no reason not to trust Kennedy. Quite the opposite, actually. She's never given me reason to do anything *but* trust her. But teenagers are a fickle breed.

He nods. "Yeah she did. Then we took a walk and she left me like an hour ago."

Continuing my quest not to panic at the simple notion of a nineteen-year-old out minding her own business, I press Asher on the current state of his appearance. "You look rough."

"I want to drink. Bad." He drags his feet behind him as he wanders into the kitchen and plunks down on a stool at the island.

"Yeah?" I say deliberately. This isn't the first time Asher's stated his case in my kitchen, and I assume it won't be the last. I fetch a can of seltzer from the fridge and slide it across the island.

He grunts, the aluminum crack of the can opening echoes in the kitchen. "I meant something stronger than this."

"So? You're an alcoholic. That's what we do... *want* to drink. But if you *really* wanted to get drunk, you would have gone to a thousand other places than your sponsor's house."

He takes a sip, looking none too happy about it. "I told Kennedy you weren't my sponsor, by the way."

With that one sentence Asher tells me that his conversation with Kennedy covered far more than her attitude. "How much does she know?"

"Everything."

I lift my eyebrows. "That's a lot. All at once?"

He shakes his head. "I hadn't planned on it, really. She knew there was more to me than I was telling her, and she called me on it. I started by telling her about the sex and the parties and then the accident but... damn it if that daughter isn't a carbon copy of you in some ways, man. She *knew* there was more. Asked me what happened earlier in the day before I crashed the car. And, just like with you, I ended up spilling it all."

"And now you want to drink," I observe. "Because you were vulnerable with someone."

Asher sets the can down on the island with a heavy thud and points at me. "You got it."

I shrug. "So why'd you come here? Why not be sitting down at Johnny's or McClarin's or wherever it is people get boozed up on a Friday afternoon?"

He faces me, the despair in his eyes shifting to confusion and a little anger. "Dude, are you serious?"

"Think the drink through, man. You tell *me* why you're here. And it's not because you want to drink."

Asher's jaw flexes beneath his skin. If I didn't already know him so well, I'd probably be afraid to push his buttons. Thankfully I know him to be a bowl of mush packed inside a huge frame.

"Well?" I press, while the back of my mind wonders exactly what Asher said, and how. And what Kennedy is doing right now. Where she is...

Asher folds his arms on the countertops and briefly lowers his forehead onto them, taking a long, deep breath. Lifting his head as he exhales, he eyes me again. "I'm here because I don't want to drink. The alcoholism wants me to. Real bad. But I don't want to. And, even if I thought I did, I couldn't anyway because your daughter prayed for me."

My heart skips a beat. "She what?"

He rises from his stool and stretches his arms overhead. "She prayed for me, man," he says again with half a grin.

"Out loud?" I question before having time to think through the words. I don't want it to seem like I'm passive about Kennedy's prayer life, but I know that praying aloud isn't for everyone. And it's not part of the spiritual culture she grew up in.

Asher laughs. "Yes. Not only out loud, but we were on a bench on Cottage St. So, pretty public. Well, I was on the bench. She was knelt down in front of me squeezing the life out of my hands."

Goosebumps shoot across my back and down my arms. God's here. Poking me to recognize the work he's doing in Kennedy's life and in those around her. "Wow," I whisper, trying not to get overly emotional. "What'd that do for you?"

"I'd been wanting a drink all day, actually," Asher admits. "For no particular reason other than I woke up."

I nod in solidarity. Sometimes the urge comes out of nowhere. Sometimes the longer it stays away, the stronger it is when it shows up.

"But," he continues, "when she prayed for me without hesitation or question or second-guessing... I knew it was God doing for me what I couldn't do for myself. It's crazy... You know I don't usually hear God's voice through other people. I'm more of a dreams and listening in my own head kind of guy. But as Kennedy went on it was like... *so* clear that God was using her as a vessel to save my sorry soul today."

I nod, swallowing hard, sending up a silent praise to God that Kennedy got out of her own way long enough to let God intercede for Asher. Whether she was conscious of it or not, she may have saved his life for today.

"You know where she is now?" I ask, picking up my cell to text her. Asher shrugs. "You need a meeting though, huh? I do too, frankly." I look at the clock. "St. Andrew's starts in twenty. Wanna go?"

"Yes. *Yes*." The color is returning to his face, which is a good sign, but not enough to bank the rest of the day on.

I find Kennedy's number in my phone and type out a quick text.

Me: Hey you, just checking in. Everything okay with Asher?

I'm grateful she has her read receipts turned on so I can see she's received *and* read the text I just sent. Waiting for her to answer takes half an eternity.

Kennedy: Weird. He's not mad at me though, so that's good.

Me: Where are you now?

I've already checked her location via her iPhone—a feature her mother has insisted she leave on, and Kennedy didn't protest. So I know Kennedy's at the University Chapel, though I don't know why, and I'm praying she's honest. It annoys me that my gut instinct is to not trust her. But it's not *her*, it's her age group. They struggle to work out their honesty muscles.

Kennedy: UC. Why?

Me: You busy? Going to be long? Or can I come by? I have something I want to talk about with you.

Kennedy: Ask a few more questions.

I chuckle before considering she could actually be annoyed. "What?" Asher asks.

"She's funny," I remark offhand before returning to the text.

"Yeah," he huffs, "a real riot. Gets into your chest and scrambles things around until they pour out of your mouth. Like father like daughter."

I shake my head, shooting Asher a grin and taking pride in a gift Kennedy might not even be aware that she has.

Me: Sorry.

Kennedy: I was kidding. Don't panic. You can come.

I find it interesting that she didn't ask to just talk when we got home, which piques my anxiety and curiosity at the same time, but I'm not quite sure why. Maybe I have to pray for the willingness to accept that being directly in charge of a young adult is going to ramp up my paranoia. More fodder to talk about with my sponsor, I guess.

"All right," I finally say to Asher. "We gotta make one stop on the way to the meeting. Let's go."

Concern for someone other than himself washes over his face, which is another good sign that he's coming out of his craving. "She okay?"

"I think so."

The creak of the heavy wooden door at the front of the chapel echoes into the vaulted ceiling. It takes my eyes a minute to adjust to the dim, muted rainbow light cast by candles and the stained-glass windows. When they finally do, I can see half a dozen people in various stages of prayer throughout the dark, wooden pews. Kennedy said she was here, so finding her doesn't surprise me, but her position in the very first pew does.

I make my way to the front, performing the sign of the cross over my chest as I do. This isn't standard practice in many evangelical circles, but something I've always just found myself doing when in more traditional churches such as this. It serves as a good reminder to myself at times, I guess. Arming myself with everything Jesus died for me to have.

"Hey," I whisper once I reach the front.

Kennedy slides over without looking up at me. Her eyes are fixed on the massive stained-glass window at the front of the church, just behind the altar. A rendition of Jesus being taken down from the cross. Bloodied and surrounded by those who love him. I always focus on the face of his mother, Mary. And I thought losing Kennedy was bad...

"Hey," she mumbles.

"I talked to Asher," I admit up front. "He told me it got kind of heavy."

She nods and gives a long blink. A tear rolls down her cheek and breaks my heart.

"Do you want to talk about it?"

Still facing forward, Kennedy speaks. Soft but clear. "Everything's inside out."

After a few seconds of silence, I ask, "What do you mean?"

She shrugs. "It's like... It's like I fell down a rabbit hole and tumbled out into Munchkinland. Only... there's no yellow brick road, and Tim Burton has taken over as mayor."

I stare at her for a moment, thanking God for her creativity and eloquence. I might have the gift of speech, but she's got a gift of words that takes my breath away.

"Yeah," I say, as if I have a clue, "life does that sometimes." Because I do. And it does.

Finally, she looks at me. Her eyes are wet, but she's composed as usual. No signs of significant distress on the surface. "The good news is that Matt and I are on even footing again. But the rest? Forget it."

"How so?"

She sighs and looks to the ceiling for a moment as if composing a grocery list in her head. "Let's see. Well, Asher's a real person. A broken, *broken* one. Classes start in a little over a week, filming for a *reality show* starts next week where I intend to *allow* barely-restricted access to my life, I've joined the university worship band, it seems, and have to do a performance with them at the end of the first week of school. Ugh. My friendship with Mollie has gone from breezy to complicated, and it barely bothers me, and *that* bothers me. Silas is being nice while Bridgette is MIA, and I really want to live with you for this school year."

She looks at me with wide, vulnerable, hopeful eyes. Eyes that stared at me through the face of a five-year-old girl in a photograph for over a decade.

Twisting my lips, I put a hand over hers as they sit folded in her lap. "Can I tell you something?"

"Sure."

"It's all going to be okay."

She rolls her eyes and I hold back a chuckle. "Are you serious right now?" she asks in a volume well above a whisper. "It's going to be *okay*?"

"Hear me out."

"Do I have a choice?"

"Yes," I say, then wait. She roams her eyes around the room but stays put.

"Fine," she finally says. "What." She barely ever says it like a question.

"You prayed with Asher," I start. "*For* him."

Her eyes widen. "He *told* you about that?"

I nod. "You may have saved his life today." It's a bit dramatic, but you must meet people on their level.

"That's pushing it," she calls me out.

"The power of prayer isn't something to be messed with. No, it's not a magic potion or spell. It's more than that. So much more. Never underestimate it, Kennedy. Whether in your head, by yourself in your room, or aloud with another person, prayer offers protection, comfort, healing, and redemption. Sometimes in the moment, and sometimes generations down the line. I firmly believe that where I am today is due, in part, to prayers your grandfather—your mother's father—shared with me and for me ever since he met me."

Kennedy's eyes flutter wildly back and forth across my face. "What does this have to do with all the other stuff? Asher aside."

I smile as broad as I can and, taking a risk, kiss her on the forehead. "Take what you did for Asher today and do it for yourself. Pray over all of those things, and I will, too. Hey, listen..."

"Yeah?" Her hair had been up in a ponytail, but she removes the elastic and allows her hair to fall across her back.

"I'm on my way to an AA meeting. It's open, meaning you could come... if you wanted to. I've been meaning to ask, just so you can... see... but, maybe after all you've heard today, and from me for the last couple of years, you want to come?"

Kennedy takes a hard breath and puffs out her cheeks. "Soon," she answers. "But, not today if that's okay?"

I nod, trying to mask my disappointment but understanding completely. "Of course it's okay. Just let me know when you're ready and I'll probably ask a half dozen times in between now and then, too." I stand, not wanting her to feel like she has to be the one to leave, and I've got Asher in the car. "I'll be home for dinner, okay? Want pizza?"

She stands and shakes her head. "I'll make us something."

Swallowing hard, all I can manage to do is nod before barely squeaking out, "Sounds great."

Turning on my heels I walk as casually as possible out of the church, when I really want to drop to my knees and thank God for this gift of a second chance with her.

"Oh, Dad?" she calls after me, this time lifting a few heads among the praying crowd. Her voice echoes through far more than the building.

Dad...

She doesn't call me that very often, and I don't ever *expect* it from her, so I take what I can get.

"What's up?" I turn to find her walking after me.

"Is Asher going to be okay?" she whispers.

I give her a tight side hug. "He is. Just keep praying for him, okay?"

She nods. "I will. See you at home."

"Yeah," I exhale a sigh of gratitude. "See you at home."

CHAPTER FOURTEEN

TO THE WORLD

Kennedy.

"JESUS never intended for Christianity to be a *thing*," Roland states, pacing in front of our New Testament class on a fresh Friday morning. This sounds like a spinoff of his message from yesterday, so I'll get to test how much I retained from his sermon. "In fact," he continues, "his early followers simply called their path *The Way*. Jesus called *himself* The Way, and his earliest followers were just that—people who were following The Way."

Classes have been underway for a couple of weeks now, with the NBC camera crew in tow and so far, I'm happy to report, there haven't been any casualties. When students arrived for move-in day, and a few days after, there was much excitement and giggling about the show. Some people were grumpy they weren't asked to be a focus, although everyone is still trying to get on camera now and then—no matter how nonchalant they try to look.

It's not as weird being in Roland's class as I thought it would be. But, we haven't had any graded assignments yet, so I have time to revise my opinion of the whole thing.

To be honest, I'm having a hard time focusing. My regular work schedule starts at Word tonight, and I've got Bible study, band rehearsal, and our first gig at Sunday's service coming up all in the next three days. I know I'll be able to balance the mechanics of the schedule easy enough, I'm just hoping I'm up to the task, emotionally speaking.

"What we're going to spend the next couple of weeks looking at, class, is all the *I am* statements Jesus made. Does anyone know what they are?"

Cue Silas.

"Yes, Silas?" Roland grins as if he heard my thoughts.

Silas, directly to my left, speaks with confidence, but not the cocky vile kind he had when I first met him. His whole demeanor has changed since last year. He's softer and gentler, in voice and manner.

"Jesus makes seven 'I am' statements found in the book of John. The Bread of Life, The Gate—or Door in some translations—The Light of the World, The Good Shepherd, The Truth, The Life, and The Way—like you said."

Roland nods astutely. "Very good. Now you've all heard these statements throughout your entire lives."

Except for Kennedy.

"But," he continues, "how many of you have given thought to what *each* of them mean for your life? Why did Jesus bother to state these seven things about himself? We're going to be breaking that down over the next several classes. And, at the end of it, each of you will be given an *I am* statement on which you'll write a personal essay."

What? I've skated through my time at CU without having to personalize a single thing in my coursework. When I first entered school, I was waiting for this moment—the time when I could throw all of my worldly "knowledge" into the faces of my professors. But now? First of all, my worldly knowledge has changed so much over the last several months that I've had to start reexamining everything I've once thought as true. Second of all, this is my *dad's* class. I can't decide if that makes things better or worse.

The shuffling of papers and the zip of zippers throws Roland's eyes to the clock. The verdict: the students are on time. Class is over. I usually participate in calling the professors' attention to the fact that class is over, but I don't with Roland. Again, the dad thing makes it confusing.

I offer a quick wave to Roland as I zip my coat and throw my bag over my shoulder. I don't make a show of lots of small talk with him after class. I don't want the rest of the class to think I'm getting some sort of extra attention or special privilege from him, though it's kind of a tough case to make since I live with him. And we're filmed what feels like *constantly*.

The TV crew.

Yes, they're sticking to the deal they made in all of our contracts that they're only here two weekdays and so far they've been able to get footage on both Friday and Saturday. It was tricky but unsurprising wording in the contract. It was written to make sure a single student didn't get filmed on both of those days, not that they would flat out choose one day. Living off campus, I haven't been involved in the nightly floor prayer sessions, and that's okay by me, but Eden says it's weird having the cameras there. She says the girl named Adelaide, who is filming in her dorm, is nice and will usually only film for a couple of minutes—but it's still weird.

As if I'd need reasons to feel more naked in public prayer. However, my luck in that department will change on Sunday with the first service at New Life that Water on Fire will be singing at. The camera crew didn't film at the first church service, per prior arrangement with Roland, so this will also be the first time they're there. Filming us in our intercessions with God.

I don't like it.

"Kennedy, can you hang back for a moment?" Roland calls after me in an overly done professor tone.

"Later," Silas says cheerfully, patting my shoulder as he scoots by.

"Later," I reply, holding my index finger up to Matt, asking him to wait for me. I'm still relieved when he responds to me, even though it's been a few weeks since we've been back on track. He points that he'll be waiting outside.

"What's up?" I ask Roland once the last of my classmates have moved on to their next destinations.

"I'm not holding you up from another class, right? You don't have one till later?"

"Right." I roll my eyes. *Literature.*

Roland chuckles. "What? Aren't you reading literature?"

"I guess. Not, like, anything relevant. We're certainly not reading *The Divine Comedy.*"

Roland twists his lips. "I heard you asked Professor Walker if that would be on the reading list this semester."

"Of course you did." I snicker and lean against the podium he teaches from. "So what's up?"

Roland tries to look casual, but it's the kind I recognize from class when he's about to discipline someone. Only, I haven't done anything out of line that I can think of, though that's never stopped demerits before.

"How are things going with the film crew around, and all that?"

I shrug. "I barely notice them." That's a total lie, but I pretend not to notice them. My theory is that the more uninterested I seem, the more uninteresting I'll be to them. Then, I can save my more talkative self for the interviews.

"You're cooperating?"

I scrunch my eyebrows. "Cooperating? Yes. No one's *asked* anything of me. Wh—what is this about?"

Roland takes a few steps closer to me before looking around the room, I look, too, making sure we're really alone.

"What?" I whisper.

He sighs. "I can't believe I'm going to tell you this," he starts, which does little to calm me. "But, some people at the network are wondering if your living with me is causing you to go into hermit mode and they're not able to get an accurate representation of what life is like for a more secular student like you at CU."

I snort. "That's rich. As if I'm the most liberal kid here." I have zero grounds for this statement. "They can find someone else."

Roland's eyes pinch at the corners.

"They don't want someone else," I say, monotone. "They *want* me don't they? It wasn't enough to get me to *agree* to be filmed... was it?"

With regret coloring his eyes, Roland shakes his head. "Apparently not. And, you yourself told me you wanted to be in control... and all that..."

"I... I don't know what to do," I say, feeling helpless. "I can't even..."

"Dean Baker isn't thrilled with the idea of you getting more screen time, either."

I arch my eyebrow and take a step back. "Fine, then. I'm in. They want more of me, they've got more of me. I will share zero allegiance with that walking blowfish."

Roland rolls his eyes. "Revenge on Dean Baker... or whatever this is... isn't a good motivator, Kennedy."

I shrug. "This isn't about revenge," I try to assure him, adjusting the straps on my backpack. "This isn't about revenge at all. This is about justice. And independence."

"Independence?" he questions.

I nod. "Dean Easy Bake Oven doesn't get to dictate what I do or how I do it."

"If you want to get anywhere with him, you're going to have to do more than countermeasures, you know. Not that I'm saying you *should* be planning *anything* in regards to him... I'm just... saying."

Oh, Roland. He's trying to be the better person here, I know he is. And I don't intend to play as dirty as the dean, but I'm not going to be a marionette of his any longer—as if I ever were.

"You've got a frightening grin on your face, Kennedy," Roland says with a nervous laugh.

I give him a firm pat on the shoulder and follow it with a wink. "*Jesus Freaks* is in need of a star, Roland. And a star they're going to get."

"You," he half-asks, half-answers.

"I either wait for the network to pervert my friends in some way, or let the administration curate a Jesus Fantasy Land that will make the students here look just as bad... trust me."

"Don't do anything that's going to get you kicked out of school or make me field middle-of-the-night calls from your mother. Please." Roland returns to the podium and pulls out lecture notes for his next class as a few students trickle in.

I stare at him for a few seconds. "You're not going to try to stop me?"

"Nope." He grins. "Because, A. It wouldn't work and B. I trust you enough not to do anything stupid."

"Thanks." I smile back at him and walk out of the building in search of Matt... and a camera guy.

I spot Matt quickly when he flags me down from under a tree on the quad.

"What was that about?" he asks as I approach.

I shrug. "Just checking in on the reality show stuff. Apparently I need to make myself more available."

Matt's eyes widen as we make our way to Mission Hall. "He *said that?*"

"God no," I reply, offering no more. "What's with the speed, psycho? You that hungry?"

He does this weird move in an attempt to flex his muscles while walking. "You can't maintain this brawn without eating every few hours."

"Yikes." I grin and he smacks my shoulder.

As we approach Mission Hall, I catch sight of a startled Eden running through the doors and toward us. It brings a queasy flashback feeling of last year when my not-so-undercover identity was revealed to the whole school right in this same setting.

"What?" I ask, studying her wide eyes.

"Joy's here," she blurts out.

I'd heard Joy Martinez, my arch-nemesis according to the Internet, was returning to CU in the fall. All attempts I made to contact her over the summer through her CU email were in vain—her account was no longer active. It's been a few weeks since the start of school and I haven't seen or heard from her, and neither has anyone I asked.

"Seriously?" Matt answers for me, as I remain glued in my spot, staring at Eden.

She nods. "She's at a table talking with a camera person and Dean Baker."

Heat rises through my neck and Matt eyes me. "Perfect." I swallow hard. "Excellent timing."

"Odd timing, if you ask me," Eden admits, perching her hands on her hips.

"Glad you said it," Matt mumbles.

"Good," I take a breath, "we're all on the same paranoid page."

Eden puts a hand on my shoulder. "What are you going to do?"

My conversation with Roland flashes briefly through my mind. I lift my chin and take a deep breath. "I'm going to take some control for once."

Neither of them say anything, which I appreciate. They just follow me into the crowded dining hall as I scan for Joy and company.

"Back corner," Eden murmurs, and instantly I spot them.

Talking over my shoulder, I say, "Let me go by myself. I'll find you after, okay?"

As I get closer, I see that while it certainly *is* Joy, her appearance has changed drastically. Her once waist-length hair has been sheared into a severely angled reverse bob—the front of her hair a few inches below her chin while the back is stacked almost boy-short. Also, even though she's sitting, I can tell she's lost a lot of weight which is concerning since I don't think she cast much of a shadow in the first place.

The NBC camera kid spots me first. I recognize him from Roland's class. He's probably five foot eleven and a little soft in the middle with one heck of a baby face underneath a mop of bouncy brown curls. His name badge says "Finn," but that's all I know of him. Either way, he clearly recognizes me by the lift of his eyebrows, which draws the attention of Joy and the dean away from their conversation.

"Joy," I open, with a smile. "You're back."

"Kennedy," she says with a similar smile but also a bit of hesitation.

And, now we're in one of the most awkward bouts of silence I've encountered in my nineteen years. Which says a lot given how the last year has gone.

"I'm not really back," she says, standing and walking to the head of the table to face me. "Not yet anyway. But... I told the school I'd be happy to do an interview about the process of getting myself ready to come back." She looks down to her fingers, fidgeting with them. Her voice is unique. A Southern-mixed-with-Spanish accent. She was adopted from Korea as a baby and grew up speaking mostly Spanish at home with her bilingual adoptive parents, but her South Carolina address is also present in her voice.

Leaning in, I whisper, "Can we take a walk?"

She nods. Dean Baker, who's been eerily silent up until now, clears his throat. "I'm in the middle of a meeting, Miss Sawyer."

Peering around Joy, I offer the most fake, polite smile I can. "We'll be just a moment, if you don't mind. I promise to return her in one piece." Giving him a slight wink, which takes about all the guts I have left for today, I turn on my heels and head for the back door.

Joy's close behind me. I can tell because every time we pass a table, the conversation ceases for the second or so we're in front of them. Except those gracious people who pretend not to care.

There's a bench right at the exit of the dining hall and, since it's clear, I grab it. It would take too long to find something completely private, and nothing's completely private in this place, anyhow.

"Can we sit here?" I ask her. She nods

I'm face-to-face with my accuser for the first time in several months. I thought I'd hate her. That I'd want to swear at her—

again—or throw something at her. Looking at her nervous face, though, I just want this to be over. For both of us.

Before I can say anything else, Finn pops his head out the back door, spots me, and grins.

"*God*," I mumble under my breath.

"What?" Joy asks.

I nod to the door. "We have company."

"Hey guys," he starts. "Do you mind if I—"

"Yep." I hold up my hand, stopping him. "We mind."

He tilts his head to the side. "Contract?"

"Shrewd," I reply, narrowing my eyes. "This is the first time we've talked since last year..." I don't know why I thought this would help my case.

"Excellent!" Finn answers. "Proceed like I'm not even here."

I huff. "Whatever. Joy," I say quietly, turning to her, then chickening out a little. "Your hair looks great. So different!"

She smiles. "Thanks. I donated it. I've done that a couple of times. My hair grows really fast, thankfully." She laughs nervously and crosses her legs. "I like your hair, too. I always wanted wavy hair, but it's too thick. Not even a curling iron works for long."

I smile, searching for something to say to thank her for the compliment, but I can't stand another second of pretend-conversation with her. "What happened, Joy?" I blurt out, shaking my head and looking down.

Of everyone here, and of all the strides I've made, I find it disturbingly difficult to look her in the eyes. She said I was having an affair with the *pastor* for goodness sake.

"I mean, what... happened? Why did you target me? What did I do to you?"

I look up and Joy looks down, our eye contact see-saw seems to be working for us right now. "I hated you." She looks up after she says it, then looks down again.

I hated you.

I assume people have hated me before, but I figured they just went about their business and said it behind my back. "But you told a lie. And you told one about Roland. And you didn't come to me with it..." I trail off, needing to take a breath to calm the brewing anger.

Tears instantly spill down Joy's cheeks. I hadn't thought her capable of tears, so I just kind of sit with my face unmoving. "I'm so sorry," Joy sobs into her hands.

I can't help it, but out of the corner of my eye I search for Finn, to see if he's enjoying any of this. He's just far enough around my side that my peripheral vision misses him.

"I've already forgiven you, Joy," I say quickly, as if I've practiced it a million times because, in a away, I have. In prayer I've asked for the grace to withstand my first meeting with her since everything went down. Maybe this is what grace looks like. Maybe it's not always harps and hugs and sunshine. Maybe it's tears on a bench in the middle of a college campus with a film crew nearby.

I put a hand on her shoulder and look around. Yep, we're attracting attention. "I just... want to know why. Why did, do, you hate me? Why Roland? And why not just talk to me about it before spreading all the gossip?"

I wonder if Joy can honestly answer any of these questions. There was this time when I was ten and was playing with a yo-yo in my living room. I started swinging it around and, inevitably, broke a lamp. One of my mom's favorites. I don't remember her reaction, which could be a good or bad thing, I suppose, but when she asked *why* I broke it, I couldn't really answer. I was being an idiot and not thinking clearly. My guess is there's a lot of hurt in this world caused by people being idiots and not thinking clearly.

Joy shrugs and looks up, wiping her tears away. She's either wearing waterproof mascara or has amazingly natural lashes, because there are no black streaks down her cheeks. "I had no idea why someone like you would want to come to Carter. You're from a liberal state, which is one thing—but there are all kinds of people everywhere." I nod slowly while she continues her character analysis of me. "But when we were in the dining hall that first week—maybe it was even the first day—you made it clear that you had no problems with liberal politics, or the homosexual agenda..."

Agenda...

Whatever, just listen to her.

I roll my eyes anyway because I can't just let that one slide.

"And," she continues, "I started trying to figure out *why* you'd want to come to *Carter*. So far from home for you in a *lot* of ways."

Tell me about it.

I keep my mouth shut, because I've learned quickly in my time here that that's the best policy right out of the gate. But, Joy has more to say. "I started seeing things that I now know weren't there. I mean, your da—Roland is a pretty divisive issue for some on campus, and you seemed pretty chummy with him. At first I figured it was just because you are both so liberal." *I hate politics.* "But, then I saw how he smiled at you, and I saw you two hug a couple of times. Not necessarily romantic hugs, but longer than is usually acceptable between staff and students."

I figured this much. Major errors on both mine and Roland's part in the effort to keep our relationship under wraps. "I get that," I say out loud. "But... the fliers? Was that necessary?"

Joy closes her eyes, tightly, and shakes her head as more tears spill. "Not at all. I had spent so much time trying to figure you out and prove to myself that you couldn't really be a Christian that I lost touch. With God and..."

"Reality?" I cut in, but softly.

She nods. "Reality. It was like I was out of control in that dining hall. When I first saw you, it almost energized me in some way, like I'd get to out you. Then you told your secret, and called me a... bitch," she whispers. "It was like a bucket of cold water was dumped over my head. I've never been so scared in my life."

I have chills watching true fear fill Joy's eyes. "I was afraid I was going to get kicked out of school, and I wanted to come here my whole life. And how mad my parents were going to be at me..."

"How mad were they?" I ask, to remind each of us that we really are still just teenagers and parents can be pretty scary.

Joy eyes me and tilts her head and gives a slight grin. "There was a *lot* of praying. And talk of disappointment."

I wince. "Ugh. Disappointment is the *worst* thing in the parent arsenal."

"I know, right? It's like they save it for the fatal blow. *We're just so disappointed in you.* Gah!" Just like that, Joy and I are having our first normal conversation ever. "But," she gets serious again, "you saying you didn't want disciplinary action..." She scrunches her eyebrows and shakes her head. "Why?"

I twist my lips and shrug. "Honestly, Joy? I have no idea what came over me. My active theory on that right now is God. And mercy. For both of us, I think. I don't want to over-spiritualize this, or anything, but I just thought it would be pointless for you to get kicked out, or whatever, for something that's kind of gone away anyway."

Her eyes widen. "Gone away? You've been on the Today Show... *twice*. And now... look around! We're basically on TV!"

"It was bound to happen," I admit with a sigh. "You might not like Roland, but lots of other people certainly do and find him just *fascinating*." I say this with some sarcasm, because it is still sometimes surreal for me to comprehend the secular/sacred popularity line Roland masters on a daily basis. "Just do me a favor?" I add, cautiously.

"Anything," she replies in an instant.

"Don't do this to anyone again. For the rest of your life, okay?"

Joys face falls a little, like she's being punished by the principal. "Okay," she agrees meekly.

"Don't beat yourself up about it. You don't have to like me, or my dad, or my politics or any of that, but you can't tear down someone's character like that."

Without direct evidence.

Dean Baker, and the skeletons I know are shoved in his closet, is never far from my mind, but I'll keep him miles from this conversation.

"I get it. I do." Joy rises to her. "I'll still pray for you, though," she says brightly.

I give her a small wave, deciding to stay in my seat for a while longer. "I'll return the favor."

"Let's talk more soon, okay?" she asks, wiping her hands on her grey skirt.

I nod, feeling a bit emotionally drained. "Of course."

Joy turns back to the door, I suppose to go in and finish her "meeting" with Dean Baker. Finn follows close behind her, but stops to offer me a thumbs up and a smile before he disappears into the dining hall.

Once the door closes, I stick out my tongue in his direction and rake my fingers through my hair, resting a hand on my head.

Despite dozens of people swarming in and out of my vision, everything goes silent for a moment. I don't know if NBC will use any of what Finn caught on camera, and I don't care. I was being as honest with Joy as possible, however brief our conversation was, and I can only hope she was honest with me, too. It was surreal, that whole conversation with her. I haven't seen her in almost a year and it's like she dropped from the sky just so we could patch things up. Or whatever it was we just did.

"Lost in thought?" Roland's voice startles me. He takes the seat vacated by Joy."

"Didn't you have a class?"

He chuckles. "It was a brief study session. I stayed for the first ten minutes and let my grad assistant take over, because I have a meeting in five minutes."

"You know," I say with a grin, snapping out of my daze, "people on the outside think you're weird because you smile all the time. Like you're a fake, or you're drunk, or something."

Roland laughs. "Well, if I was drunk you'd know it. It would be far from the polished exterior you see before you now." He gestures to his always-pressed clothing while smiling broader. "I'm glad you mentioned being drunk."

Will we ever have a normal conversation? "Because...."

"Because," he takes a deep breath, "I'm coming up on my fourteenth anniversary of being sober."

"Oh, that's right. And awesome," I say with a smile, trying not to think of him drunk on the floor staring at my picture.

"One of the meetings I go to has asked me to be the speaker on my anniversary date. I've spoken a few times before, but this time I'd like you there." He leans forward, placing elbows on knees, arching his eyebrow slightly.

I swallow hard. He's asked me before and I chickened out. I don't now why. "It's allowed... right?"

He nods. "It's an open meeting, for one thing, meaning you don't *have* to identify as an alcoholic to come. Also, I've asked the meeting if they minded if I brought you. Everyone said it was fine. And my sponsor thinks it's a great idea... if you want to."

A sponsor. Of course. I know what sponsors are, but hearing Roland mention his at first strikes me as funny.

"What?" he asks as I fail to respond.

"It's just... weird to me to hear you talk about a sponsor. Because, like, you're *everyone's* sponsor at church sort of, right? I mean... you, like, help them get in touch with God and themselves, and all of that." I shift in my seat, crossing my legs before leaning back in the chair.

Roland laughs a little. "I guess. But, that's why anonymity is so important in the program. I don't know what most of the folks do for a living. And, most people don't mention what I do. When we get together we're all just a bunch of drunks."

My eyes widen. "That's a little... something. Self-deprecating?"

Roland plants his hand on my knee. "It's just a fact, is all. Nothing to be ashamed about. Have to call a spade a spade once in a while."

"I have no problem coming with you," I say. "But... why do you want me to? I know your story."

Roland leans back in his chair and takes a deep, thoughtful breath. "It's not so much for you. It's for me. To remind myself that the program helped me get you back, and I'll do anything to keep you *and* my sobriety."

I'm still uncomfortable with his excessive vulnerability and obvious parental affection toward me, but not as much as I used to be. I just don't know how to show him that I feel the same way... sometimes.

You could go to the meeting with him.

An eerie thought swirls into my head. "Pardon my general adolescent self-centeredness for not considering this before, but, did everything that happened when our relationship status was outed cause you to want to drink? That was wicked stressful."

Roland shakes his head. "I suppose it could have, but it was kind of everything that happened in the fourteen years *before* that made me want to drink. I haven't had to white-knuckle it regularly in years, but there are plenty of things about our relationship—my guilt, actually—that pose a risk for me. Like your birthday, the day I got your picture, any time I would wonder what kind of young woman you were growing up to be..." he trails off and I study the rarely-seen vulnerable face of Pastor Roland Abbott.

"Did Jesus really come save you on the kitchen floor that day?" I sit frozen, contemplating what exactly constitutes a miracle.

Roland licks his lips and looks skyward. Heavenward, maybe. "Kennedy," he says, looking back at me, "science can't even explain what would make someone like me—a low-bottom, hope-to-die drunk—*want* to walk away from the bottle. Just like there's no thermometer for love, hate, sadness, or joy, there's nothing scientifically measurable about the force that lifted my sorry behind from the cold floor that day. It wasn't my will, I can tell you that. I'd long since drunk that well dry by the time I got sober."

Goosebumps spring up along my arms and down the back of my neck. I haven't felt a kiss from God like this in several weeks, maybe more. But, staring at Roland and knowing his story, my mom's stories of him, and seeing the man he is today, there really *isn't* anyway to explain it besides *miraculous*.

"I'll come," I finally say. "I'd love to."

CHAPTER FIFTEEN

OKAY?

Kennedy.

"**D**O we really need an audience for *practice*?" I glower at Matt and Eden as they causally take their seats in the sanctuary at New Life, where Water on Fire is rehearsing before tomorrow morning's service.

"It'll do you some good," Eden quips. "Multiply us a couple of hundred times and, voila! Tomorrow's audience."

Matt chuckles and I shoot Jonah a horrified glance. "Why'd I let you talk me into this?"

Jonah laughs. "It wasn't a tough sell."

Far be it from NBC to leave us alone for rehearsal. The "camera kids," as I've come to call them, are twittering around. There are more of them, along with a half dozen more important-looking people playing with the lights and measuring the acoustics of the sanctuary. We're all preparing for tomorrow, it seems.

"Ready, guys?" Max Walker, the drummer and lead of the band questions. He doesn't sing much—most drummers don't—

but he's been in the band the longest, knows the sets like the back of his hand, and is an incredible percussionist.

"Yep," Jonah answers for the both of us, taking a swig of water before slinging his acoustic guitar over his shoulder. An electric one sits on a stand a few feet away, though he doesn't use that as often.

While the rest of the group gets their act together, Jonah turns off his mic and steps closer to me. "You okay?" he asks.

"Sure," I say, uncertain. "I mean... it's just practice, right?"

He chuckles and hands me his water. "Here, take a sip. Your voice is all raspy."

I arch an eyebrow. "Some genres of music require that."

"Maybe so." He winks. For the love of God, he winks. "But for safety's sake, let's stick with the set as arranged."

I can't peel my eyes away from him as the cool water coats my throat. My chest and neck feel like they're on fire and I'm sure they've turned red under the dreamy gaze of Jonah Cross.

Wait, what's happening?

"Here. Thanks." I hand him the water and wipe my disconcertingly sweaty palms on the back of my skirt.

"Hey," he whispers after setting the bottle down.

He stares for a few seconds, not saying anything.

"Yeah?" I draw out slowly.

"We want you to sing with us permanently," he blurts out.

My eyes bug. "That's awfully confident of you since I haven't even performed in front of an audience yet."

He laughs, looking down as if he's nervous. "I know, but you've got a real joie de vivre on the stage."

My mouth slacks open. "Jonah Cross, do you speak French?" I joke.

"Yeah," he says without offering more explanation.

Suddenly I can't even feel my tongue.

"Sorry," I sigh, setting my hands on my hips in the hopes I won't fall over, "but all the books I've read tell me I should stay away from boys with guitars. And there are at least two on the stage right now. It's an anti-drama policy I'm trying to adopt since my life is one giant fiasco..." I give him a wink to try to lighten the thick air between us.

"Well that's a bummer," Jonah says. Out of the corner of my eye, I catch Lucas—the bassist—shaking his head and fiddling with his strings.

"What's that?" I ask of Jonah.

"That your policy is to stay away from guys with guitars," he says with a grin.

Oh the warmth. The warmth in my chest that spreads to my cheeks the longer he stares at me.

He's flirting with you, you fool. Step up your game!

"Boys," I correct him with a smile. "I said *boys* with guitars."

"Ah," he replies with a nod. "Guess we're safe, then."

I lift my eyebrows and can't help from licking my lips. "Guess so..."

Jonah looks down at his guitar for a second, then slowly brings his gaze back to me. "Kennedy," he starts.

Here it comes.

I nod. "Yes," I reply in response to what he has said and what he's, hopefully, about to say.

Lord, don't fail my flirt signals now.

He clears his throat and shifts on his feet.

"Are you okay?" I whisper, suddenly well aware of how public this is. In front of Matt and Eden no less.

Matt!

Eden!

Maybe they're not eavesdropping.

Ha!

He smiles at me, even with his eyes, and says, "I think so."

I'm not okay. My throat is so dry I feel like it's squeezing shut. I'm plagued by all the thoughts I've had about Jonah over the last couple of weeks that I've kept one hundred percent to myself. I haven't even told Mollie, or my journal. Because this is nonsense. He's my best friend's ex-boyfriend. And, while relationship rules are wildly different in this world, some things never change. Like dating your best friend's ex-boyfriend.

Oh, man, though. This is *Jonah*. Even in my head I say his name in a sigh with birds and butterflies fluttering around it. It's like he always has a soft-touch haze around him, and I half expect to see woodland animals hanging around him. He's Prince Charming, is who he is, and now I'm rambling about it in my head as loud as I ever have and I half expect my ears to act as loud speakers to all of those around us—projecting these embarrassing thoughts.

Breathe.

"Okay..." I say slowly as he stares at me, tongue-tied.

"Guys," Max calls out, causing Jonah and I to jump nearly in synch. "We'll start in ten. Sorry, we just have to fix a sound thing with the TV crew."

"Okay," I say before nearly leaping off the stage and running to Eden. "Can we talk?"

She traces a line with her eyes between me and Jonah and back again. "You betchya." And, like the best friend she is, she shoots up from her seat, grabs my hand, and races up the stairs to the seat in the sanctuary farthest from the band.

Eden grips my shoulders and her wide eyes match the intensity of her springy curls. *"He. Likes. You!"* she says like she just came across a social goldmine.

"Shh!" I beg her, thanking God we're not mic'd up like those hardcore reality shows. The last thing I'd want is for my *romantic life* to be broadcasted on TV. I'd take a million biological father reveals any day.

Eden rolls her eyes, still speaking with a high-pitched whisper. "Oh it's so *obvious*. We're not discussing top-secret info here."

"Um! Yes we are! What are you talking about? And he's your ex-boyfriend for goodness sake!" Now I'm doing the high-pitched whisper. From the corner of my eye, I watch Jonah plunk down in the seat Eden just occupied. Next to Matt.

"So?" Eden waves her hand. "We weren't engaged or anything. Yes, I had a crush on him for a long time. But, you know what? We liked the *idea* of each other more. We just figured since we'd crushed on each other for so long that we ought to give dating a shot."

"And?" I ask, needing more information. "Why wouldn't this be weird for you?"

She shrugs. "Because he's not mine, Kennedy. In order to have a clean heart for the man who will someday be my husband, I can't be emotionally bound to anyone I date, even casually, between now and when I meet him."

In five seconds, my entire view on Christian dating has changed. I'm certain Eden doesn't speak on behalf of all Christians who date, but I know her well enough to know that she's pretty up on what's going down in modern evangelical circles. She's fierce, that girl, and practical.

"Do you like him?" she asks, sounding hopeful.

I open my mouth to answer, and find my eyes stinging with self-conscious tears. "I can't," I admit. "It's *Jonah*. He's... the son of a preacher man," I say with just enough sarcasm to keep me from crying. "I'm not his... material."

Eden's face darkens. It's never been dark as long as I've known her. Her eyebrows shift downward and her lips form a tight, thin line before she speaks. "Wow," she whispers. "Sounds like someone's been spending a little too much time around Matt. You're stealing his lines."

I swallow hard against the rough reality of her words. When Matt said those words to me, when he told me *he* wasn't good enough for *me*, I internalized that and thought it was more about me than him. Now with my turn in the hot seat, it crosses my mind that Matt might *actually* feel like he's not good enough for me. I know his "reasons" why, but since we come from different dating worlds, they're not good enough for me. Well, weren't good enough. I'm thrilled to no longer have those back and forth conversations with Matt now that our relationship is signed and sealed as *friends*.

"Do you like him?" she asks again as if the last few seconds never happened.

All I can do is nod.

Breathing out a small sigh, Eden moves a hand to my shoulder. "You deserve happiness, you know. Don't punish yourself for who you *think* you are. Love yourself for who you *are*. Haven't you been telling all of your friends back home about how *not* different we are from them in some ways? Don't you see how twitchy and weird Jonah gets sometimes around you? Even him, Mr. Confidence. Don't you think he's hesitated to ask *you* out because of what he thought you might say? The reasons *you* might say no?"

Grinning, I point at her accusingly. "He's talked to you about this already. You've *known* about this?"

Eden lifts her chin like a queen in her castle. "I don't gossip," she states as regally as possible. "But I also don't lie... so... let's just say someone has asked me if they should even bother to ask someone else out."

"Even bother?"

She smiles. "We've all got insecurities, no matter how we grew up. Just think about it, okay?"

I nod as Max thumps the bass drum a number of times to get our attention, calling us back from the break. I'm careful on my way back to the stage because my nerves feel like rubber bands, and the last thing I want to do is a somersault down the stairs and land at Jonah's feet.

Max counts us in to our first song right away, leaving little time for Jonah and me to say much more than "hi" to each other before we head into twenty minutes of nearly nonstop worship music. The band is flawless, if I do say so myself. The songs are primarily set in keys attainable to even the most tone-deaf of worshippers. That's the idea, and it makes total sense. You *want* people singing along with you and feeling like they *can*. One thing I do love about this life is the worship music. I find myself humming or singing the words to these songs all week, and I can't for the life of me remember a single hymn from my more formal churchgoing days. Except the big holiday ones.

I think this is the first time Matt and Eden have heard me sing with the band, and they both look pleased throughout the whole set. Matt even tosses me a thumbs up after we belt out a rendition of Matt Redman's "10,000 Reasons." I try to keep my thoughts on the songs, but find a very tangible energy coming from my left, where Jonah stands. I want him to ask me out, I do. But I don't want him to do it here.

After the set is finished, I check my phone and realize I've got just enough time to beg Roland to drive me to work or lend me his car.

"Hey Kennedy?" Jonah asks as we shift things around on the stage to be exactly where we need them in the morning.

"Yeah?"

"Can we talk for a sec?"

My heart swan dives into my stomach. "Work," I blurt out.

His face twists up in confusion. "What?"

Now mine is beet-red. I can feel it. "Ha," I chuckle nervously. "I mean I have to work. In like fifteen minutes, so I have to run. Literally. I'm on till ten, though, so come down and see me?"

Also, the cameras won't be there thanks to Asher barring all production at his establishment. I don't even care why, I'll take it.

Jonah smiles an uncertain smile and picks up his backpack. "Of course. I'm going to head to the library for a while to work on my chemistry homework."

I nod and he turns toward the door, looking back once to give me a wave. I wave back and then Matt's suddenly at my side.

"Well, that was awkward," he says with a charming grin.

I smack his shoulder. "I don't know what you're talking about. And, I'm gonna be late."

"I'll walk you to your dads," he says, following me.

I peer around his shoulder to find Eden, but she's chatting it up with Max, offering me a small wave with a goofy smile.

Weird.

"If you must," I say to Matt of his insistence to walk me home.

"I must," he replies with mock chivalry.

"I don't know what you're talking about," I say as we walk across the back lawn of New Life, which will drop us in Roland's side yard. "And, even if I did, nothing was awkward."

Matt shakes his head. "Jonah's got it bad for you."

"Shh!" I smack him again.

"Stop hitting me! I need this body for the team!"

I roll my eyes. "What would they *ever* do without your brawn," I tease.

Matt lifts his eyebrows, trying to look serious. "Not much, I can tell you that."

"Anyway," I redirect us. "I don't know about *bad*, but I do know that he wants to ask me out. And, I also know I don't want to be having this conversation with *you*," I say as we reach

Roland's. I suppose I could call it my house now, but I'm trying not to be too possessive.

Matt slaps his hand across his chest. "I'm hurt," he says with a laugh. "Why don't you, though? I'm your friend, right?"

I crinkle my nose. "But you're a *boy*. And, as liberal as we all know I am, some things are better left for friends of the ovary-carrying variety."

Now Matt crinkles his. "Nice image."

"See you at church tomorrow? New Life, I mean. I know you've been cheating on it with the UC."

Matt drops his hand and throws his head back in a laugh. "Yeah, that's when I was throwing my massive temper tantrum. And it's easier to nap during the UC services."

"You can nap at New Life, too, I guess."

Matt arches an eyebrow. "With you up on stage? Not a chance, K. Sawyer. Not a chance."

Rolling my eyes, I reach for the door. "I've seriously gotta go to work. But thanks for walking me home." I turn the knob and slip through the side door. "Oh, Matt?" I ask, poking my head back out.

He turns around, hands in his pockets. "Yeah?"

"You're okay with this, right?"

He shrugs, silently asking, "What?"

"I mean, it's not, like, weird? I've asked you out before, you broke my heart." I laugh, making the whole thing sound matter-of-fact. He gives a half grin. "I just want to make sure you're, like, okay with this whole Jonah thing. Though it's not even a thing. I'll stop rambling once you answer..." I arch an eyebrow.

Matt walks a few paces to reach the door, nudging it open with the toe of his boot. Placing his hand on my shoulder, he looks into my eyes for a few long seconds. Saying nothing.

"Of course," he finally says in a near-whisper. "I *am* your friend, and Jonah's a *good* guy. I want you to be happy, Kennedy. Of *course* it's okay."

Placing my hand over his, I give it a light squeeze before he walks away.

CHAPTER SIXTEEN

Matt.

No, it's not okay. It's not okay at all.

CHAPTER SEVENTEEN

ALWAYS

Kennedy.

"**R**EADY for your big performance tomorrow?" Asher asks over the loud coffee grinder. He lifts the impossibly heavy bags and I push the button. It's a system I'm happy with.

I stick out my tongue. "It's not a performance, you know that. It's *worship*."

The overriding theme in many of our practices has been how to keep ourselves humble. How to keep the attention on worshipping Jesus and not expecting accolades for our abilities. This, admittedly, will be hard for me. I was pretty competitive in high school and couldn't, for the life of me, understand why someone would want to get up and sing in front of people and be happy with no applause.

But, I've been told it really is about worshipping in our faith, and the music is one avenue to help people get in touch with God.

Asher grins. "Sounds like you're invested in the group."

We haven't talked about his big revelation since it happened. Including the street prayer. Asher looks the same to me as he always has, just with a slightly gaping wound in the center of his chest. I find his ability to keep his act together a miracle in and over itself.

I shrug. "I guess, though I still have no idea what I'm doing. Ever. Anywhere. I'm kind of just, I don't know, praying that God sort of leads me along."

"That'll do for a while," he says. "But eventually you've got to be an active participant."

I huff. "I can't seem to get out of my own way most of the time."

"You'll get the hang of it. A big part of college and young adulthood in general is making mistakes that you won't want to repeat later. But at some point the rubber has to meet the road of our relationship with God."

I release the button on the grinder and put my hand on my hip. "Meaning?"

He shrugs. "Meaning there will come a point where God will ask you to act. He won't lead you around like a blind sheep. At *some* point, he will expect you to simply listen to his commands. He will give you harder challenges. Things won't be laid out so neatly."

"Neatly?" I say with a sharp laugh that silences half the cafe for a second. "Yes, my journey thus far has been defined by its *spotlessness.*"

"You're feisty," Asher says with a broad grin. "I like that."

"I think you're wrong," I say as he turns away for his office, causing him to turn back.

He's wide-eyed as though I've challenged him to a dual. "Oh yeah?"

I nod. He crosses his arms, and I cross mine. "Yes. I don't believe God can lead anyone anywhere they're not willing to go. If so, this world wouldn't be such a hole sometimes. It's not about things being laid out so neatly. It's about *willingness.* People talk all the time about a sixth sense or a conscience. Do you think that inner voice is biological? I don't, but I know a ton of people who chalk it up to *whatever*." I take a deep breath before closing my case. "I'm just saying that simply listening, or at least feeling around in the dark for the thing I know is there, is what's helping me here. Sometimes I *am* blind, but I can still feel. Still hear. As long as I have even one of those three things operating at full capacity, I think I'll be okay."

Asher stares at me for a couple of moments, long enough that it catches Chelsea's attention as she tries to clock in for her shift and has to ask Asher to move.

"The hell are you doing, Asher? Move!" She hip-checks him out of the way and enters her ID number.

"Sorry," he says as if startled out of a daydream, gesturing to me. "Just listening to Kennedy preach over here."

My mouth drops open. "Shush."

He shakes his head. "Never. Get back to wor—oh *Lord*," he cuts himself off. "*Try* to get back to work."

"Wh..." I turn to face the counter and see Jonah saddling up to the open stool near me. Turning back to Asher, I shoot him a serious gaze. "I'm never telling you anything again," I hiss, regretting sharing the prospect of being asked out.

Asher leans in close so only I can hear. "You've seen me cry. We're far from even."

He winks as he backs away and finally turns to his office, letting me know that, while we haven't talked about our walk since that night, he hasn't forgotten all he shared with me. I didn't expect him to, I guess, but I wasn't sure how to continue the conversation. What do I say? *"I'm sorry everything sucks for you"? "Thanks for letting me pray for you on the sidewalk"? "Please don't tell anyone I did that"?*

"Hey Jonah, what can I get you?" I say with the flirty casualness of a waitress from a diner in a 1950s comedy. When, in actuality, I feel like a baby deer walking across a frozen lake.

"The usual," he says with a grin before biting his lip.

My heart races as I go through the motions of his vanilla latte, remembering not to tell anyone that's what he orders—with an extra pump of vanilla no less. I'm grateful it *is* a *usual* so I can perform the drink making duties by rote. My nerves are a bowl of rubber bands migrating to my knees.

"Easy," Chelsea whispers into my ear as she froths some milk. "It's just a boy."

My face heats under her observation and I wonder how many other people in the cafe know that Jonah and I are in the middle of a *very* serious non-conversation.

"Relax." She laughs, patting my shoulder. "Asher hasn't said anything to me, it's just obvious. The way he paws around here like a puppy all the time."

"All the time?" I whisper. "I've been back to work for like two weeks.

Chelsea rolls her eyes. "And all last year. No worries, I won't tell anyone." She gives me a devilish grin and sticks out her pierced tongue before returning to her customer.

Walking a casual few steps back to Jonah, I gracefully set down his latte in a tall ceramic mug. "Here ya go. That'll be fifty dollars. Three for the drink, and forty-seven for the stellar service."

Jonah leans forward, reaching into his back pocket for his wallet. His mouth is a frightening few inches from my face. "You sell yourself short," he says before handing me a five dollar bill. "Can I owe you the rest?"

I've gone mute.

Swallowing hard, I fumble my way through opening the register and shakily handing Jonah his two-dollars in change.

He holds up his hand, shaking his head. "Keep it."

"I... I was just kidding about... you don't have to tip us, you know."

"Yeah he does," Chelsea shouts from the other end of the counter. "Especially with the way Asher pays us."

"Watch it, Chels," Asher calls from somewhere else behind me.

I clench my teeth at the thought of an audience.

"Sawyer, take your fifteen," Asher says close enough to make me jump.

Turning, I say, rather impatiently, "I just clocked in. It's not time for my—"

"Go," he commands, arching his eyebrow. "I need two baristas on tonight, not one and a mess."

My mouth drops open. "I'm... I'm not a..." I widen my eyes, begging him to shut up.

Asher chuckles, cupping a hand over my shoulder. "Just go, kid. Fifteen. If you're not back in twenty, I'll send the purity police after you."

"I hate you," I hiss, untying my apron and tossing it on the table beneath the time clock. "Hate." Asher simply rolls his eyes and waves me out from behind the bar.

I nod Jonah toward the door, where I'm grateful that the still-warm air allows us at least the illusion of privacy at the outside tables. I situate Jonah and myself at a table in the back corner. In fact, it's the table Dan and I sat at when he told me he was certain my mom would always love Roland. I saw Matt and his dad sit there once, too. It's the heavy discussion table, making me and Jonah perfect cases regardless of if anyone gets asked out on a date.

"Are you okay, Kennedy?" Jonah asks after he pushes my chair in and takes the seat opposite me. His back is to the cafe—his face lit by the quaint streetlights that almost confuse this setting for Paris. I was only there for a few days in high school, but it was just enough to sweep me up in this moment.

I nod. "I'm sorry," I start. "I just... I think you're—we're—flirting. That's what's happening, right? It's... been a while."

Stop talking, Kennedy. For, like, several minutes.

Jonah's eyes widen and he laughs. "Well..." He blushes, looking down.

Something in me wants to give Jonah an out of this conversation. Maybe Eden had an identical conversation with *him*. Maybe she told him that *I'm* the one who might want to date *him*. That hadn't occurred to me until this very minute, and now I'm panicked. Maybe he's stalling because he's waiting for me to ask him, or he's trying to preemptively shoot me down.

No! You're a catch! And, this is Jonah. He's good. And, come on, look at him.

I take a deep breath. "Jonah," I start, but am cut off by his polite hand-lift.

"Kennedy... I like you," he says with shaky confidence. His eyes meet mine, and I want to say yes before he's even said anything.

I smile, *needing* to say something like, *I like you, too*, like we're fourteen or something. But I can't. I just sit and let the moment happen without any input from yours truly.

He swallows hard and I just want to kiss his face. I don't know how this happened, me fancying Jonah. But, maybe when I leave things well enough alone, something good really *can* happen. Maybe when I stop telling myself I'm not good enough at something—like singing, or for someone like Jonah, God can move. It seems like God likes it best when I get out of my own way. Just like I tried to tell Asher earlier.

See?

He clears his throat and is so obviously nervous I wish I could put him out of his misery. But, maybe we both need this moment to happen just the way it is. "I know we see a lot of each other already," he starts, still shifting in his seat. "But... I was wondering if you'd like to go out to dinner with me sometime. On a date," he adds quickly.

My ears are hot. "I'd love to," I say softly, barely able to speak through such a wide smile.

"Awesome." He bites his lip, still smiling, and looks down for a moment. I wonder if Eden felt this giddy when Jonah asked *her* out. I understand on a new level why she agonized so deeply about breaking up with him. He's just so... *good*.

Just like that, I get in my own way. I panic again about my qualifications here. "You really want to go on a date with me?" I ask, trying not to sound as cynical as I feel.

Jonah's eyebrows pull in for a second. "I do," he reassures me softly. "I've wanted to for a long time, Kennedy. But I was scared."

I grin. "I *am* pretty scary."

He chuckles, nervously. "Not just that. Sure, at first you were just this neon sign right in the middle of what I expected to be a dull first semester of college. But, once I realized you were just as confused as the rest of us, I set that all aside and just became... intrigued by you. You're fierce, you know."

I tilt my head side to side, allowing a small smile. "I guess so."

"And how you have handled everything with Roland, and Matt... Kennedy, I would be honored to be able to call you my girlfriend—if that's where this goes." He sets his hands in his lap and brushes them against his pants. I've made him sweaty-palmed.

Honored.

Girls where I come from typically only hear the word *honored* in movies when men are proposing to their girlfriends. Even when reporting his desire to acquire my virginity, Trent never once indicated that it would be an honor... for *him* anyway. To have a great guy—a friend—like Jonah talk about dating me and *honor* in the same sentence makes me thankful, no matter how briefly this feeling will last, that I kind of *do* go to school on a different planet.

I allow myself to forget for the time being that dinner with Jonah won't be a date like I'm used to. Mainly, it won't be just me and Jonah. Friends will be with us as chaperones to ensure we keep the Word of God forefront in our communication. And, you know what? I don't have anything snarky to say about that right now. I'm sure I will once we're halfway through the to-be-planned date but, for now, I'm grateful that I'll be safe, not pressured, and with someone who gives a damn about what I think and how I feel.

In the meantime, I've got to clean up my mouth. I've been letting that slide for a while, and I'm sure my grace period in that department is running out. And, really, having a real date to go on in the near future makes me want to up my game. Be a lady, and all of that.

"There's this French restaurant around the corner I've been eyeing," Jonah says, pointing in the direction of the eatery. "Some of the guys have recommended it. I'd like to take you there, if you're okay with French food."

French food. Paris. My mouth waters at the thought. "What's not to like!" I try not to drool. "Cheese, meats, bread, *chocolate*."
Calm yourself.

Jonah smiles and stands, offering his hand to me. He often does this. Extends a hand when I'm standing or sitting, or holds a door for me. I thought this was just how guys around here did things. Then I realized, no, it's not. Yes, they're all incredibly polite and respectful, and hold doors, but... it seems as if Jonah's been courting me a bit longer than I realized.

"Thanks," I whisper, new heat in my cheeks. "I have to get back." I nod toward the door. This time to go in.

He nods. "I know. I've got to meet up with the guys who went to the sports store so we can get back to campus."

I grin. "Did they go to the store so you could ask me out without them gawking at us?"

Jonah shrugs, then blushes, then I faint inside. "I guess," he mumbles a little. "Is next Thursday evening okay for you?"

I nod, not having to check my social calendar since I don't have one.

"Great. I'll pick you up at Rolands?"

I nod again. "Chaperones?" I ask, slowly. "How does that..."

Jonah waves his free hand, since his other is still covering mine. "I'll take care of it." He gives my hand a gentle squeeze before walking to meet his friends, a slight bounce in his step.

Meanwhile, I'm left to float back behind the coffee bar and finish out three *whole* hours with this dizzying high.

"Young love," Asher teases once I tie on my apron and get back to work.

I smack his forearm. "How do you even... know that..."

He laughs. "If he didn't ask you out by next weekend, I was going to ask him for you."

"It's true," Chelsea cuts in, while my mouth hangs open. "Ash was really getting tired of his pussyfooting around." She tosses me a wink, then returns to flirting with a nearby customer. "And he left his coffee on the counter."

Asher shakes his head. "It was just a prop, anyway."

Trying to get back to work, I'm interrupted again by Asher's burly tone.

He clears his throat and speaks in a low, careful voice. "Here comes bachelor number two."

Looking up, I find Matt shuffling his way to the right side of the bar, taking the stool Jonah occupied only moments ago. The steaming latte shifted just to the side.

"Hey!" I walk toward him and pour his coffee. Just coffee, black. Diner style without the frills. "You doing okay? I thought you weren't gonna show." He always comes in at least once when I'm working.

Matt grins, but I don't really believe it. After a long sip he says, "I wanted to give Jonah enough time to ask you out."

A small child could knock me over. "Oh?" I say, shaky. I don't know why I'm nervous. Matt didn't want to go out with me when I asked months ago.

He chuckles. "You look like you saw a ghost. Are *you* okay?"

I stumble around for enough words to make a sentence. "I just... didn't realize news travelled so fast."

Matt shakes his head. "It hasn't. I got here a minute ago, but saw you two talking outside. *Anyone* walking by would know what was going on in your little conversation," he says with a smile.

"We're going to dinner next Thursday," I say, slowly. I've had guy friends my whole life. But only one with whom I talked about *other* guys... and he was gay. Even if I never dated my guy friends in high school it just seemed poor form to bring up other potential suitors. Then again, I've never had a guy friend as close as Matt. "Is this weird?" I say out loud.

Matt laughs, sounding relieved. "A little?"

"I mean," I ramble on, "before at my dad's, you said..."

He waves his hand and looks at me with his pulsing grey eyes. "Don't worry, K. Sawyer. Every guy has to have a girl that's the one that got away."

And, for reasons I don't fully understand, I die a little inside.

CHAPTER EIGHTEEN
FROMAGE

Kennedy.

"ANY plans this week?" Mom's voice is genuine, if a little tired.

"For once." I snicker.

She pauses a moment, then asks, slowly, "Such as..."

I clear my throat, pausing for a second to decide what to tell her. Our conversations have only recently returned to normal, and I'm not sure how protected she is from all the bombs I'm about to drop. "Well, next week I'm going with Roland to one of his meetings. It's an anniversary meeting. Fourteen years..."

"Ah, yes..." she says with about as much excitement as someone waiting for a colonoscopy.

"Mom..."

"What?" She sounds wounded.

Pressing my lips together, then releasing them, I check the freshly applied color in the mirror and back away to check the full effect. I look good. *Really* good. As scheduling would have it, I have lots of plans coming up.

"Wanna know what I'm doing tonight?" I deflect the conversation away from Roland.

"There's more?" she asks brightly.

"I know, right?" I laugh, relieved at the easy way we can slip back into our normal selves.

Wow, I think to myself as I twirl in front of the full-length mirror in my bedroom, *I do look good.* I had to borrow a dress from Eden because I arrived at CU with nothing date worthy, I came to find out far too late—when I got out of the shower and stared at my closet. Thankfully, she responded quickly to my panicked phone call, racing over to Roland's with a lovely deep purple dress in hand. It falls just below the knees and has three-quarter-length sleeves. The skirt folds deliciously when I twirl, though I doubt there will be much twirling tonight. One can never be sure, though, so I'm glad I'm prepared.

Mom interrupts my private twirl in the bathroom. "Kennedy? Your plans?"

"I have a date."

"With Matt?" It rolls off her tongue as normally as any conversation we ever had before my enrollment here.

There's a tiny twist in my stomach when she says his name, but it doesn't last long because, hello—*Jonah.*

"Jonah," I say with a Disney-princess sigh.

Eden coos along with me, fluffing my hair as she grins at me through the mirror.

"By the way, I talked with Joy and things are fine," I blurt out, changing the subject once again.

"Okay," she says slowly. "Continuing with random facts then... in two weeks I'm shipping you out to D.C., and you're meeting me there for a rally."

Staring at my reflection, I watch my eyes light up. "Really? For what?" I shriek.

Eden leans in and whispers, "Can I grab a seltzer? Want one?" I nod and she slips through the door and down the stairs.

"Kennedy Lucille Sawyer, do you have no idea what's been going on in the news?"

The dreaded full-name attack.

"What do you mean the news?" I ask, sitting at my desk and opening my computer. "What's going on?"

"The *Republicans*," she always says the word like it tastes moldy, "are going to back *Howard White* ."

She's right. It *does* taste like mold. The black and green kind. Fuzzy. Howard White has been the face of many behind-the-scenes battles Mom has fought for the last several years. Each time she suits up to campaign for the rights of women across the country, that asshat with his douchey smile is ready and waiting with his band of merry right's-squashers. All men, mind you. I mean, most of them have wives who stand behind them and dutifully smile.

Would Eden... No. Don't even go there right now.

"He's been the frontrunner for some time, Mom."

Ever since Mom's revelation that she'll be heading up Liz Baldwin's campaign—which I've still told no one about—I've been keeping my ear on the ground regarding politics again. Naturally, this involves a lot of Internet research since CU isn't really a hub for bi-partisan and equally representative information. I tap Howard's name into the search engine to see if there's anything about him I've missed in recent months. Like an underage prostitute hiding in his closet, or something. No dice. Just your general search that provides loads of his heinous decisions from one side, venom from the other.

"How many political events have you attended on campus this year, Kennedy?" Mom asks, almost impatiently.

I let out a sharp laugh, then quickly cover my mouth. "About as many times as guys I've had sex with." Eden returns at this exact moment, looking horrified with her wide eyes and slacked jaw.

"I'm joking," I whisper to her, talking her off the ledge of cardiac arrest.

"Cute," Mom muses. "Do you go on your school's website often?" she asks.

"Not if I can help it." I can tell she's chomping at the bit about something, but I can't even begin to tell what it is.

She takes a deep breath. "Howard White is Mormon."

"Yep, him and his eleven-hundred kids. Not FLDS, though, right? Doesn't he speak out against the whole polygamy thing?" Leaning back, I twirl a strand of hair around my finger. From the corner of my eye, I spot Eden doing a horrible job of trying not to obviously eavesdrop. So polite, even though I couldn't care less.

"Seven kids, and yes not FLDS, but that's not the point," she cuts in. "Carter University has, for a long time, had a page discussing the ill-advised tenants of the Mormon faith."

I nod. "That makes sense." Oddly enough, it does. At the beginning of last year, Eden had made a comment about Mormon's not "really" being Christian. I set out on a broad Internet search and found out what she was talking about. False prophets, and all. If there are any practicing Mormons on the campus of CU, they're about as well hidden as a pregnancy would be around here.

Recalling Asher's voice as he shook through his own story about pregnancy throws my thoughts far from that analogy.

"Type in this address." She rattles off a university web address that is supposed to take me to their "statement" on the Mormon faith.

An error message pops up, so I try one more time, double-checking the address. "There's... nothing."

"Now go to the main site, Love."

I type in the school's address and my jaw flies open so fast it hurts. "What?" I whisper. Hiss, really.

Carter University President Supports Howard White as Potential White House Candidate.

"Mmmhmm," Mom says, quite satisfied.

"What the... hold on." I look to Eden, extending my laptop. "Have you seen this?"

She has the audacity to look at me like I'm covered in flies. "Where have you been?" Eden asks. "Everyone's split about it."

"Everyone's split on it," I relay to my mother. "What about?" I ask Eden.

She shrugs. "I mean... he's Mormon which, theologically is a problem. But... what choice do the Republican's have? He's clearly in the lead and he has the values we... the country... the Republican's... want."

Well, here we are. Not once since the first week of school have politics been discussed inside the walls of our friendship. The homicidal rage I have toward Eden's views reminds me of why I enacted the silence around politics rule in the first place.

"Mom," I break eye contact with my best friend, "I've got a date. I have to go."

I want to club everyone in the head.

Which is why I need to keep my mouth shut.

"Bet you're going to be a lot more politically aware for the next couple of weeks, aren't ya?" she teases.

I snort. "I feel like you sent a heat-seeking missile to my—"

"Soul?" she interjects.

"I hate you," I laugh, happier than ever to be having a normal—truly normal—conversation with my mother for the first time since I enrolled at Carter.

"What are we doing in DC anyway? What's your plan?"

"Women's rights," she says as if I asked what the sun does in the morning.

Rise.

"I... I'll have to get back to you. School schedule. Rules. I don't know..."

She sighs. "Lie and tell them you're going to go hand out Bibles."

Now I sigh. "Yeah..." Because her assumptions aren't far off. Looking at Eden, I'm quickly reminded of the literature she handed out at Planned Parenthood last year.

Mom laughs while I remain trapped between two worlds. Universes. "Have fun on your date. What are you wearing?"

I stand, looking to my feet. I tell her about Eden's dress, and the addition of my grandmother's pearls.

"Sounds beautiful. And, really, have fun. Jonah seemed like a nice boy."

There she goes using the word "seemed." Only, this time I don't correct her. He does *seem* like a nice boy.

But I've never asked to see his voter registration card.

Eden left moments after my mom and I got off the phone, leaving me just enough time to stew myself into a mini panic attack before I receive a text message from Matt.

Matt: Have a good time tonight. Your boy looks fresh.

Me: Nope. Weird. Stop.

I roll my eyes but am grateful Matt texted me, for some reason.

Matt: Sorry, you're right. I just wanted to tell you AS A FRIEND that I'm happy for you two.

Me: Slow down, killer. This is just dinner.

You don't even believe that.
I giggle, hitting send.

Matt: Will it be weird with the camera person there?

My heart skips several beats. In the glorious rush of preparing for my date, I'd forgotten that on top of chaperones, we'd have NBC in our faces. I growl as the doorbell rings and I tap back a quick text.

Me: And, just for fun, the first episode of *Jesus Freaks* airs tomorrow.

Matt: Yeah, a bunch of us are going to watch it in the student union.

Me: I hope by "a bunch of us" you mean that you, Jonah, Silas, Eden, and Bridgette—if she climbs out of her hole—will come to Roland's for pizza and relative seclusion.

"Kennedy!" Roland hollers up the stairs. "Jonah's here."
"Coming!" I call back, giving myself one more look-over in the mirror.

Matt: mmm. Pizza.

Me: He's here. Wish me luck! Night!

Matt: You don't need it.

I slip my phone into the small silver wristlet I've selected for the evening, and descend the stairs with held breath. I'm grateful NBC can't film here, though I'm sure if they're not in the car they'll be waiting for us at the restaurant.

As soon as I see Jonah in his charcoal grey dress pants and black, button-down shirt, though, it's easy to reassign my attention.

"Jonah," I remark a bit breathlessly, "you look so handsome."

Let's be honest. This boy has looked nothing less than catalogue-ready since I met him. But, this is a new level. And, it was done for me.

Jonah approaches me with his hands out, taking mine into his. His eyes meet mine and my knees feel a little drunk. In real life, this is where he would kiss me. Not necessarily on the lips, but maybe on the cheeks. Instead, he smiles and gives my hands a squeeze.

"You look exquisite," he says quietly, clearly trying to keep this conversation between us. "Shall we?"

I cast a shy glance to Roland, who's looking at me. Beaming, really. "Bye." I give a small wave as I wait for his response.

He simply nods and takes a step back as if forcing himself not to impose. "Have a great time tonight. Back by nine," he says, reminding both of us of Jonah's campus curfew. I don't technically have one since I live off campus, but I couldn't really finish our date without him, so nine it is.

"Absolutely, sir," Jonah replies with a firm nod. "Thank you," he says for reasons I don't understand before he links his arm through mine and escorts me out of my house and down the broad front steps.

It hadn't occurred to me *how* we'd be getting to the restaurant until my foot hits the sidewalk and Jonah leads me to Roland's Prius. He dangles the keys in front of me with a broad grin.

"He lent us the car so we wouldn't have to walk or take the bus."

I nod in approval. "Great. Want me to drive?"

Jonah laughs as if I've told a joke, then opens the passenger door for me. "Your chariot awaits," he says in a mock-royal tone. Maybe it's not mock. I don't know. I've never been on a date with him before.

"You were excellent on Sunday," he says for the fourth time this week as we wind down to the restaurant.

I blush, looking at my hands. "You've mentioned."

Sunday was pretty spectacular. I *saw* all the people in the congregation. All five-hundred-plus of them, but I didn't let them into my head. The songs all stitched together seamlessly and I didn't even notice the camera crew, though I knew they were there. I assume a big portion of tomorrow's *Jesus Freaks* premier will focus on church, school, and where we all come from. Silas mentioned the other day that some crew members from NBC had spent a weekend with his family at home, filming some of their day-to-day life as they did mini profiles on him and Bridgette.

Still not many real words from Bridgette, but she doesn't shoot daggers at me with her eyes anymore. And, at lunch on Monday she nodded and said "good job," when Silas brought up our lineup the day before.

"I had fun up there," I say.

"You sound surprised."

I shrug. "I thought I'd be more nervous, or that I wouldn't take it as seriously as I wanted to, or something."

"How so?" Jonah questions, turning onto Main St.

I tilt my head to the side, winding a strand of hair around my finger before shaking my hand free and setting it on my lap. *Stop Fidgeting.*

"I don't know." I sigh. "It's all my judgments... you know. I thought I'd be too nervous, or people would think I shouldn't be there, or whatever."

"I love how honest you are," he says quietly, effortlessly parallel parking right in front of a restaurant called *Fromage.*

Any restaurant simply called "cheese" is going to be okay in my book.

"I'm serious. It helps me stay honest with myself." He opens the door for me and leads me out of the car by the hand, holding open the restaurant's door as we walk into the tiny space.

Jonah speaks to the hostess, who leads us to a table for two. I stop, staring in confusion at the configuration.

"What is it?" Jonah asks, pulling out my chair. "Would you rather sit somewhere else? I thought this table would be nice because it's near the fire—"

I put up my hand. "No, no this is fine. Lovely. I'm just confused," I whisper, "about the chaperone seating situation."

Jonah's face relaxes and he points over his shoulder. "They're sitting over there."

I turn around, and in the back corner of the restaurant I see Silas sitting with a female camera crew member who has both a GoPro camera and a hand held nearby.

"Just Silas? And, oddly, the camera girl who was at my dads?" I say of Sophia.

"Sophomores don't have as many restrictions as freshmen as far as going off campus. Chaperones are still required for dates," Jonah explains. "But, both Silas and I are in good enough standing to kind of be one-off chaperones. And, with a camera..."

I suppress an eye roll. "With a camera that's like ten thousand chaperones. But... I thought... don't they have to sit with us?"

Jonah shakes his head. "Not technically. They just kind of have to be... near."

Somehow, this information makes me more nervous. This has turned into less of a group experience and more into an actual date. With a real, beautiful guy.

"Oh." I exhale and thank him for pulling out my chair as I sit.

Fromage is clearly exclusive, and I'm terrified at how expensive it must be. There can't be more than ten tables in here, and my date experience is occupying two of them. Twenty percent of the restaurant seating is dedicated to my date with Jonah.

Breathe.

Taking a second to look around, I note that the place is a narrow rectangle, with a few-seat bar in the center against one wall. The kitchen is partially open, and I crane my neck to see that the kitchen space is roughly the same size as the dining space. I thank God for how good it smells in here. Not just because of the cheese, which nestles into every pore of the walls, but the fresh bread and the thick aroma of butter.

The floors are a dark hardwood, and the walls and linens are a crisp white. It's clear that the star of the show here will be the food. And I am so hungry. I shouldn't have come to a place like this on an empty stomach.

"You're fidgeting," Jonah remarks softly.

"Jonah, I don't know how to tell you this," I start. His face freezes, but I chuckle. "I'm really nervous."

He exhales for a long time. "Me, too."

We both let ourselves laugh nervously for a few seconds before our waiter comes to take our drink order. I order a club soda with lime, and Jonah orders the same.

"You like that, too?" I ask when our waiter vacates our space.

Jonah shrugs. "Kind of, but I didn't really know what else to order. I'm bad at this, aren't I?" He lowers his head and his cheeks pink with embarrassment. It occurs to me that Eden never mentioned any nerves on Jonah's part. He was always "smooth" and "put together."

I bite my lip and grin. I've made the boy come undone.

"You're perfect," I admit. Because in his imperfections, Jonah Cross might actually be close to such a standard. "Have you been here before?"

"No, but there's a restaurant like this near my house."

I grin, wondering how many lucky girls have fumbled their way through first dates with Jonah Cross. I don't ask, though. I want to be the center of his attention for tonight. It's nice to be at the center of attention that doesn't involve scandal. Though, to be honest, me dating a preacher's son is a sort of a scandal all on it's own.

You're a preacher's daughter...

Glancing at the menu, I'm relieved to see that the French menu items are helpfully subtitled in English, as I haven't taken a single language class in a year and a half. *Cheese* I understand, but some of the descriptive words are buried in the deep recesses of my brain.

We start with an appetizer of baked Brie with melon and berries and, I have to tell you, it's divine. The hot, creamy, slightly bitter cheese swirling through raspberries and strawberries is enough to almost make me moan out loud. Cafeteria food can really trick a person into thinking it's *actually* food.

"This is like Heaven." I say between bites.

"I hope so," Jonah answers. "Here, you take the last bite."

Jonah loads his fork with puff-pastry encrusted Brie and extends it toward me.

My lips part and I catch myself needing a deep breath. He's just... offering me his fork. His face is flushed as I lean forward, opening my mouth just wide enough to let him slide the hot bite in. I close my mouth and forget to chew for a second, staring at Jonah who has forgotten, it seems, to lower his fork.

Leaning back, I work the food around my mouth in slow motions, savoring more than just the flavor of the bread and cheese. I shoot a quick glance down the alley of tables and catch eyes with the camera girl while Silas seems to be intently staring at the table, giving us the respect of privacy. Her quick eyebrow arch and half-playful pointed look tells me she saw our interaction, but I'm too blissed out to care. I know the physical contact rules of this place like the back of my hand because I'm a girl who wants to be kissed, and am aware that it's allowed. Fork sharing isn't depicted in detail in the rule book, but I'm sure we're safe.

"Thank you," I say, refocusing on Jonah, who looks like he's recovered his senses.

Before we can come up with any graceful conversation to follow that last bite ordeal, our food comes. I wanted the seafood dish, but since we're far, far away from any ocean, I questioned the validity of such a plate. So, I went with the braised portobello mushrooms topped with mashed potatoes and Gruyere cheese. Jonah ordered the rib eye special, which fills my senses as the plate hits the table. It's topped with horse-radish and a Bordelaise sauce that smells like the rich butter and peppery wine used to make it.

"This is so good," I say slowly after a bite. "Yours smells fantastic."

Jonah nods. "This beats Mission Hall any day of the week."

I grin. "Tell me about your family," I make myself say. This is a date after all. I know where he's from, but not *where* in the emotional sense. "Dad's a pastor, I know that. Do you have siblings? I can't for the life of me remember."

Between bites, which forces me to focus on his mouth, Jonah considers my question. "I have an older sister, Kylie, who is twenty-one."

I furrow my brow. "Does she go to school here? I haven't seen her."

He shakes his head. "She goes to Dartmouth."

I widen my eyes. "Wow. Good for her. That's an excellent school."

Lucky. I have an acceptance letter from them in my desk drawer at home.

"Why'd you think she went here?" Jonah sips his club soda and leans back.

"I just... kind of assumed this was a family sort of school. There's a much more specific demographic that attends here, and there aren't many schools like it." I talk faster, worried that I've offended him via categorization. "I mean... people can go wherever, I guess... I just..."

Jonah chuckles. "It's okay, I'm just teasing you. My parents actually wanted her to go here. Or Bob Jones. Or anywhere other than a big university."

I laugh. "Dartmouth has like half the undergrads as this place."

"I know. They mean big in like..."

"Ideas?" I blurt out, then cover my mouth. "Sorry."

"I'd be offended if you weren't exactly right, Kennedy. You don't offend as many people as I think you think you do."

Despite sounding a bit Mad Hatter-like at the moment, I find comfort in Jonah's words. "Do I offend you?" I challenge, biting my lip again.

He swallows hard. "Not in the least. I find you challenging, but not offensive. It's not even because you have all of these other ideas about the way things should work, it's that you admit you don't have a damn clue." Jonah's voice quiets as he nears the end of his sentence. He leans forward. "That's what attracts me to you, aside from your stunning beauty."

I mirror his lean, resting my elbows on the table. "That I don't know anything?" I tease in a whisper.

Though I thought it was impossible, Jonah leans even closer. I can feel his breath on my lips. "That you don't think you know everything."

My heart is racing. His mouth is so close I can nearly taste his thirty-dollar steak. "Jonah," I whisper, feeling dizzier by the moment.

"Yeah?"

My eyes flick upward and he's staring right at me.

"I'd like very much to kiss you. Right now."

The tip of Jonah's tongue traces a thin line of moisture along his bottom lip. "*I'd* like to be the one to kiss *you*, Kennedy."

If he says anything else, I don't hear it. I just feel. The heat of his hand as his fingers curl around the side of my neck, and the warmth of his lips and the smoothness of his skin when his mouth connects with mine. And, in the back of the tiny French restaurant, Jonah and I share our first, fantastic kiss.

...*Two, three...*

CHAPTER NINETEEN
THE HANGOVER

Matt.

"**J**ONAH, you going to Pastor Roland's house for the show tonight, or are you heading to the Union?"

Jonah stretches out on the couch in the floor lounge, clicking off the TV. "Roland's," he says, quite relaxed.

"Have fun last night?" I chuckle, forcing myself to ask the question as I would any other guy who's gone out on a date with a hot girl.

Jonah sits up, resting his forearms on his legs. "It was great. Thanks for being so cool about this, by the way."

I hold up my hands in defense. "Nothing to be cool about, man. Kennedy's a great girl and you're an awesome dude. She's my friend. Just don't hurt her or I'll have to bury you."

"I believe you," he says, chuckling as he stands. "How's... everything going for you?"

Purity. Lust. Temptation. Masturbation. That's what lives in the pause between his words. I don't regret having Silas and Jonah as accountability partners as I work through my lust issues—the history of lust in my family runs deep and I'm desperate to overcome it for whoever my future wife is. Wherever she is, she deserves better. But, it's a little awkward talking about it with Jonah now. I know he would never say anything to Kennedy, but... I don't know. Let's just say I plan to lean more on Silas during the course of Jonah and Kennedy's dating.

What if they...

Internally, I shake my head, not letting my thoughts run down the aisle of a church with Kennedy dressed in white walking toward Jonah.

"Things are fine. Solid," I finally answer. "Keeping it between the goal posts." I bring in football, which thankfully Jonah understands, since Silas has limited knowledge of the sport.

"Awesome," he says with a firm slap to my shoulder. "I'll keep praying for you. See you tonight?"

I nod. "Thanks... yeah. See you tonight."

Jonah disappears down the hall to his room and I find myself wondering about his date with Kennedy. *What did they talk about? Did he hold her hand?* This isn't just about Kennedy—it's about me needing to get my thoughts right about all women. None of them are mine, including Kennedy. I don't need to be watching them naked on the TV or a stage, and I certainly don't need to be thinking about whether or not they hugged or, God forbid, kissed one of my best friends.

It's none of my business, but as soon as I start thinking it is, I risk getting myself into trouble. So, I make a beeline down the opposite hallway to Silas' room. He's proven excellent at helping me redirect my thoughts to where they need to be. Away from lust and temptation and toward God, my family, friends, and schoolwork.

As always, I just turn the knob and walk in, since Silas and his roommate always tell everyone to just "come on in," because they're two of the friendliest people I've ever friggen met.

Except, I'm betting they wished they locked the door today when I find myself standing in their doorway and they find themselves lying—fully clothed—in Silas' bed next to each other, Silas' head on Brett's chest.

"Shit!" one of them hisses as they scramble out of the bed and I turn on my heels, mumbling a garbled apology, and walk back to the lounge.

"Matt!" Silas calls after me, hurrying into the hallway, running his hand over his hair.

I hold up my hands. "Sorry, dude." My hands are shaking so I shove them in my pockets.

Silas looks paler than usual as his eyes plead. "Can we talk about this?" He gestures to his dorm room, eyes darting everywhere.

My mouth opens, but I take a second to say something. We certainly can't continue this conversation in the lounge, but I don't know if I want continue it at all. Do we *need* to talk about it?

Maybe he needs to talk about it.

"Okay," I finally say, wishing for a number of reasons that Kennedy was here. From her history, I gather she knows how to handle these kinds of situations. But, even though it's killed me to keep this secret from her, I have. It's just *none* of my business.

Well, it *wasn't*. Until I walked in on it. Lord knows what I would have walked in on if it had been a few minutes later. Or earlier. Whatever.

Lord.

Yes, the God piece. I think about that on the too-short walk back to Silas' room. Of all the things I learned at every youth group and camp and even in some sermons.

Sin.

Clearing my throat before entering his room, I shake those thoughts from my head. This is Silas. He's my friend, as unlikely as it seems, and he looks scared.

"Hey," Brett says when I get in there. Looking far less terrified than Silas.

I wave and stand awkwardly while they seem to silently converse.

I've long assumed Silas was gay—or at least bisexual. That's part of the reason I wanted him as an accountability partner. Not just because he's a strong Christian, but because I knew he wouldn't tempt me to looking at girls because he never looks at them.

It didn't take me—or most of the guys on our floor—long to figure it out about him. That "rocks" thing he does with Bridgette is great, and a lot of people do similar things, but every once in a while as he "warned" her about a guy that she shouldn't be looking at, I'd catch him take a long look. Far more than a casual, passing glance.

It did, however, take me a while to bring it up to anyone else. In an all-male setting anywhere, discussion of homosexuality is touchy—let alone in a place like this. I had to do my research on my floor mates to determine who was a safe ally to run my theory by, in case we should ever need to help him, or whatever.

Jonah was the prime candidate. Honest, trustworthy, and rational. Not a nasty or violent fiber in his being. He's the only one I've talked about it with, and honestly we haven't talked about it much. He's told me a few other guys have also brought it up here and there, and while we haven't all sat around and had a meeting about it, it just kind of seems like it's an unspoken but accepted facet of our floor makeup. There's a gay guy. Two of them, who happen to be roommates, in fact.

Makes a lot of sense why they requested to be roommates, I guess. Though most of us just requested friends...

To be sure, there are several guys on our floor who *don't* know this as fact, and who I *literally* pray never find out. For Silas and Brett's sake, and theirs. Because I'd hate to have to do time for pummeling a bigot who tries to hurt one of my friends.

"Uh," Silas finally starts. "I just... I don't know what you saw, but..."

"Nothing I didn't know already." It just comes out. It's the truth, but I didn't mean it to cause Silas to turn that shade of grey.

Brett leans into him. "I told you." Silas leans away, almost wincing.

"Does everyone know?" he chokes out.

I raise my eyebrows and eye Brett—a star member of the CU basketball team. Long and lean like Silas, but with a bit more muscle. Not as big as me, but he definitely takes care of himself.

"No," I say, as if Silas should realize this since he hasn't been harassed. "Not everyone knows. I don't talk about it with anyone. The only person I've talked to about it with is Jonah." I hesitate to say even that much, but I don't want to lie, and Jonah's nonthreatening, which I hope somehow gives Silas some comfort.

Silas sits on the edge of his bed and hangs his head. Taking a deep breath, he looks up at me with a lost look.

"This doesn't change anything, Silas," I say, sitting on the bed next to him. I never imagined I'd be in a situation like this, so I'm just kind of going through the motions and begging God, if he's listening to me anymore, to help me do and say the next right thing.

"It changes everything," he whispers. "I've been lying to you this whole time and posing as a worthy accountability partner for you—"

"Posing? I asked you even after I suspected..." My heart thuds like crazy in my chest as I talk.

"Sexual immorality is not a qualification of an accountability partner."

Brett crosses his arms, clearly annoyed as he taps the back of his head against the wall. "Si, we've been over this..."

Silas stands, pacing the length of the room. Agitated. "It's still sin. And the more people who find out, the more watered down my testimony."

They've clearly had this conversation before, and I feel like an eavesdropper despite being invited in. "Your walk with God is your walk, no matter where it takes you, Si," I say.

Brett huffs and heads toward the door. "I'm taking a walk," he says before slamming the door behind him, leaving Silas and I in deeply awkward silence.

"He's upset," Silas finally says. "Because I'm ashamed of what I am."

I want to tell him he didn't look that ashamed. Not grotesquely. But that when I walked in their room, he looked like someone lying next to someone he cares about. I'm surprised at how unfazed I am about it, but I get it, somehow. The need to care for and be cared for. But I don't say any of that to Silas. Because I understand the shame, too. I want to tell him that the months I spent paying to watch women undress was about as immoral an act as one can get, but I don't say that either. Because both of us come from places where what he's doing *isn't* okay, and I haven't been armed with the vocabulary to tell him it doesn't bother me. I have no scripture in my head to comfort him, only to confront him. Which I don't want to do.

I'm *really* wishing Kennedy was here. She'd know what to say. Or do.

"Self condemnation doesn't get any of us anywhere, Silas," I start with. "You saw what happened to me..."

"You *know* it's different," he hisses, growling at himself.

And he's right. It is. Even if it's *not*. Even if we've been taught that "sin is sin," there's *always* sin counted worse than others in different communities. Always. Murder, divorce, and sexual immorality rank far higher on the "yikes" scale than taking the Lord's name in vain, vanity, greed, any of that.

"I've tried to change," he says, nearly in tears. "I've prayed for healing. To be different." He shakes his head. "But it's not working. I think I might need some stronger therapy, or something."

"What does Brett think?"

"He's comfortable with who he is. He says this is how God made him. That God knew he was gay when he made him."

I nod, taking all of this in. "And what do you think?"

Silas looks forward, unblinking. "That people wrapped up in any kind of sin can take it for granted—for who they are. I don't believe God makes mistakes, Matt. People do. And if He said homosexuality is wrong, then I know He wouldn't make anyone that is an abomination."

I pull my head back at the word. *Abomination.* Such a fire-and-brimstone word used with gusto throughout many churches to drive home how deeply awful something is. A word thrown like a thousand daggers at my father by some members of his own church as he struggled with his own brand of sexual immorality.

The difference is, my dad wasn't born to cheat on his wife or feel up call girls. It wasn't part of his makeup. It was a clear choice bred from discontentment and sin. One that blew apart my family.

"You're not an abomination, man. This is different."

This *is* different. But I don't know how. No one's taught me that it's different, but so many of us here on campus know it is. Not all of us, of course. And most of us won't be heading to any marriage equality rallies any time soon, but a lot of us just don't care. Ask some of our families and they'll say it's because we've been numbed by a culture of sin. Which is why so many of us had restricted access to TV and the Internet. Well, what they *thought* was restricted access. There are always ways around everything.

"Don't tell anyone, okay?" he asks. Begs.

I shake my head. "I won't. Again, it was just Jonah-"

"Don't tell Kennedy I mean."

I swallow hard. "Okay. Why her specifically, if you don't mind my asking? She'd be the absolute last one on this campus I'd worry about."

"I can't risk my sister finding out," Silas answers flatly. "She'll go insane."

"Seriously?" I'm not wondering if Bridgette will go insane; I'd say that's pretty likely. But I'm surprised she doesn't know.

"She suspects," Silas sort of answers my unasked question. "But any time she's brought it up I've just talked about struggling. And for a while I think she thought what I wanted her to—that it was with girls."

"What makes you think she doesn't?"

He shakes his head, standing and stretching his arms overhead. "Paranoia," he answers honestly. "There's nothing she's said or done to make me think that. And it's not like free-range dating before marriage is allowed in my family anyway, so she can't gauge my interest in girls by how many I date..."

"How do you know, then?" I ask with trepidation. "That you're... gay?"

Silas turns to face me, a bemused grin on his face. "How do you know that you're not?"

"Fair enough," I say, though I'm fighting through almost two decades of scripture jungle to see his point. "If so, then why... why worry about changing yourself?"

"Don't you think it's a sin? The Bible says it everywhere."

Brett walks back in, giving me a chance to escape a conversation I can't finish. One I don't have any answers to. "Come to Roland's tonight," I say, talking mostly to Silas. "We're all going to watch the show together.

Silas looks at Brett, who holds out his hands. "I've gotta work tonight anyway. You might as well."

"Seven." I nod to punctuate. "We're gonna order pizza first and stuff. Show's on at eight."

He smiles for the first time since I walked in on them. "Eight o'clock on a Friday night. How'd we get that lucky with a time slot? That's huge!"

"Yeah. Luck." I roll my eyes and head out of their room.

I make it a few steps before Silas sticks his head out. "Matt?"

"Yeah?"

"We'll talk more later, okay?"

I nod, walking back toward him. "Look," I say quietly. "I don't have all the answers. Or any, really. But I know you're not a bad guy. I know you're a guy I look up to and one who's been helping me crawl out of the hell that is my own head. Whatever you are... it's not an abomination, okay?"

Tears well on the edges of his eyes before he takes an exaggerated deep breath and clears his throat. "Thanks."

What the hell now?

"Matt... you're early." Kennedy steps aside as I push through the front door. "I know you love pizza from Tony's but three hours is a bit excessive, no?" She giggles, following behind me as I pace into her kitchen and around the island.

I left the dorm and came straight here. With no plan.

"Oh, and you're being weird," she says, standing in the broad doorway to the kitchen, staring at me. "How new and exciting for us."

Setting my hands on the island, I lower my head and take a deep breath before facing her with my question. "Why don't you think homosexuality is wrong?"

She stares at me. Wide eyed and blinking like a startled owl for several seconds before replying. "Why do *you* think it is?" She places her hands on her hips as if ready for battle.

I shake my head. "I don't know if I do. I'm... collecting research. Opinions. Everyone around here is going to get crazy with the election next year and... just... I want to know. I know we said no politics but this isn't really *us* talking about it. I'm just curious."

She folds her arms across her middle and gives a heavy sigh. "I don't know, Matt. I don't know if we should even talk about this. I'd hate to have to hate you." I can't tell if she's joking. I can never *freaking* tell with her. It's maddening.

"Please." I cross in front of the island and approach her holding out my hands. Setting them on her shoulders, I ask again. "Just... come on. Please?"

With her mouth still closed, she runs her tongue across the front of her teeth. "Promise not to talk?" I nod. "Promise to let me just tell you what I think and know before you say a *thing*?" I nod again, grateful that the election rouse is working. "Fine," she concedes. "I'll get my laptop and be right back down." She grins before turning for the stairs. "I thought you'd never ask."

A minute later she plunks down next to me and I can almost feel the electricity coming off her. I take a deep breath and remind myself to calm down, though, because this might be our only chance to make this a discussion if one of us gets heated.

Tread lightly.

"Perfect timing," she starts with. "I'm going to a women's rights rally in DC with my mom in a couple of weeks."

I raise my eyebrows. "Really? How you gonna get away with that?"

Kennedy waves her hand in the air as if shooing a fly. "It'll be fine. I'll ask for pamphlets to bring, or whatever. I'm just going to lie."

"Casual." I chuckle. "But I'm asking about gay stuff."

"Oh, right. Well at these things there's typically representation from all sides. It's Liz Baldwin's event and she has support from everyone and there *are* gay women, you know," she teases and I let it slide. "I figured if people on any side questioned why I'm there, I'd need to be able to defend myself at least somewhat Biblically. Where do you want me to start?"

I rub my hands on my jeans. "I don't even know."

She tilts her head to the side. "Let's start with the verses thrown around talking about homosexuality as a sin?"

"If you think... that'll help."

She nods quite seriously as she navigates to a document she seems to have been working on. "Let's start with good ole Sodom and Gomorrah. Right in Genesis. I'll never forget when I pieced together where the word *sodomy* came from. Real clever..."

I shift nervously in my seat as she pulls up the story in another window.

"Read the story," she says of Genesis nineteen.

"I've read it. Over and over." I don't want to get into detail with her about what I've been fed. I'm interested in her biblical diet at the moment.

"All right. Verses four and five show a group of men show-ing up at Lot's house, demanding he turn the two men loose so they can have sex with them. Look how angry they were."

"Yeah... and?"

Kennedy huffs. "Nowhere in this verse does it talk about homosexual attraction or relationships. This is about rape. A gang rape. When I read this, I think, *Good*. God is against gang rape. Not that gay men should be burned in their city. These were *bad* men because they were propagating sexual *vio-lence*, Matt."

Holy...

I take a minute to let my eyes scroll through the story that's typically used more than any other one to illustrate the conse-quences of homosexuality.

"Oh," she cuts off the thoughts she can't hear. "And for further confirmation, the business with Sodom and Gomorrah was brought up again in Ezekiel. Verse forty-nine says, 'Now this was the sin of your sister Sodom: She and her daughters were arrogant, overfed and unconcerned; they did not help the poor and needy.' So," she says with a frustrated breath, "looks to me like Sodom's sin was against helping the poor and needy. Spoiler alert: Jesus talks about the same thing when he busts onto the scene."

"What about Leviticus," I spit out. "That calls homosexu-ality an *abomination*." It killed me to hear Silas use that word on himself.

Kennedy's face falls as she navigates to that verse. "Yeah," she says solemnly. "Leviticus is a real pain. It says homosexuals should even be put to death."

I nod. "What do we do about that?"

She scrolls through the online menu and pulls up Leviti-cus twenty, which is the verse containing the punishment for homosexuality.

"Look," she whispers, pointing to the very first verse in chapter twenty and running her finger down the screen. "Anyone who curses their mother and father should be put to death. Adulterers and adulteresses. Death. If a man marries both his wife and her mother he should be burned. Or if he has sex with an animal. But look at this." She scrolls back to chapter nineteen. "Don't plant two kinds of seeds in a field or wear clothes of two kinds of material. Don't eat fruit for three years after planting a tree? Seriously? Don't eat any animal with blood still in it? Jewish custom, Matt. I've got tons of kosher friends. Don't cut your hair," she continues with the list of commands. "Don't tattoo yourself..."

"Okay," I say slowly.

Kennedy looks down for a moment, thoughtful. "Didn't Jesus come," she says, staring at her keyboard, "to complete the prophecy of himself and abolish the law? In at least Romans and Hebrews it is said that Christ came to end the law and that the old law is dead or obsolete, or something."

"I..." I start but have nothing to say.

Kennedy closes her laptop and turns, facing me on the couch. "I could go on," she says. "There are more verses I could pick apart, but when it comes right down to it there's one thing I know for certain."

"What's that?" I say in a near whisper as the light from the front bay window highlights her face.

"You trust my dad, right?" I nod. "And his sermons lately have been about following Jesus. The man. The Divine. Doing as he did and loving as he loved, right?"

"Yeah." Roland's sermons have been tying in nicely to our New Testament class. I don't think that's an accident. Focusing on the "I Am" statements Jesus made, and walking those out.

Kennedy leans in close as if we're in a crowded room and she doesn't want anyone else to hear this but me. "Jesus never once spoke against homosexuality. He did speak about a whole lot of other things that are really hard, and things I still don't know how I feel about, but there *is* that piece that I know. He talked about sexual immorality, yes. But he talked about it in the form of prostitution and adultery. In fact, even the barest mentions of homosexuality occur less than ten times in the Bible, while there are hundreds of verses regarding how to treat the poor. And look what *Howard White* focuses on—the *impeccable Christian* that he is. Is it feeding the poor? No, it's taking away food stamps and abolishing gay marriage. Jesus, the man and the Divine, never talked about homosexual relationships. What then, are we to do about that?"

My mouth opens with no words ready to speak. Her eyes are sad as if she's seen some of the effects of those scriptures thrown at friends. I bet she has; she's mentioned a gay neighbor once or twice, I think. I can't for the life of me figure out why Silas doesn't want Kennedy to know. If I were in his shoes, she'd be the one person I'd *beg* to be in my corner.

"Why did you want to talk about this now, anyway?"

Her question startles me. "I told you—"

"I know you told me what you wanted me to believe, but not what the truth is. And, I know you're not gay... right?"

"No!" I shout with an uncomfortable laugh.

She puts up her hands. "Chill, I didn't ask if you made out with cats."

I feel bad for my indoctrinated reaction, but it is what it is. Luckily, Kennedy is the forgiving type. After all, she still wants to be my friend after all the crap I've put her through.

"Sorry," I say, standing and walking to the kitchen to help myself to a soda. She's told me for weeks that Roland's house has an open door *and* open fridge policy. And, I'm grateful for the brief, sugary distraction.

"Did someone put you up to this?" she asks, holding out her hand and silently asking for a soda. Which I should have offered her anyway.

I shake my head. "No. And I'd never do that to you even if they did."

"So... this was just a general fact-finding mission?"

I tilt my head side to side and give her a mischievous grin. "Information collecting. Let's not go calling things facts just yet."

"Fine." She huffs. "So, what are you going to just loaf around here for the next three hours and not ask me at all about how my date went last night? It was wonderful, by the way, thank you for asking."

Internally I roll my eyes, but plaster on a grin for her. "I wasn't going to ask. Didn't need to. Jonah gushed all about it during floor prayer last night."

Her face flushes. "*What?*" I can't keep a straight face, and she punches me in the shoulder. "Jerk!"

"Ow! Psycho! I have a game Sunday."

She shakes her hand. "I'm sure I hurt myself more than you, you brute."

"What happened on that date to make you change color like that?"

"None of your damn business, Wells."

I laugh. "Gonna be eventually if a camera crew was there. Might as well spill the beans now."

Her face flushes again and it's clear she's forgotten until this very moment that she had extra guests at dinner.

"Dinner was just last night," she says, color returning to her face. "Nothing will be on tonight anyway. You'll have to wait to next week to figure out if Jonah proposed." She winks, clearly trying to deflect attention away from the subject and, honestly, it works.

I don't ever want to know what happens between the two of them.

"You're probably okay," I joke. "Jonah's too ugly to be on screen anyway."

"Jerk!" she shrieks again, this time slapping my stomach.

"Ugh!" I pretend she knocked the wind out of me. "That's it, Sawyer. You're *dead*!"

As if she spent a life living with brothers, which I know she hasn't, she skirts to the other side of the island, putting the large slab of granite between us.

"I don't know what your game is, Kennedy, but I'm an athlete."

"Yeah?" She sticks out her tongue. "I'm an athlete, too. *And* I'm a girl. What are you going to do about it?"

Without giving it much thought I press my hands into the counter and swing myself across it like it's a pommel horse. Kennedy screams in surprise and makes it only as far as the couch before I tackle her against the white cushions and tickle her.

"Stop!" she squeals. "Not... fair! I hate being—ah!—I hate being tickled." She laughs harder than I've ever heard her laugh in the entire time I've known her.

"Doesn't sound like you hate it." I'm out of breath from restraining her wiggling body. "People don't laugh at something they hate." I let up for one second and start in again. Her laughter is like music. Why doesn't she ever laugh like this?

She growls before contorting herself into the fetal position. "Not fair! You have to laugh when you're being tickled, *freak!*" She wriggles a hand free and drives it right into my armpit, giving me a taste of my own medicine.

"Ah!" I fall back in broken laughter as she gains position over me and strikes the other armpit.

"Oh," she teases, menacing little thing she is. "Not such a big tough football player after all, are you?"

Before I can exert any force for defense, the front door swings open, which throws Kennedy off me in one swift motion.

"Oh," she says breathlessly. "Hi Dad."

"Kennedy," he starts, scanning the situation. "Matt. Nice to see you..."

"Don't worry," she says passively. "We weren't making out or having sex. Matt's a child and thought he could tickle me and win. He underestimated my strength." She chuckles. "A mistake he's certain not to make again."

I clear my throat and offer Kennedy a handshake from the couch. I can't stand yet, anyway. "You were a formidable opponent. You should try out for the team," I tease back.

She sticks out her tongue and I'm increasingly uncomfortable by Roland's still presence in the entryway.

"Matt came over to talk about homosexuality," Kennedy blurts out. "Is this against the rules? We're not in dorms. We're also not freshmen..."

"I..." Roland starts, his eyes staying on me for longer than on her. "I don't know. Just... don't make a habit of it, I guess."

Kennedy walks over to her dad and it's finally safe for me to stand without causing a scene.

"Sorry," I hear her whisper. "I didn't ask if this was okay with *your* rules."

I rarely see them in their father-daughter context, and I still feel a bit like I'm spying even though I knew about their biological ties before anyone else on this campus did.

Roland puts his hand on her shoulder. "It didn't occur to me until this moment that we needed to talk about it. Fun! New stuff for us to talk about! Matthew, I trust you were respectful?"

I nod. "Of course, sir. I didn't mean any disrespect. I was just asking Kennedy for some scriptural stuff."

He lifts his eyebrows. "Okay, then. I see I've walked in on something with more layers than I have time to dissect between meetings. You'll be back tonight for the show, right?" he asks, effectively dismissing me for the next few hours.

"Yes, sir. See you then. Kennedy, thanks."

She smiles, the tops of her cheeks still pink. "You're welcome. For kicking your butt, too." She winks and I stick out my tongue.

Slipping by Roland, I exit as quickly and gracefully as possible before jogging back to campus. I have to get my clothes and head to the gym to ward off the impending massive Kennedy hangover.

CHAPTER TWENTY
JESUS FREAKS

Kennedy.

B Y the time everyone starts trickling into the house around seven o'clock, I feel like I've fully recovered from the bizarre afternoon with Matt. And, it wasn't just about the weird tickling fight—which was fun, but... weird. It's how invigorated I felt using biblical text to show Matt why, my feelings aside, the Bible doesn't, in fact, say that homosexuality is a sin. Studying and then presenting that information gave me the confidence I'll need heading into election season dealing with my mother. She's still in a very "those people" sort of place regarding Christians—evangelical ones particularly—and when the time's right, and when I feel she won't misuse the information, I'll show her exactly what the Bible really has to say on the issue. Or not say at all, as the case may be.

Of course I don't know everything, and I need to pay attention to how the opposition uses the text for their gain. And vice versa. On more than just this issue.

God, how complicated can humans make things?

From what I've read and heard for the last year, Jesus came with a simple, but not easy, message. For us to love one another as he so loved us to give his life for our salvation. No, it's not easy to love them with the same love of someone who would *die* for us. But, I feel like maybe, just maybe, everyone has it a little wrong.

And, this isn't a new problem, either. For centuries wars have been fought, governments have been built and destroyed, and countless lives have been lost in the name of two sides claiming they know *exactly* what the text means.

"Do you ever think," I say to Eden in the privacy of my room before heading downstairs to join everyone else, "that things wouldn't get so awful if we really *could* just love each other the way Jesus loved us?"

"Wow." She giggles, "You *really* don't want to talk about your date with Jonah, do you?"

Rolling my eyes, I give her a teasing smile. "A girl's gotta keep *some* things private."

"Did you two kiss?" she doesn't hesitate to ask.

My cheeks flush before I can even answer.

"You did!" she shrieks.

"Shh!" I beg, pointing to the door. "I promise to tell you *all* about it. *Later.*"

"Fine." She sighs and heads to the door.

Before she makes it through, and against my better judgment, I stop her. "Eden, can I ask you something?"

"Of course."

Taking a deep breath, I give myself one more chance to back out of talking about it.

No dice.

"Matt came over this afternoon."

Studying my face, Eden slowly closes the door and sits in my desk chair. "Okay," she says slowly, proving she's read my face correctly. "And?"

I tell her about the whole visit from beginning to end. Every detail without missing a minute. From going through the Bible to my dad walking in. She's quiet for a while, taking several deep, pensive breaths before looking up at me. To my relief, her gaze isn't one of judgment or disappointment. It's a calm resolve.

"Well," she says as if she's been waiting years to have this conversation, "I guess it's time for you to set some of your own boundaries with Matt."

"Meaning?"

She shrugs. "He's set some with you, although they're admittedly sloppy. I know you said it was like brother and sister, but you guys *aren't* brother and sister, which means there is *always* a chance for that line to be crossed. Or erased and redrawn somewhere you don't mean for it to." She rises and steps toward me, placing her hands on my arms. "You need to take time to pray about your relationship with him. If his friendship is that important to you, you need to set clear and defined boundaries, or you'll risk losing him one way or another. And hurting other people, besides yourself."

"Jonah," I say inside a breath.

She nods. "Or anyone you might be dating. I personally don't have a problem with guys and girls being besties. But it always has to be different than two girls or two guys. And, to be honest, there are a lot of guys on this campus for whom your relationship with Matt would present a huge problem."

"Do you think it would with Jonah?"

"I don't know," Eden whispers. "If you feel convicted about it, talk about it with him. If not, let it go."

"Do *you* think it's a problem?"

She twists her lips, flicking her eyes away from me once or twice before answering. "I don't know. I mean, my first reaction is, yes, it's weird. But I don't know if it's *actually* weird, or just what I've been trained to believe is weird."

I can't stop myself. I step forward and wrap her in the tightest hug I can. "Thank you," I whisper. "This is why you're my best friend. We don't know anything, do we?"

"No," she whispers back. "Not a thing. Now, let's go get awkward and watch ourselves on TV."

Stepping back, I roll my eyes. "Do we *have* to?"

She nods. "'Fraid so."

We arrive at the bottom of the stairs at the same time Roland closes the door with three pizzas in his hand, next to Matt and Jonah who are hoisting chips and soda in plastic bags.

"Hey," Jonah greets me with a toe-tingling grin.

"Hey," I whisper, trying not to focus on the fact that everyone's attention is now on me and Jonah. Including Silas and Bridgette, who have made themselves at home in the living room. "I'll go get glasses and plates and stuff."

Eden follows me in to the kitchen, and I'm surprised when Bridgette joins us.

"Hey Bridge," I say as cordially as I can. "Glad you could make it. I've... I've kinda missed you."

"It's been a crazy start to the school year," she says as if she hasn't been actively avoiding me.

"Yeah," I agree, deciding to let it go for now. "This whole TV thing is crazy, isn't it?"

Bridgette smiles. "Yeah, but it's kind of exciting to be able to be part of some wholesome Friday night TV on a major network. I know my family will be watching, and normally it's really hard to find something to watch that's not, well, you know..."

Eden agrees with a sympathetic "mhmm," while I just nod because I disagree, but am not in the mood to go any number of rounds with her tonight.

"I heard you and Jonah had a date," she says.

Of course she did. Silas was our chaperone.

I nod. "We did. We went to Fromage. It was delicious."

"Is dating like this weird for you?"

"Like what?" I ask, sensing Eden tense a bit by my side.

Bridgette shrugs. "I don't know. Slow—"

"With chaperones? That's weird. I don't know what's slower or faster about it because I didn't really *date* much before. Trent and I went to dinner and movies and stuff, but it wasn't formal. We just hung around each other and made out a lot. Grab the napkins?" I say, walking to the living room with a heated face and a stack of paper plates."

"That went smoothly," Eden says under her breath.

"Maybe I should go," Bridgette announces, setting the napkins down on the coffee table.

With an eye-roll so deep I can almost see my brain, I grab her hand and take her to my dad's office for relative privacy. The room behind us goes silent as our friends and my dad undoubtedly try to eavesdrop.

"Stop it," I snap, shutting the door behind us most of the way.

Her eyes widen like a baby deer. "Stop what?"

I point between us. "This stuff. The getting offended and poking me first to ensure it happens. Stop. You *know* I've never dated like this before because we've talked about it before, back when we were roommates before you and your family decided I was too-risky of an influence for you to live with."

She opens her mouth, but I cut her off gently. "I know you don't like me, and that's okay. But we need to figure out a way to get along, okay? We have mutual friends and with this TV show thing, we're probably going to end up around each other even more."

She puts her hands on her hips and huffs. "How self-righteous of you."

"Try again." My ears are on fire.

Bridgette grins. A cocky, mocking grin. "Not everything is about you Kennedy. I know that might be hard for you to believe, but even this show isn't about you."

"I suspect not since I've avoided being on camera as much as possible."

"Even if the network was first interested in it because of your story it's not about the poor liberal, unchurched girl from Connecticut. It's about all of us, and how God works through us and our families. I asked if it was weird to date like this for you because I *did* pay attention to you in the past and I was *curious* as to how you were adjusting to a different way of doing things. I'm not out to get you, for goodness sake."

"Unchurched?" I barely heard anything else she just said.

She huffs again. "You know what I mean."

"Yeah," I huff. It's my turn to huff. "I guess I do. A self-righteous, unchurched girl..."

"Maybe I *should* go."

I point my finger inches from her face. "No. You're staying as we planned and we'll just keep our distance, okay? If I'm not allowed to run away from my discomfort here, then neither are you."

Her impossibly blue eyes gaze into the distance. I hate how pretty she is. Because she'll probably get a load of airtime from NBC and people will fall in love with the innocent, Jesus-loving girl when, in actuality, I think there's something way darker beneath it all.

God, please help me not judge her like this.

"Fine," she agrees. "Let's go watch the show."

I follow her out of Roland's office where we walk into a living room full of people pretending to not have just strained their ears.

"Everyone good?" Roland asks as diplomatically as possible.

"Yep," I say at the same time as Bridgette chirps an airy *yes* that makes me want to choke her.

Okay. It's clear she gets under my skin. Let's admit that and move on.

Jonah slides over on the couch and pats the seat next to him. "Here," he says, handing me a pizza and chip-filled plate.

"Thanks," I half-whisper, feeling quite on display in the middle of my dad's living room.

"Is everything okay?" he whispers.

I nod, waving my hand dismissively. "Yeah," I whisper back amidst lots of side chatter in the room. "She thinks I'm self-righteous and I think she's fake."

Jonah's eyes double in size. "Did you guys really say that?"

"She did," I say, taking a bite of thin-crust Greek pizza. "I didn't. In so many words anyway."

He puffs out his cheeks. "What are you gonna do?"

I shrug. "There's nothing to really *do*. I'm just going to avoid her as much as possible, I think. She hates me."

"I don't know if she ha—" he starts, but I cut him off.

"She does. Trust me. I'm a girl. We have all kinds of silent, and not so silent, ways of letting another hen in the henhouse know that we're less than thrilled by her presence."

Eden plunks on the arm of the couch on the other side of me. "Was there bloodshed?" she whispers.

"No. I'll tell you about it later."

Just before eight o'clock, my phone buzzes with a text.

Matt: You gonna kill her?

It makes me laugh out loud as I'm texting back.

Me: Not today. That's all I can promise.

Matt: Good. It'd be awkward to be serving you at the prison ministry.

Me: It's a men's prison only, remember?

Matt: Oh, that would be even more upsetting then, wouldn't it?

I cast him a smirky glance and slide my phone onto the couch next to me.

"Everything okay?" Jonah asks, clearly trying *not* to ask who I was just texting with.

"Yeah. Just a friend."

That was a weird non-lie...

At eight on the dot, the credits to *Jesus Freaks* roll, with an interesting opening montage of scenes from campus, various churches, and a collaboration—collision, really—of dialogue over them all. Voices talking over each other. Scripture, opinions, sound bytes from politicians and movies. All centering around one thing: Jesus.

The voice-over silences us.

"The quaint, quiet campus of Carter University, founded in 1925, has withstood nearly a century's-worth of trials and change as the Christian landscape of the United States has morphed and shifted."

Bridgette's face pops on the screen first. *"I think it's exciting to be part of a university that has remained true to its values—the values of Christ—in the middle of the cultural turmoil of secular America over the last several decades."*

"Bridgette Nelson," the narrator continues as the camera cuts to a shot of the front of a sprawling homestead, *"is one of fourteen children here in this rural Tennessee family. While she and her twin brother, Silas, are the third and fourth oldest in their family, they are the first to go to college."*

It turns out that many of my superficial assumptions of Bridgette's upbringing are holding up. The girls in her family all have waist-long hair, are dressed in long dresses or skirts, and have meek smiles on their mouths all the time. The boys all look like politicians in training. While Silas clearly belongs with them, as the boys all look alike, and some even have red hair, too, he seems out of place somehow. Like he has this restlessness. I begin to wonder if my assumptions of *him* were all wrong. Maybe he'll break free of the family that looks more like a round hole to his square peg charisma.

Charisma is not a word I would have ever thought to use to describe Silas, but watching him interspersed with his family, it's clear that's what he possesses. He's boisterous and smiling for the camera, making frequent eye contact, while the rest of his siblings seem to be exercising excessive restraint.

Look how humble we are...

It's Silas' turn for formal introduction. He's quite photogenic, like his sister. There are giggles throughout the living room as our friends get their screen time. I keep my eyes and ears glued on the set. From the corner of my eye, I can see that Matt and Roland are on my wavelength.

Waiting. For... something.

"It's a big step for me," TV-Silas says. *"Leaving home for the first time was a big deal. Of course there has been a lot*

of temptation along the way, but my strong roots in God and my family have helped me avoid disaster."

Disaster...

At this point, the announcer discusses some of the "disasters" that evangelical Christian kids can often face their first times away from home in a college or missions setting, or the job force. Sex, drugs, and alcohol—in no uncertain terms—are the main concerns highlighted. Then, naturally, the show cuts to *my* introduction. Because, why wouldn't I follow all the warnings?

Jonah slides his hand in my direction, shaky as he weaves his fingers through mine and gives it a squeeze. My cheeks flush, and not from seeing my face on TV. I've seen it there twice in the last year. They burn with the realization that Jonah has just taken our fledgling relationship rather public. Right in the middle of my father's living room.

And I'm okay with it.

Looking down for a moment to get my bearings, I take a cleansing breath before returning to the out-of-body experience that is watching myself on TV.

"It's been a big adjustment," I say in an interview taped a couple of weeks ago. With Finn, I believe. *"Everyone's so different than back home."*

"Kennedy Sawyer, formally estranged daughter of beloved and world-renowned pastor Roland Abbott, is no stranger to controversy," the narrator remarks before showing small clips of each of my Today Show interviews. *"Hailing from a liberal, and predominately Jewish community in a wealthy Connecticut suburb, Kennedy might just have the biggest culture shock of all the students here at Carter. For the next couple of months, we'll get to follow these students as they navigate a post-high school world free from the watchful eyes of their parents. Carter is known across the Internet*

for their strict guidelines of student behavior, including chaperones for off-campus activities."

Pieces of the Student Code of Conduct are either shown or spoken. Interestingly enough, this is not something that's easily accessible to the public. By going on Carter's main page, one can only access the document, along with other academic-related things, when they're logged in. Meaning you've got to be a student or faculty member to get the whole shebang. Thanks to the Internet, though, enough of it has been leaked in pieces to be stitched back together on various blogs. There are a bevy of anti-Carter blogs floating around the Internet. I haven't spent a ton of time on them, but thinking back to my conversation with Asher, and the previous meeting with *The Resistance,* I realize a search of those blogs might provide me and us with exactly what we need to uncover the dark belly of this university—witnesses.

Matt and Jonah fill the screen next, sitting next to each other in their dorm's lounge.

"The rules aren't any different than they were for me in high school," TV-Matt says.

"Does that bother you?" an invisible voice that sounds like Finn's asks.

Matt shakes his head and shrugs. *"It is what it is."*

"Yeah," Jonah adds on the screen. *"It's just kind of more of the same."*

"And in light of your struggles, Matt?"

The show then cuts to *the* picture, which I haven't even seen since it was first smeared across the media many months ago. Me, Matt, and Jonah leaving that strip club. Though, at first, Jonah and I are blurred out of the picture as Matt discusses his struggles when the camera cuts back to his face. His eyes are down.

In real-time, I look over to Matt, who locks eyes with me. His eyes fall to my lap, where my hands are locked with Jonah's. He shoots me a wink before looking back to the TV.

"Turns out it's a lot harder than I thought it would be," Matt answers as Jonah looks on sympathetically, and, out of the corner of my eye, I catch him shoot Matt the same glance in Roland's living room as the volume around us dials down to near silence. *"I'm lucky to have friends who are helping point me back to God."*

"Back to God," Announcer-Man says, *"is the whole focus of the student body here at Carter University."*

Nausea fills my stomach when Dean Baker fills the screen. Quite literally. *"It's not uncommon for young people to slip and slide. We're not expecting perfection in performance here at Carter. What we do expect, is for these students to fight for God in their lives, and for their salvation. The administration, staff, and everyone else here at Carter are in place as guardrails and lifelines for these kids. To help them transition from home life to real life."*

My mouth drops as I listen to the complete bull falling from his putrid mouth. I cast a quick glance at Jonah, and another at Matt, who are looking as skeptically at him as I am, while Bridgette beams as if Christ himself is giving an interview.

After a few more snapshots of life at CU, the announcer says, *"Join us as we take an in-depth look at a side of America most Americans don't know. A side, they say, is the foundation for America as we know it—one where God is the center of everything."*

"I'm a Jesus freak," Jonah says proudly as the long intro begins to wrap up. *"And I want to make my life about serving Him."* Then, much to my own dismay and eye-rolling, the camera

cuts back to me. *"I mean, when I first got here, I wondered how I'd survive around all of these FREAKS."*

Jesus Freaks, the screen shows as it fades to commercial, and the room buzzes with chatter and giggles about how everyone looked on TV, and how they felt about it.

"Well," I whisper to Jonah. "I think it's safe to say that they're going to cover our date in this episode with that nice little set up."

"Really?"

I nod and excuse myself to the kitchen for more root beer.

"You okay?" Matt follows behind me, holding out his cup.

"Are you really thinking of leaving CU if you get a football scholarship somewhere?" I blurt out as if this root beer is less root and more beer.

Matt gives an impish grin, holding out his hands. "And miss all this?"

Tilting my head to the side, I sound impatient. "I'm serious."

He shrugs. "It's such a minute possibility that it's not even worth thinking about."

"Not minute," I respond. "You guys are good. *You're* good," I say, immediately trying to figure out how to explain sneakily watching a couple of their practices. "And I know you've thought about it. You're a guy, and an athlete. There's always that goal."

"I don't know," he sighs. "We'll deal with that when the time comes. But, are you okay? You're weird."

"I should be asking the same of you," I ask, the hiss of the root beer filling his cup and the silence between us.

He shrugs. "I was there for the interviews. I knew they'd use a bunch of it. That's my angle, remember? The broken kid clawing his way back to God."

I eye him curiously. "Are you comfortable with that? It's intensely personal."

"Are you comfortable being the cynic?"

"I am," I answer quickly. "With them portraying me as that."

"Are you?"

I swallow hard. "I believe in God. And Jesus. And the crucifixion and rising from the dead. And that Jesus did that for us. The ultimate sacrificial lamb."

Matt tilts his head. "Do you believe Jesus is *the* way to God? Like those I Am statements we're studying in your dad's class. I am The Way, Jesus said. Do you believe that?"

My pulse pounds through my neck. I put my hand there, begging it to calm down. "I don't know," I admit in a whisper. "Please don't tell anyone. I just don't know if there's *one* way." I think about my Jewish friends, and the ones I made at the temple this summer. Rao, especially. One of the best people I've met in all my life.

If they don't believe, then what becomes of them?

Matt makes a claw with one of his hands. "It's life or death for me, Kennedy."

I feel sucked into a vacuum—as if I'm really seeing Matt for the first time this year. His eyes are the same—vulnerable and pleading. But there's a fight in them that I don't quite recognize. Before it was against himself. Fighting who he was and where he came from. Now, it really seems like he's fighting for his relationship with God, just like he stated on TV. In front of the whole nation.

Why does it make me uncomfortable?

Why is he asking me about my salvation beliefs?

"I'm proud of you," I force myself to say, extending my arms for a hug. "This takes a lot of guts. Admitting it. Doing it. Letting cameras film it."

"Thanks," he says, pulling me in for a hug.

One...

Just one. Then he lets go.

Pulling back, I catch Jonah sauntering into the kitchen with his hands in his pockets. "Hey guys." He smiles, eyes scanning between Matt and me.

If you feel convicted about it... I replay my earlier conversation with Eden.

Casting a quick glance into the living room, I let my eyes fall for a second on each of my friends, and on my dad. Are they all as sure as they seem? As sure as this show has so far portrayed them to be, regardless of what struggles and poor decisions they find themselves in?

Am I really the cynic? Not just made-for-TV, but in the flesh?

Grabbing Jonah's arm, I eye him, panicked. "I need to talk to you," I whisper, whisking us past Matt and into the hallway between my dad's office and the front door.

My heart is still bass-drumming my pulse through my body, and I'm starting to get dizzy.

"Are you okay?" Jonah asks, seeming to accurately assess my mental state by my physical appearance.

"Are you?" I ask in earnest. "With my friendship with Matt."

He pulls his head back, eyebrows drawn in. "Where'd that come from?"

"The hug," I spit out. "The one you walked in on. It was just a second—"

One second.

Jonah cuts me off. "Hey," he says softly. "It's fine. I know you guys are friends."

"He's one of my *best* friends, Jonah. If not *the* best. Also, I don't know if I believe Jesus is the only way to God."

"What? What... what are you doing? Who brought that up?" He looks around as if searching for a third party pulling the strings on this conversation. "Where's this coming from?"

This must be what a mental breakdown feels like.

I point to the living room. "The show. It's a bad idea. They're going to do the thing I knew they would. Make me the doubt-filled heathen. But I can't prove them wrong... because I have so many questions, Jonah. I'm not like you. I'm not like my dad, or Eden, or even Matt." I shake my hands in a futile attempt to return feeling to my fingers.

"You think I don't have questions?" Jonah's tone is borderline uninterested. "We all have questions."

"What about Jesus being The Way? Capital T, capital W? That's a definitive statement."

He nods. "And, one under which I'm currently operating. Because it works. And because I believe what the Bible says. I believe God left it for us, through the men he used to write it."

Leaning against the wall, my brain is sucked straight into the black hole it's apparently been fighting against for the last year I've been in this land. "It's all chicken and egg, isn't it?"

Before Jonah can speak, Roland ducks his head into the hallway. "Everything all right? Show's starting."

With my mouth hanging open, and eyes wide, I address him. "In order to believe what the Bible says is truth, I have to believe that God wrote it through those men. They're just words on a page until someone believes, right? The Bible in and of itself can't prove itself, can it..." I trail off, my eyes floating to the ceiling. "It means nothing unless someone can believe God meant for those words to be written."

"Kennedy..." Roland says with the kind of caution I'd imagine he'd use to talk someone out of jumping from a seventeenth-story window. "This is kind of a lot for the hallway on a Friday night, don't you think? Why don't you come back in the living room—with your *caffeine-free* root beer—and just watch the rest of the show?"

"You're making fun of me," I pant.

Roland scans my face, then glances at Jonah. "Jonah? Can you excuse us for a moment?"

With a silent nod and a slight brush of his hand against my shoulder, Jonah retreats to the living room. Before I lose all control of my senses, I can make out that the show's restarted and seems to be focusing on faculty, and the history of CU.

"Kennedy," Roland says as if he's calling me again. "What's going on?"

My eyes flood with tears when I finally manage eye contact with him. "I don't know if I believe what everyone else does!" I sob, quietly like the good New England Protestant I am, sliding down the wall and drawing my knees to my chest and resting my forehead on them. "I thought," I say between labored, stuttered breaths, "that if I came here, I'd be able to figure it out. Figure out what changed your life. What turned you around. What thousands of kids my age build their lives around."

"And?" Roland asks, positioning himself next to me, bringing his knees up, too. "What have you found?" he asks as calmly as if he's teaching class, not cleaning up his mess of a daughter from the floor.

"That I have more questions than ever. Matt's *really* healing, but for some reason I can't believe it's just through prayer. And I don't know why. And," I admit sheepishly, "I really *don't* think I'm good enough for Jonah. He'll probably have to lie to his parents about dating me."

Roland leans his shoulder into mine, lowering his voice to ensure we're the only ones to hear. "There's no one too good for you, Kennedy. It's quite the opposite."

"You have to say that. And that's not the point, anyway."

He breathes a heavy breath. "How long have you had all these questions? And why haven't you talked with me about them? Have you talked to *anyone* about them?"

I blink away the last of my tears with a growing embarrassment of the scene I must be causing. "All my life. Because you're my dad. And, no," I answer his questions in order.

"I'd be happy to walk through this with you, you know. And not just because it's my job as a pastor. It's my responsibility as your father."

It's the first time he's been so bold about his role in my life, biological or otherwise. But there's no hesitation in his voice or on his face this time. He means it. He's staking his claim in my life.

And I'm paralyzed.

"I need to take a walk. To the coffee shop. Can I?" I take it slow rising to my feet to avoid getting even more lightheaded than I am already.

"Stay," he commands, soft but firm. "Until the end of the show, and then you can go. You can take my car. I don't want you wandering around after dark."

I roll my eyes. "Because I'm a girl?"

"Because you're my daughter, you're upset, and I care about you. But I respect you enough to know that when you say you need space you mean it."

"Thank you," I whisper, placing my hand into his, calling him to help me stand.

Back in the living room, my overly polite friends try not to pay attention to the fact I just had a crisis in the hall. Jonah squeezes my hand when I take my seat next to him, Eden sends me a text asking if I'm okay, and I reply that everything's just a bit much but I'll be fine, and Matt stares at me every few seconds. Stern. Concerned. I shoot him a quick text.

Me: It's okay. I'm fine. I'm just overwhelmed all of a sudden. TV was probably a bad idea for me.

Matt: Promise? You don't look good.

Me: Eh. What's a little existential crisis? And, I look just fine.

He grins and slides his phone back into his pocket when the show comes back on. We don't see much of the angry kid I saw in the network meeting weeks ago, but the other girl, the freshman, is all wide-eyed and full of hope. She talks about her dreams of being a church worship leader, preferably married to its pastor, whoever and wherever that might be. It fits the stereotype I had of this place before arriving, but this *is* TV, and they need that.

Within a few minutes, my sense of equilibrium has returned, but, interestingly and maybe a little disturbingly, only because I've been focusing my thoughts on the peace and serenity I found when I was at the Buddhist temple this summer. How I had the silence to pray, to develop my spiritual relationship with God. I wasn't bogged down in rules and theology. I had a few quotes from the Bible taped to my wall, along with some thoughts from C.S. Lewis, but other than that it was just me and the Big Guy. Day after silent day.

Maybe the Buddhists are onto something?
But Jesus said "I am The Way," didn't he?
What becomes of them, then?

When my thoughts begin their slippery descent down that path, I quickly refocus my thoughts on the chimes. The incense. The colors, the sunlight, the soft music. And, all at once, I'm okay.

Jesus Freaks blends a montage of pictures and sound bytes together again as it begins the close of tonight's episode. My friends stifle chuckles when their faces flash across the screen, and most of them are tapping away on their cell phones, no doubt responding to text messages from friends and family watching across the country. One of the last scenes promises coverage of an important football game taking place this Sunday. A rare Sunday game for CU students, but one for which an exception's been made due to conference-type issues I can't begin to understand.

"I'm *so* stoked," Matt admits, bright and masculine at the same time. "They're going to film it Sunday, the world will watch it next Friday, and I'll be famous by midnight!" He thrusts his fists into the air in preemptive victory as the TV shows the football team working out in the weight room and on the field.

"Sweet. My first football game," I remark, winking at Matt.

"You're going to come?" He sounds hopeful, and I instantly feel like dirt for not making attending the first few games this season a priority.

"Of course. Jonah, want to go with me?"

A weird tension flickers between Jonah and Matt as if each of them is holding an empty soup can with a tattered string between it, trying to converse, but no one else seems to see or sense it but me.

Jonah gives my hand a squeeze. "Of course, I'd love to."

"Count me in," Silas chimes in, reminding me that this isn't really a private conversation.

"Oh!" Eden squeaks. "Me, too!"

"Oh I see how it is," Matt starts, dramatically with a smile on his face. "All I need for an audience of support is for Princess Kennedy to come? Then you all come?"

Everyone laughs, as my cheeks grow hot.

"Shut up." I try to be light, but I'm really struggling with over the top attention these days. Again confirming this show was a bad idea, and I make a mental note to accost everyone who supported me.

The conversation switches gears on a dime as an image of Jonah and me in a restaurant bleeds across the screen.

"And," the announcer says. *"We'll get a look into what it means to have a dating life when God is riding shotgun."*

I cover my face with my hands, allowing my fingers to separate some.

I wish I hadn't.

Because as the final credits roll, the entirety of my father's living room—never mind the nation—are feasting their eyes on my first kiss with Jonah.

"Oooooooh!" Silas and Eden giggle with each other.

Bridgette blushes, but her face is approving, somewhat. I can't for the life of me look at Roland, so I bury my face in Jonah's shoulder for a few seconds, allowing the attention to ebb and flow throughout the room.

Matt shows up behind me, identifiable by the large, warm hand he places on my shoulder. "Suck it up, K. Sawyer," he says into my ear. "With a kiss like that, you can guarantee a *lot* more airtime. You're a star, baby."

A muffled growl crawls out of my throat and I look at Jonah. "Everyone saw."

He looks nervous. Maybe a little nauseated. "Yeah." He swallows hard.

Then, it hits me.

"Even your parents," I say. He stays silent, looking to the ground. My stomach sinks. "Who don't even know you went on a date with me."

He shakes his head, still looking down. "It's... it's not like that."

I was going to leave for the coffee shop anyway, immediately following the show, but it can't hurt to have a few more reasons to storm off tucked in my back pocket.

"I'm going to get some coffee. *Alone*," I say, slipping away between Matt and Jonah while Eden and Bridgette discuss hair and makeup for the coming week, now that they've seen what they look like on camera, and Silas and my dad are holed up in a corner discussing something that looks serious but I don't care enough to eavesdrop on.

I grab the keys and I pull out of the driveway before Jonah and Matt can even make their way to the front door.

CHAPTER TWENTY-ONE

MONSTERS UNDER THE BED

Kennedy.

FIVE seconds after I leave the driveway, my phone chimes with several incoming text messages. I ignore them all for the time being. I just need to make it to neutral ground. To one of the few places in my life without a camera, or anyone who knows much about my personal life, since they're all in my dad's living room. Except Asher, but he's not there every Friday anyway.

Pulling into the parking lot behind *Word*, I finally check my phone, and see not only messages from my friends at Roland's— all wondering what happened—but from Mollie as well.

Mollie: You look good on camera, lady. You might as well get a job in TV now, since you can't escape it.

Me: God. You watched?

Mollie: You bet your ass.

Me: I just rolled my eyes at you.

Mollie: And I just rolled mine at you. Why didn't you tell me you were in the WORSHIP band?

Me: That was like a 3 second clip.

Mollie: Who are you, and what have you done with my best friend?

I don't know...
I don't know anything.
Ignoring Mollie for a moment, I check my other messages. Jonah's sent three. *I'm sorry. Where are you? Your dad won't tell me where you are.* I mentally give Roland ten imaginary "Awesome Points" for respecting my space.

Me: I'm fine. This isn't just about you. It's mostly not. I'm overwhelmed and need a second to breathe.

Jonah: We have to be able to talk things out with each other.

I pause, my thumb hovering over the screen. He's right. *We* do. But I don't know if I'm ready for a *we* with him if he can't be honest with his parents about dating me, *and* if our fledgling relationship will be followed as closely as our first date was.

Me: We will. But you also have to respect when I need a second. You know my quick tongue. I need to chill it before I say things I don't mean.

Jonah: Fair enough. Please text me when you're back home.

Me: I will.

Of course, there's one from Matt. But just one. To the point.

Matt: What was that about?

Me: You heard Jonah. He can't even tell his parents about me.

Matt: Nice try. Text me when you want to tell me what's really going on.

I crinkle my nose at his text, heartened and annoyed that he knows me as well as he does. But, what am I supposed to say to him? Tell him that, in reality, his sudden turn around for the better makes me uncomfortable? What kind of person doesn't want their friend to get well? And that, in thinking that, I've convinced myself that maybe I'm not the believer I'd hoped. That maybe I want to go back to the Buddhist temple and see what they're so calm about all the time.

Instead, I breathe.

I set my phone to silent and slide it into my back pocket.

Only when I've entered Word do I realize I'm in a more disheveled state than usual. I *was* just sitting at home and watching TV, after all. I'm not unkempt by societal standards, but I certainly wouldn't be wearing this outfit around campus: dark-washed bootleg jeans—not too tight, though—and a fitted black T-shirt with white dandelions on it made to look like the wind is blowing the little puffy seeds off the shirt.

I quickly tie my hair up into a ponytail. That's fancy talk for *my hair looks like crap and I don't want anyone to know. I mean for it to look like this.* Walking into the coffee shop, I couldn't be more grateful for the absence of TV's. Of course, there are plenty of students clearly watching the show via some pirated TV website, because I'm greeted with a few smiles and knowing glances. Luckily, for now, people seem to have the social grace to leave me alone.

"You're a star!" Chelsea exclaims with sarcasm when I reach the counter.

"You're a jerk," I mumble back.

She puts on a dramatic pout. "That's not very Christian of you, you know."

I know she's teasing, but it's hard for me to stomach at the moment. Luckily, she senses my not-in-the mood aura. If auras are a thing.

"Usual?" she asks.

I nod and wait awkwardly at the end of the counter, scouting the place for the most secluded seat available. Then I spot Caitlyn, member of *The Resistance*. There's a seat by her, deep in the front corner, which might not seem secluded, but it's well away from the door, and not near any window. After thanking Chelsea for my drink, I make my way to the girl I've only spoken to a few times, and all of the conversations we *have* engaged in have centered around Dean Baker and how we can take down his oppressive, secret empire.

The main problem is we have barely enough information to make much of a case against him. Caitlyn's sister was raped, that much I know. And, Caitlyn says Dean Baker was more interested in a cover-up and moving on than he was in actually helping her or bringing justice to the man who raped her. That's an impressive accusation to make without evidence.

Further, and I haven't said this out loud to anyone, I'm more than a little convinced that the dean was *somehow* involved in the pictures taken outside of The Pink Pony. But that's purely speculation and paranoia. I just let the thought

doggy-paddle around in my head while I search for the life pre-
server of evidence.

"Kennedy!" Caitlyn half-gasps, sounding startled when I
reach her booth.

"Mind if I sit?"

She gestures to the seat across from her. "Not at all. I figured
you'd be hanging with Jonah." She gives a wink and I roll my
eyes.

"Matt and Jonah and all them are at my dad's right now,
actually. I just... had to get out of there. It was kind of... too
much... or something. And I had this existential crisis in the
middle of it all. It was the ultimate panic attack."

She nods slowly, almost knowingly. "I promised my sister I wouldn't watch. She's pissed enough that I go here, but
doesn't want me supporting anything that brings attention to
the school."

I take a sip of the steaming latte and contemplate my next
words. Careful. "Caitlyn," I start. "Why do you go here? If
things were so bad with your sister. Why come?"

Without hesitation, she answers, "Because then I'd have to
tell my parents what happened."

"They don't know?!" I gasp, setting down my mug and causing Caitlyn to look around as if scouting for ears on our conversation.

She shakes her head. "Of course not. Would you believe if
your daughter told you one of the most well-liked and powerful
men at your alma-mater raped her?"

Did she...

"Wait. *What* did you just say?" My ears are ringing as all the
blood in my body feels like it rushes to my head.

Caitlyn's eyes grow wide. She catches her mistake mid-
thought.

"*Dean Baker* raped her?" My whisper is strained, unbelieving of the words. Breathing is hard—harder than it should be for sitting and drinking coffee.

"I... I..." she closes her laptop and slides out of the booth, slow as if trying to avoid being.

"No!" I command, grabbing her wrist and pulling her back down. "No. Why didn't you say anything? This is a..." Adverbs and adjectives collectively fail me.

Across from me, I watch Caitlyn slowly unravel. Her wide eyes fill with what looks like two year's worth of tears. "Because," she whispers, "it gets even worse."

"Tell me," I beg as if she has any reason to trust me. She doesn't know me. I'm public. My dad's a pastor and I'm a mediocre Christian at best.

Reaching across the table, I set my other hand on hers. "Caitlyn, *please*. You have to tell me. I can help. We can figure this out."

"There's nothing to figure out." She swipes at her tears in vain. They're not stopping despite the resolve in her voice. "We can't tell."

I shake my head. "No. *No*. That's the lie he told your sister. One that continues to rape her to this day. People don't start out that extreme. If it happened to your sister, I can *promise* you it's happened to others. A man like him? All the years he's been here? It's almost a guarantee."

This must be what shock feels like. My mind and body are unable to process the information all at once. All I really know for sure is Dean Baker is a *bad* man who has *literally* ruined someone's life.

Something breaks in her face. A shield of some sort that finally lets me see her for who she is. Not some bitter sister of the victim of a horrible crime. An actual broken person.

By something much deeper. Much, much worse, as her words promised me.

Caitlyn gets out of her seat and slides in next to me, tightening the space between our words to each other. "He got her pregnant."

My mouth waters, full of bile as I search for a place to throw up. But, she's not done.

"He... he *made* her get an abortion," she squeaks out before collapsing her head onto my shoulder.

I wrap my arms around her. Tight, as if to squeeze away all the pain, the memories. For both her and her sister. "That *bastard*." My teeth grind together so hard I'm afraid they might break. "It's okay," I try to comfort her. "We'll figure this out."

She pulls back. "How? No one will believe us. Courtney doesn't want anyone to know."

"She's afraid. Still," I assess, thinking back on the many, many victim-impact statements I've heard over the years at various women's rights rallies I've attended with my mom.

Rape doesn't happen just once. Even if it only happened one time. One woman I recall from an event last year said that you don't get over something like that. You move through it, and it becomes part of who you are.

Caitlyn nods. "He said she's never to say anything or he'll—"

"He'll what?" I snap? "What could he *possibly*—he's lying. He's playing on her naïveté and yours. This isn't okay. This isn't normal, and it has to stop. If he did it to your sister, he's done it to others."

She scrunches her eyebrows. "How do you know?"

"Because," I sigh. "Serial killers never start with a human. It's usually bugs, small animals, or other deviant behavior. Dean Baker didn't start by raping girls and making them get abortions, followed by holding them eternally emotionally hostage.

I'd bet my life on it that he's done this before and is still doing it now, on some level."

"You would?"

My teeth press into each other. "My life, Caitlyn. My *life*." I take a deep breath. "Who else knows about this? Jonah? Matt?"

She shakes her head. "Neither. They know what you know... knew. You're the only one now. Besides Courtney."

"What is she like now? Courtney. What does she do? Did she finish school?"

Caitlyn pulls her laptop across the table, opening it to face us where she left off: Facebook. She types her sister's name into the search bar.

"She tries," Caitlyn says, apologetically.

I focus my attention on the page and stare at the almost-pretty blond girl staring back at me through her profile picture. Almost. If her eyes weren't dead. It's so obvious to me I almost have to look down. I try again, to see Courtney as others see her. Those who don't know. Yes, she's pretty. Lost-looking with fair skin and blond hair in stark contrast with her sister's dark brown. Is there a visual descriptive for someone who looks like they need an eternity's-worth of hugs? Courtney defines it.

"She finished college back home and is slowly working her way through her master's degree so she can teach. She wants to teach little kids," Caitlyn says with sweet pride in her voice.

"Does she, or has she, done any volunteer work or anything for domestic violence or rape victims?"

"No," Caitlyn answers quickly. "She just pretends it didn't happen."

Same story. Different woman. It happens too often.

"How's that working for her?" I ask in honesty, wondering if I'll ever be able to find someone for whom "forgetting" actually works.

Caitlyn clicks through some of Courtney's pictures, going back to an album that took place when she first arrived at CU, before she ever met Dean Baker. The light in Courtney's eyes reminds me of the doe-eyed, bright look I saw the first day I came to campus and met Eden and Bridgette for the first time. Hopeful, excited, loving. The girl staring at me from the past has rosy cheeks, manicured nails, and looks to be held together by far more than forgetting her past. One focused on her future. One who had a future in mind that didn't include fate doled out by an evil man promising to have her best interests at heart.

"How'd she meet the dean?" I ask. "I mean, everyone knows him, but did she work for him? Volunteer? I need you to know, Caitlyn, that rape isn't about love or sex. It's about power. He took advantage of your sister in the worst way possible. I'm just trying to figure out how premeditated his attack was."

Caitlyn shrugs. "She volunteered in student affairs almost from the beginning. She was captain of the cheerleading team for our high school and was involved in way too many activities. It was never too many for her, though. She thrives—thrived--in organizing, planning... everything. And, you know the activities office is under the Dean of Students, by a few rungs anyway. I think she was around him from time to time, but I do remember her talking about him more as her last semester here wore on. That they had been planning dinners at restaurants downtown. Even just pizza, or whatever. She felt like she was going to get promoted to a position of significant responsibility by the end of the year."

It sounds like Caitlyn is giving a eulogy, the way her grey words swirl around us. Choking. And, in a way, she is.

"Anyway," she continues after a breath, "one day she just stopped talking about him. And about anything to do with school activities all together. Within weeks, it seemed, she was home on the couch recovering from a mental breakdown."

"No red flags for your parents there?"

Her face grows grim. "The school threw out all kinds of explanations. Over-worked, stressed, needs more prayer, saying she'd been partying and had demerits and it all became too much."

"Had she? Been partying?"

She shrugs. "Just as much as everyone else, I think. Once in a while. Experimenting."

Clearly I need to learn more about this CU experimenting scene. Not because I'm bitter that no one's invited me anywhere, but because I don't doubt there are faculty—Dean Baker included—who use this information to manipulate students. The system is set up for that *perfectly*. Demerits, privileges, everything. I'm willing to bet most of my friends would do just about anything to avoid their parents finding out about demerits and violations due to risky and reckless behavior.

"I've got to go to the bathroom," Caitlyn says, wearily. "Watch my computer?"

I nod. "Do you mind if I keep looking through Courtney's pictures? Maybe look through old statuses?"

"Whatever. I've been doing that for more than a year. Maybe you'll find something I haven't been able to see."

"It'll be okay," I assure her as she slides out of the booth. "I don't know how or when. But it will be."

Looking fatigued as if just in battle, Caitlyn offers a weak smile before shuffling to the bathrooms in the back.

Taking a deep breath, I refocus my attention on Courtney's page. I scroll through some recent pictures, which show no sign of partying, drinking, or anything. There aren't any with her and friends either, though. So, I go back. To the person she was. *Is*—deep down.

Friends, awards, pep rallies for the football team—for which she was a cheerleader—all paint a picture of a young, all-American girl who had everything going for her. All the while, a predator was watching, and I need to be able to talk to her to figure out what happened. How it happened.

Maybe you don't.

Maybe it's enough *that* I know what happened. What he did. There's no way I can bring this to my mom right now. Not yet anyway. She's just gearing up for the biggest career move of her life, and if I know one thing about her—she'd drop everything to come help me fight this. And I love that about her. And I'll use that if and when I need to. But, maybe for now it's just enough that I know.

What he did.

I was able to hold Roland off on talking through what happened tonight when I got home. I promised we'd talk in the morning over donuts and coffee. It was too much to see him, almost. How much do pastors know about the depth of the hurt in their churches? I don't even know if Courtney went to New Life, but I know that she can't be the only one, and there has to be people hurting just as bad under my dad's leadership week after week. I wanted to hug and kiss him when I walked through the door, but I was afraid that I'd lose my mind and spill everything about what Caitlyn told me.

He can't be involved because I'm not sure what it is Dean Baker has on him—or thinks he has on him—that makes him hate my dad so much. And, until I have enough evidence to blast that guy out of the water, I need to keep collateral damage to a minimum.

Sliding into bed, I text Jonah, as I promised I would.

Me: I'm sorry about tonight. Thank you for giving me space.

Jonah: No, I'm sorry. I shouldn't have acted weird about my parents. They're super critical of anyone I date, and I wanted to see if you and I were going somewhere before I brought it up to them.

I grin, remembering his soft lips against mine. The aroma of French food lingering between us.

Me: Do you see us going somewhere?

I hold my breath, watching the three dots as he types back.

Jonah: If you'll have me.

If you'll have me...
I'd die right here of romantic overload if that wouldn't leave him hanging.

Me: Are you asking me to be your girlfriend, Jonah Cross?

Jonah: I'd never do that over a text message. Lunch tomorrow?

I kick off my covers, welcoming the cool air across my back and cheeks.

Me: Tomorrow.

Interrupting my flirty text is a text from Caitlyn. A group text, actually, to me, Jonah, and Matt.

Caitlyn: Can we meet at noon tomorrow at Word? It's important.

Me: Yeah. See you then.

Jonah: Of course.

Matt: You got it.

Jonah texts me in our private conversation.

Jonah: Wonder what's up.

Me: Yeah. Seems urgent. We'll meet her then do lunch?

I try to keep all knowledge about Caitlyn's potential motives out of my words.

Jonah: I'd love it. See you then. Sweet Dreams.

Me: Stop making me blush.

Jonah: I've never seen you blush in person.

Me: Keep talking like that and you will.

I giggle at myself, alone in the dark, staring at unassuming stars from my bedroom window. Tilting my head, I set my sights on the unseen heaven and offer up a prayer.

If you're really up there, why is this happening? Why Courtney? Why any of us? Why is Dean Baker here, proclaiming your name?
Fix it.
Now.

CHAPTER TWENTY-TWO

HIDE AND SEEK

Roland.

"**W**HEN did you start drinking coffee anyway? It's not good for you."

Kennedy licks the sugar glaze of a donut from her lips. "Says the person who's on his third cup."

"Touché."

"I don't know... somewhere in high school, I guess? Mom and Dan worship at the House of Nespresso, so our kitchen always smells like fresh-ground heaven. I wanted to partake, I guess. Look cool, hip." She winks and I'm reminded of how much of her life I've missed.

Since she's been part of my day-to-day it's been easy for me to forget the void. The nearly twenty years before I got to see her on a regular basis. I can see it now—the daily stuff. When she tries a new lipstick or wears her hair differently. When she bends the rules of the dress code ever so slightly or slides her lip ring in the second she's done with classes and home for the day. Those are all things I'd miss if I were still meeting her for lunch one afternoon every several months.

"Why don't you call him dad? Dan." I ask before I have enough time, or coffee to consider if the question is a good idea.

"Because he's not," she answers matter-of-factly, if not slightly annoyed.

I decide to drop it, but she picks it up.

"Sorry," she says. "Just... I don't know. He was always Dan. Which pisses me off a little, because my mom wouldn't really acknowledge much of your presence in my history, but always referred to Dan as "Dan." It's like she didn't *want* me calling anyone "Dad," or something."

I don't want you calling anyone else dad.

"I get it," I say, meaning it. "I put her through a lot."

Kennedy nods, then comes the thick silence.

"Anyway," I say, cutting it, "want to talk about last night?"

"Hardly."

I twist my lips, trying not to laugh as she lays the teenage angst on thick. "Was it just a lot? Seeing yourself and everyone on TV?"

She grins. "Kind of. I don't know. My little breakdown didn't help matters, either."

"Do you want to talk about *that*?" I ask about her spiritual questions.

"I just don't get it. If, as we're learning in your class, that Jesus is The Way, as he stated, then what becomes of the people who don't follow that? Who either choose not to or don't know, or... whatever..."

I take a deep breath, not knowing where to start. So, I prepare to go in easy, but she has more to say.

"Never mind that," she says. "All of *that* aside, if God is who he says he is, then why do such *shitty* things happen to people. Good people. And, yeah, I know that Jesus said there would be trials. But trials and devastation are different, no?"

"Not necessarily," I answer honestly. "Devastation is another trial."

"It's bullshit," she says, and I choose to ignore her current slide into mild profanity. This stuff can be heavy. Especially when you get it all at once.

"Ugh," she says like a seventy-year-old man shaking his fist at the youth of America. "I just can't today. Can we continue this later?"

Her detachment, while on par for adolescents, is rare for her. "Sure, but are you okay?"

She *looks* fine. Put together as usual, no dark circles under her eyes and her hair is straight down and tucked behind her ears. Whatever's going on seems to be situated in her brain and heart and hasn't *yet* manifested to the rest of her. Hopefully I can get it out of her before then.

"Yeah," she says apologetically. "I'm actually going to meet some friends at Word, then Jonah and I are going to grab lunch somewhere. As long as we can procure a *chaperone*." Bitter.

"You like Jonah?"

Pink fills her cheeks instantly. "Do we have to do this?" Her face is fixed on her coffee mug as her eyes move up.

"Yes," I say with a bright smile, bringing my dishes to the sink. "Does he treat you right?"

Her eyes widen. "On the one date, yes. And every other second. He's a regular Prince Charming. Come on, it's *Jonah*."

"I know, but I'm going to keep checking in. All kinds of people can look good on paper."

She stops chewing, her eyes flashing to me. Accusing and questioning. It's only for a second, so short I feel like I imagined it when I watch her sip her coffee. But it was there. Something I said triggered it.

All kinds of people can look good on paper.
Is she hiding something?

"I've got meetings at the church most of the morning, then I'll be working on my sermon this afternoon. Meet back here for dinner? I'll cook."

"Sure, but I've gotta work. Early dinner?" Her eyes are eager and I mentally rearrange my schedule.

"Of course. See you at five?"

"See you then." She slides from her stool and places her mug in the sink before turning to me. "I know bad things happen," she says, reaching for my tie. "But does God offer *no* protection on this side of the grave?"

I'm silent as she loosens the knot, straightens the tie, then reties it as if she's done this a million times before. Giving the knot one last tug, she puts her hands down and gives an approving nod when she takes a step back.

Tilting my head, I give her the best answer I can. "It's so, *so* complicated."

Tilting *her* head, she hits me back with a retort. "I don't think Jesus meant for it to be."

"We'll have to talk about the *it* sometime soon, okay? Because I can say with some certainty we're not talking about the same *it*."

"Okay. Go, you'll be late. Go be the super hero for Jesus today."

I give her a quick hug, stopping short of kissing her forehead. "You, too, kiddo."

Walking over the small hill where New Life comes into view, I flash back to my early walk with God, when I had the same questions as she does, only I had a bottle in my hand while asking them.

If I can spare her *that* pain on her journey, I will.

At all costs.

But, I won't get anywhere with her if I push. Especially with how much like her mother she is. So, I've got to back off.

Or she'll never tell me what she's hiding.

CHAPTER TWENTY-THREE
BREATHE

Kennedy.

A S soon as Roland left, I hooked my iPhone to the stereo system in the living room and cranked up my "Rage" play-list. It helps me think.

An hour later, I'm left with few answers regarding what to do about Caitlyn's sister. I'm not on Facebook anymore, but I did hunt her down on Instagram, and saw more of the same. Pictures of food she enjoyed at a restaurant, forests, sunsets... no mention of God, though. Anywhere. No inspirational quotes. Nothing even defaming. Just... nothing. She posts very few pic-tures of her face, instead focusing on her shoes or accessories, or skipping herself all together and targeting her surroundings. A carefully curated page designed to prevent anyone to get to know her on any sort of substantial level.

Huffing, I pace the floor, unable to even attempt schoolwork until I get this pow-wow with Caitlyn and the guys over with. Jonah's sent me a few cute texts about looking forward to see-ing me later, and I've responded with a similar tone, but I can't shake the doom. The dread that lies before us. Caitlyn was right. It's *much* worse than any of us could have imagined.

And, she's right in saying we can't really *do* anything without her sister's consent. I'm sure there are anonymous ways to handle such situations, but that's simply not my area of expertise. That will involve bringing my mother in, or at least one of her colleagues. Because we can't force Courtney to go through this again. And that's what doing it without her consent will bring.

The doorbell rings, which is odd since I've never once heard it used. I just noticed there was one. Rolling my eyes, I shut off the music and pad toward the door, preparing to ward off any salesman that might be there.

I was wrong.

The quivering of my nerves registers his presence before my brain does.

It's *him.*

"Hello, Miss Sawyer," Dean Baker says in a fake-friendly tone. "Is your father home?"

"Sorry," I answer through the screen door. "He's got a board meeting at the church. I don't know when he'll be back."

One side of his bloated mouth twitches into something like a grin. "I didn't come here to see him. May I come in?"

Not a chance.

"Um..." I falter, wishing someone was here with me. "I don't..." *Don't know what you're doing here. What you want. Why...*

"This will only take a moment, Kennedy." He nudges the door open. His tone is bright. Like he's always called me Kennedy. Like he's my friend.

Shocked at his boldness in my own home, I take a step back—and a moment to get my bearings. If there were ever a poster for "stranger danger," this guy would be the headshot.

All the warning bells going off in my head make it hard to concentrate on what he's saying. Because it's not paranoid warning bells this time. This time I know. I know what's inside that barreled chest of his.

Darkness.

Evil.

"Did you enjoy the program last night?" he asks of *Jesus Freaks.*

"Sure. It was fine. A good representation." My voice trembles as he paces through the hall and into the living room.

"That was quite an award-winning performance you gave with Miss Martinez the other day."

"I don't know what you're talking about." I fold my arms in front of me. "We had a talk that was a long time coming. Were you spying on us?"

I'd all but forgotten about Joy. I know it was less than a week ago, but it's like time on this campus operates differently than in my head. It speeds up and slows down to accommodate its own agenda.

He chuckles. The first time I've heard such a noise from him. Though, if he had a handlebar mustache, he'd be twirling it between two of his greasy fingers. "Spying? No. I've seen some of the footage they'll be airing next week. Not all of it, but enough."

Enough for what?

"Alrighty then, thanks for the talk." Dropping my arms, I gesture to the door.

"You know what I find amusing?" he continues, with no clear plans to leave.

I shake my head, my throat squeezing in on itself. "I don't."

"That you've got everyone fooled."

Ice runs down my spine as he takes two steps in my direction. His face is grim, menacing almost.

"Fooled?" I swallow hard.

"You think you're going to win everyone to your father's side, perverting the gospel and this school on your way down."

While I don't know what he's talking about in regards to my father, as I've never heard Roland talk about being on anything other than the side of Jesus, hearing him use the word "perverting" lets loose from its cage the one thing in me I've worked so hard to keep locked up since I got here.

My tongue.

"The only thing perverted around here, *Dean*, is you." My nerves are trembling with such force I can barely feel my hands.

"Resorting to name-calling Miss Sawyer? I thought it would be beneath your intellect."

Taking one solid-despite-myself step toward him, I let it fly. "And I thought it would be beneath a self-professed man of God to rape a student, and *force* her to have an *abortion*."

Like a large mouth bass, his lips sag away from each other for a brief moment, but it's enough for confirmation.

Got him.

"I don't know how many have suffered at your hand," I continue. "But mark my *word* I will find out." Taking a deep breath, my voice lowers to that of a villain. Talking to him on his terms. Surly and laced with vengeful promise. "And, I will *delight* in watching your little empire tumble block by block as each woman comes forward from your closet of secrets and tears you apart."

"You sound awfully sure of yourself, little girl. Sounds like someone has spent a lot of time watching TV and scouring the Internet to fabricate some—"

"Courtney Braverman." I summon the name of Caitlyn's sister. It works. Dean Baker's eyes widen and his teeth clench. As an act of self-preservation I back toward the door, holding it open. "Good day," I say, praying this is enough to get him out of the house.

But for the moment I have an angry rapist staring me in the face. And I'm alone in the house.

Please, please, please.

Dean Baker clears his throat, pacing toward the door as if it's his next victim. "Ah, yes. A troubled young girl. It doesn't surprise me that she'd blather on about—"

"*Don't*," I snap. "Don't you *dare* blame her. For *anything*." Then, I lie. "The truth is about to come out. And, wouldn't you know? We've got cameras and eager TV interns ready to make their name in the business. It's just a matter of choosing who the lucky one will be to air your filthy, wretched laundry."

He lunges forward, pinning my back against the banister of the stairwell. His sweaty hand locks around my throat. So tight I can't tell if the pulse I'm feeling is mine or his.

"You put a stop to it," he commands, wild eyes moving across my face. "Or those same interns will be privy to the shameful sexuality of your friend Silas." A grin spreads across his mouth as my frightened eyes collide with the confusion of his statement.

I can't breathe.

I can't breathe.

"Ah, so you *don't* know everything." He tightens his grip around my throat enough that I start to panic, clawing at his hands and working on a scream, "Trust me, little girl, in this world, that knowledge leaking out would prove to be a certain social death for your friend. If not literal. Don't you *push me*." His hand tightens again and my field of vision takes on a soft edge as oxygen struggles to reach my brain. "You're not the first mouthy pain in the ass that's crossed this campus, and I'm sure you won't be the last. But I promise you, I'll keep you quiet."

Finally he releases me and turns for the door. I lunge after him, gasping, choking, coughing. But I plow my hands into his back anyway as if I have any hope of knocking him off balance.

"Oh," he turns, unfazed. "And this meeting never happened. Or not only will Silas go down, but I'll make your life a living hell." He takes one long step in my direction, dropping his head to be in my eye line. "I recommend you don't test the ways I can accomplish this, *Miss* Sawyer. I can make you *wish* you got off as easy as Courtney. Now, I bid *you* good day."

Just like that, he's gone and I collapse in the entryway, exhausted from adrenaline and oxygen deprivation.

I *knew* Courtney wasn't the only one, but I had no way of knowing how deep his reign of terror ran. Because I didn't do my research. My mouth got ahead of me and I have no guarantee that he won't somehow screw with Caitlyn now, or contact Courtney.

Silas? What?

Silas' sexuality? A resurgence of adrenaline brings me to my feet as every interaction I've had with Silas thus far paints an obvious picture I would have seen out in the real world within minutes.

Of *course* Silas is gay.

My hands rub over my face several times as I clear away the cobwebs between what's true and what's not. Standing, dazed, in the entryway, I'm left questioning if Dean Baker is bluffing, but I don't think he is. It was too specific, too real and unreal at the same time.

I have to tell Caitlyn what I've done. I'm going to have to talk to my mother, I think. And probably Roland. Because the trapdoor has released me into the most terrifying free-fall I could have imagined.

What have I just done?

CHAPTER TWENTY-FOUR

HOUSE OF CARDS

Kennedy.

'M late to my meeting at Word with Jonah, Matt, and Caitlyn. When I approach the same booth Caitlyn and I sat in yesterday, it's evident by the withdrawn looks on the guys' faces, that she's filled them in on the gist. She has her computer opened toward them, showing them pictures of her sister pre and post Dean Baker.

I don't remember the walk down here. My adrenaline crash seems to have been counterbalanced by a protective shock. The kind that prevents athletes from fully realizing they've got a bone protruding from their skin after a fall, only for my emotions. My spirit.

Matt's the first to notice I'm here. He always is and I wonder if he will always be.

"Kennedy?" His eyes sear right into me. "What's wrong?"

I tried to put on my game face. Seems it was strangled out of me.

"I..."

I sit next to Caitlyn, and Courtney's bubbly image staring back at me through the screen.

I'm sorry I betrayed you.

"Kennedy?" Jonah slides his hand across the table, reaching for me. But I don't move.

Instead, I start with the selfish part. The part I hope will soften the blow when they discover I've actually ruined everything.

"Dean Baker came to my house. My dad wasn't home." I speak in short, broken sentences to keep the important information at the forefront. "He was saying how I didn't know anything and I don't have anyone fooled... and he attacked me."

Jonah and Matt jump forward as if there isn't a solid wood table between us. Jonah leaves the booth and kneels beside me. "What happened?" He eyes the computer, and me, silently asking the unaskable.

"Not that." I shake my head. "I have to back up... and tell the whole story," I eek out, tears blurring my vision. I eye them all carefully, ending on Caitlyn, pleading. "Just please stay seated and silent until I can tell the whole thing. Promise?"

Because they have no idea what's coming, they all nod enthusiastically.

"Promise," they say in unison.

"You *told?*" Caitlin's mouth hangs open. Her eyes fill with tears.

"Don't blame her," Matt snaps. "She was cornered in her own home. Attacked by the same man who... you know... Courtney." His jaw works, furious as he looks between me and the table. Like he's trying to fight coming to my side. And I'm trying to fight wanting him there, too.

Caitlyn looks down in disbelief. Trapped between allegiance to her sister and the facts that lay before her.

"Are you okay?" Jonah remains kneeling in front of me gripping both of my hands.

I give one nod. "But, what he said about Silas..." I trail off.

Jonah turns slightly, facing Matt as they share a tight glance.

"You know," I state. "It's true. How long have you known?"

Matt shrugs. "A while. I don't know. I didn't really write it down."

"Same," Jonah answers.

"He's known for longer," Matt adds.

"But why does Dean Baker know?"

Jonah runs his tongue across his teeth, looking down and shaking his head as if the horrible answer to a riddle just made itself known. "I told him to be careful."

"Explain." I nudge Jonah, encouraging him to retake his seat across from me. He complies, still shaking his head.

"His family is close with the dean. You saw the day we had that meeting with NBC," Jonah gestures to me and Matt. "They idolize him. Silas was going on about how great and supportive the dean's been, and I told him to just be careful but I couldn't tell him *why* because I'd promised you guys we wouldn't go forward until we had *something* to go on. I just told him that, in general, the less people knew about his sexuality until he knew what he wanted to do about it, the better. He could seek counsel, of course, but I reminded him that we have awesome peer counselors, and there probably wasn't a reason to get the administration involved. I didn't realize he told him..."

"Baker's gotta be bluffing then, right? If Silas' family trusts him that much, there's no way he'd make enemies out of *them* right?" I scramble, trying to find a way to make sure Dean Baker pays for his sexual crimes without ruining Silas' life.

Caitlyn slams her fist on the table. "So what are we supposed to do now, then? Let Silas in on all this? Make him a martyr for our cause? Because Dean Baker *will* use Silas. Look what he did to Courtney... and you..."

"I'm so sorry, Caitlyn," I whisper. "He... "

"I know," she cuts in, unconvincingly. "I know. Just... what the hell are we going to do now?"

The table falls silent. What *are* we going to do?

"You've got to tell Roland," Matt says after a long few seconds. "I hate to say it like this, but we've got to bring a grownup in."

A grownup.

What college sophomore doesn't run around their own life masquerading as a grownup only to be brought to their knees by the reality of the dark corners of life? Corners where actual bad guys lurk. And, bad guys of the worst kind—the ones parading as heroes.

"My mom might be a better choice," I admit, internally waving a white flag.

"Or both," Caitlyn suggests. "I've read up on your mom. We need her."

I bite the inside of my cheek, uncomfortable that my family can be "read up on." But it's a truth I've got to own, there are too many uncertainties swirling right now. I need truth. I need anchors.

"Okay," I whisper. "I'll call my mom tonight." My throat hurts and my voice is slightly hoarse. I try to clear it, but it doesn't work. Dean Baker's handy work has gone deep.

"And your dad?" Jonah asks, wide, innocent eyes casting nervous pity onto me.

I shrug. "Over dinner. Before my shift." My chin quivers and I dispel a few tears. Overwhelmed. Scared. Shock wearing off.

Asher's boisterous voice and personality fill the space around us, but do little to revive. "Who died?" he asks jovially. Ignorantly. "It's an awesome fall day, football team has a heck of a game scheduled for tomorrow, and—" his voice cuts off as he tilts his head, eyeing the computer open between me and Caitlyn. "What.... What are you doing?" He eyes me.

He's not the grown up we mean to tell. "Nothing. We're just... angsty college kids," I try to reassure. "Nothing to see here."

"No," he points to the computer, nearly touching it, "that. What are you doing? How'd you find her? That was *private* information, *Kennedy*." I'm failing to connect the dots, but his tone leaves something to be desired.

"What's wrong with you? It's Caitlyn's sister. She's a few years old—"

"Courtney's your sister?" He's breathy as he addresses Caitlyn.

Dots.

Connected.

"No," I slur, a moan-wail combination working its way through my throat.

"How do you know her name?" Caitlyn asks. Oblivious.

Can this be true?

Is anything true? Any goodness?

"This has to be a mistake." I'm panting, a few seconds from passing out.

"What's going on?" Matt asks. Jonah stares, valiantly trying to assess the situation in silence.

It can't be...

She killed our baby! We killed it!

Asher's story, one I buried deep in my heart the night he told it, comes flooding back. One of a girlfriend he occasionally partied and slept with. One who got pregnant and had an abortion before bailing on school. A story with no happy ending and multiple ruined lives.

"*What's* going on?" Asher growls, eliciting stares from several nearby patrons.

Could it all have been a lie? One that nearly destroyed Asher?

Is anything true anymore?

I stand, swiping Caitlyn's laptop and addressing the four of them. "The back office. Now."

"I told you that story in *confidence*, Kennedy," Asher nearly yells in the confines of his office. Jonah, Matt, and Caitlyn stare slack-jawed at us.

"Asher," I say with as much calm as I can muster despite the swirling in my head. "It's not what you think. Please. Listen."

"Do you know my sister?" Caitlyn asks, looking annoyed, confused, and stunned.

"And you prayed for me!" Asher continues, slamming his fist on the desk. "You prayed for me and then you ran off and told all of your little friends like this is all just some game to you. I knew it..."

"Hey!" My shout causes everyone but Asher to jump. Matt takes a step toward me, his hand out. A second later, Jonah follows his lead, except he makes contact, touching my shoulder. I shrug him off and walk over to the desk, my voice trembling. "You listen to me. Something has gone very, *very* wrong here, and if we're all yelling at and accusing each other of things, we'll never get the pieces in order." My voice is raspy and trembling and I've had about enough of absolutely everyone.

I knew it.

No doubt Asher's been as suspicious of me as I feared everyone else would be. Only he really stuck his neck out and all but ignored his feelings, allowing me shelter and employment here in the coffee shop. Why do I feel so betrayed by his reaction? I shake my head, taking a deep breath to get the feeling of Dean Baker's fingers around my neck out of my head.

"Caitlyn," I speak slowly, like approaching a wild animal. Because this whole situation is proving to be just as volatile, "please just tell your sister's story. The basics. What *you* know. It's okay," I reassure her, taking a seat next to her on the tattered leather couch in this metal box of an office.

She does as I ask. Brave for someone who's only told the story out loud once before. To me. She tells us all how her sister's downward spiral seemed to come out of the blue, and it was a year before Courtney was able to tell her what had gone on. What fate befell her at the hands of someone who was supposed to care. The Dean of Students.

"Asher," I say when she's done, my voice hoarse.

"That's your sister?" he points to the computer, though it's no longer open. Caitlyn nods. "It doesn't make sense."

"None of this really does," Matt interjects, Jonah nodding along.

"Asher," I say again. "Can you tell your version of things? Please?"

"Version?" Caitlyn questions.

I nod, rising, moving toward Asher. Tired from adrenaline depletion and emotional bludgeoning.

Asher's eyes meet mine and, inexplicably, they're more broken than the day he first told me of Courtney and their hidden physical affair. Of the baby that never was. The guilt that's eaten him to this day. And, just like Caitlyn, he summons the courage to tell of the dark secrets. Words he swore he'd keep hidden.

"Jesus," I hear Matt mumble as Asher talks about his arrest and departure from CU.

Exactly.

Where was Jesus when all of this was going down? Where was the hand of all creation when these lives were inextricably linked and simultaneously torn apart?

"So what's true?" Caitlyn asks, sounding as small as a six-year-old.

"If I had to wager a guess," I start, then hesitate, wondering if anyone even wants to hear.

"Go," Jonah encourages. "Even with all you know, you're the furthest outside the situation. No history with the school or administration until last year."

I sigh, the weight of my words pushing me into the seat across from Asher. "I think the dean did rape Courtney. I think that before he did, he knew about her... interactions... with Asher. I think that when she got pregnant, Baker not only co-erced Courtney to get an abortion, but then forced her to use Asher to take the fall."

"But why?" Asher cuts in. "What did I do to him? What could I have possibly done?"

"Collateral damage," Matt offers. "It was convenient that he knew you and Courtney had slept together. Then he could make her tell you she'd been pregnant with your baby, and... you know... and it covered his tracks."

I nod. "Yeah. I don't think he gave you much thought at all, Asher. It was never about you. It was about him."

He shakes his head, staring vacantly into a past I know he wishes didn't exist. "How do we know the baby *wasn't* mine?"

My gaze falls on Matt, who's already looking at me through heartbroken eyes. It's clear he knows what I'm about to say. But I don't want to, even if I have to.

"We don't," I force myself to say. "We can't."

It finally catches up with me. The realization of what happened in my dad's house, with no witnesses, the pain of Asher's story and how it is also the pain of Courtney's. I sink to the floor and bunch my knees close to my chest, letting out deep sob after full, deep sob.

These are all good people, damn You, why are they hurting like this? Why? Why did you do this?

Only, I'm not saying it in my head, I'm screaming it into my knees.

"Kennedy," Matt's voice pleads, but it's Jonah's hands that wrap around my shoulders. It's Jonah's lips that find my forehead.

"It's okay," Jonah says, like he's trying to mean it.

"You don't have to tell her that," Matt talks over him, sounding concerned and annoyed. "Not after all that's happened today."

Between my cries, my arguing with God without regard to my audience, I hear Matt tell Asher about what happened at Roland's. About the dean's hands on me. Choking me.

He tried to choke me.

I can still feel his hot, thick hands. I still can't breathe. In a moment, Asher's kneeling next to me. I dry my tears, looking up into his eyes.

"I'm sorry," I blurt out. "I didn't tell anyone. You put it together at the same moment I did at the table. I never told."

"Shh." He pulls me into a hug, Jonah graciously backs away. "I know. I'm sorry for what I said. I didn't think you'd tell anyone. I trust you, that's why I told you in the first place. I'm sorry I said that. I'm sorry he touched you. I'm just sorry."

Caitlyn's empty voice centers us. "What are we supposed to do now?"

"You need to call your sister," I answer plainly. "I have to call my mom."

"And you need to talk to your dad," Jonah says.

I stand, taking a deep breath. "Yeah. I do. Look, my mom will be here like three seconds after I tell her. Matt, I know you have a huge game tomorrow and NBC's crew is covering it. Let's... let's try to keep our acts together until at least Monday. We've got to at the very least let Courtney know what's happening, okay?"

"What about what your mom told you?" Matt interrupts. "You told me a long time ago. That we have to know the size of the giants on Baker's side before we go after him?"

I sniff, rubbing my shirtsleeve under my nose. "Yeah," I huff. "But his skeletons are much, *much* bigger."

"Don't we need more information? More victims before we take this public, or whatever it is we're doing?" Jonah looks frustrated, defeated.

I shake my head. "Between Courtney's story, if she agrees to it, and mine from this afternoon, that oughtta be enough to get the ball rolling."

"What ball?" Caitlyn asks.

"There are more victims, Caitlyn. I know there are. There *has* to be. As long as one or two people say 'this happened', we just need one or two more to say 'me too' and... you'll see. People just need to feel safe in their pain. Safe from it happening again."

"How can you be sure?" Jonah asks. "How can we be sure that the two of you won't look like you're making it up? What if no one else comes out?"

Oh no...

"Oh God," I say, panting. "Silas."

"We're back to where we were out there." Caitlyn points to the door.

"What *about* Silas?" Asher asks, folding his arms across his chest.

How many good people are going to have to hurt to get this one guy to fall?

✝

Silas is pale as death when I finish, telling him the tales of Asher's Courtney, Caitlyn's Courtney, and how they weren't separate at all. We're alone in Roland's house, and I keep looking over my shoulder. To the door, the banister, and the sweaty ghost of Dean Baker connecting it all.

"Is that why you asked to do it here?" he asks, reaching for his glass, slouching in his stool at the island. "So no one would hear this story?"

I'll never be able to thank Roland enough for negotiating no cameras or microphones at his house.

"Sort of. Si... there's more."

He lowers his head, as if praying, though I don't know what good prayer would do now. Or what good it's ever done anyone in this story.

"Dean Baker was here earlier today, after my dad left for meetings. He started out with vague threats about my character and how I was *fooling* people on TV... and then I blurted out that I knew how awful he was. He put his hands on me. He grabbed my throat and told me if I dare told—"

"He *what?*" Silas jumps from his seat and walks to where I stand, against the counter. His hand caresses my shoulder in the most tender way. "Are you okay?"

My eyes brim with tears, and I ignore his question. "He told me if I told anyone," I whisper, "that he would make sure everyone found out about your sexuality."

Silas' hand falls to his side. He takes one step back as his face takes on the same dazed look I've seen in too many of my friends' faces over the last twenty-four hours.

Inexplicably, he laughs, his eyes doing their best to cover up their betrayal. "What is he even talking about? That's stupid."

I tilt my head to the side. "Si..."

"You believe him?" He laughs nervously. "You believe him."

"I... it's true, isn't it?"

"You think I'm gay?" His neck turns red. Soon the rest of him will.

I want to run to him, to tell him it's okay, that no one is judging him. At least not in this house. But he's not even operating in reality right now. Just his own.

"Silas, at the coffee shop earlier, from the story I told you... I talked to Matt and Jonah. They—"

"*They* think I'm gay, too?! They told you that?" His yell bounces off the cold, black granite of the countertops.

I shake my head. "No. They didn't. *Dean Baker* told me."

He drives his fist down onto the counter.

I yelp, startled, which seems to startle him. His eyes dart to me. Through me.

"Did you not just hear everything that Dean Baker has done?" I ask. "And that's only the stuff we *know*. He *will* tell, Silas. He *will* out you."

"No!" He growls through clenched teeth. "No." His eyes fill with rage as he paces the floor. "Do *you* know what that would do to me? To my family? There's nothing to even tell!"

"Silas," I whisper. "I'm telling you this because I want you to know we're going to do everything we can to make sure that none of this gets out. About you. He's playing a game of chicken with me." It's not lost on me that Silas still hasn't confirmed the giant elephant in the room. I need to defuse this situation. "I keep secrets, Silas. And I'll keep this one as long as you need me to."

"I'm not gay, Kennedy, so keep whatever secrets you want." He grips the edge of the island and hangs his head.

I nod. "Okay. Noted. Nothing to worry about then."

"You're going to tell? About Courtney and you?" he asks with his head down.

"We have to," I whisper. "He's a dangerous man."

With renewed resolve, Silas raises his head and stands tall. "Okay, then. Good luck." He heads for the door.

"Si?" I follow after him, catching up as he puts his hand on the knob. "Look at me."

He does. Barely. All clenched jaw and wild, roaming eyes.

"I'll see you at the game tomorrow," I confirm. "We're not doing anything until after then."

Silas nods, and just when I think I see tears forming at the base of his eyes, he smiles, erasing them. "See you," he says softly. Disappearing through the door, leaving more confusion, anger, and hurt in his wake.

CHAPTER TWENTY-FIVE

KIDS

Kennedy.

"NOW that you've scared the absolute... whatever... out of all of us, can you *finally* tell us why we're here?" Mom paces Roland's living room, trying to watch her language it seems. I sit next to Dan while Roland leans against the mantel, his eyes flickering between the flames and my mom's panicked strut.

It wasn't that hard of a sell to get Mom and Dan to drop everything to fly here. It might be after midnight, but I never get to tell all of my parents anything at the same time, and the telephone gets old. I assured them I was safe, which isn't a complete lie, but that it was too important to relay over the phone or, even worse, email.

"There's been some... stuff going on," I start. The worst start ever, giving no information. "It didn't involve me at first. But, now it does. And I can't go on not saying anything anymore."

Dan rubs his hand down my back. "You're kind of freaking us out here, kid."

I nod. "I know. I'm... okay yesterday, or whatever, like twelve hours ago when Roland was at a meeting at the church, Dean Baker stopped by."

Roland looks confused. "What'd he want? I didn't get any messages from him..."

I shake my head, swallowing the lump in my throat. "It wasn't you he wanted to talk to."

"What's this about?" Mom asks, in the dark more than she even knows.

"Mom," I start. "You should know that this guy is bad news. Don't freak out yet until you know all the things. But, he just... doesn't like me. Or Roland, for that matter, and he goes out of his way to remind me of that any chance he gets."

"He threatens you?" She nails it.

I shift, uneasy. Dan tries to calm my nerves. "It's okay, Kennedy, just let it out."

So I do.

"He what?!" Roland slams his fist against the cold marble tile around his fireplace. Mom reaches for her phone.

"This is bullshit," she hisses. "Why didn't you tell me this was going on," she spits at Roland.

He runs a hand through his shaggy, dirty blond hair. "I didn't *know*, Wendy. And just because someone doesn't like you doesn't mean they're going to show up at your house and choke you!"

"Stop!" I yell. "Please."

"Why didn't you tell us sooner. Like immediately?" Dan asks. Calm as his hand runs the length of my back.

"Mom, put the phone down, please!" I beg again, ignoring his question. "There's more," I say softly. "It's so complicated..."

"What more could there be?" she snaps. "This man parades around preaching *Christ's love* and he does this! *This. This* is why I didn't want you here."

"Because you knew an administrator was a sexual deviant?"

She waves her hand. "At a school that forces women to be submissive to their husbands and heavily monitors their students' sexual lives. Yeah."

Roland's mouth drops and I stand, nearly toe-to-toe with her. "There is no *they* here, Mother. Don't blame Dad. *Please.* He had no idea. I know I maybe should have said something sooner, but we didn't really realize what a monster Dean Baker was. "

"We?" Mom and Roland say at the same time.

"Yeah," I say in a sigh. "We."

The Resistance.

It really is kind of a shame my parents couldn't work things out. They make an incredible team, honestly. Though, they make a great team comprised of the people they are now, not who they were then. And, then Dan wouldn't be in the picture. And the four of us wouldn't be sitting around in choked silence after my telling of all the stories that weave together. Caitlyn's sister, Asher's girlfriend, for lack of a better term, Courtney's rapist, and my peripherally shady dealings with the dean, all the way back to the meeting we had in his office last year that was never documented in my file.

"We'll get you to a doctor right away. If there's any damage, even a bruise, we'll need you taken care of *and* it documented," Mom says between deep, angry breaths. Pacing.

"Mom... You always told me not to lace up for a fight until I knew exactly who I was dealing with. Now, I might not know everything about this guy—though we tried to find out—but I know some of what's shoved in his closet. It's enough."

"Damn right it is. NBC thinks they've got a story on their hands now, just *wait*—"

"No!" I cut her off, drawing concerned looks from the three adults who call me their daughter.

Dan makes a clicking noise with his tongue. "There's more, isn't there..."

I nod. "Silas."

I don't want to keep telling his secret.

Roland shrugs. "What about him?"

But I have to.

So, in one breath, I let it out. "When Dean Baker was here yesterday he told me that if I told anyone about what had been going on, he'd tell everyone about Silas' sexuality. Which was news to me. But I talked to Silas, who I think is in denial, but he knows we have to tell..."

I turn my attention squarely to my mom. "You have to understand that in an environment like this, Silas isn't likely to get a parade for being gay. He doesn't want one. He's—"

"Scared," Roland cuts in.

"You knew?" I whisper.

He stares blankly at me, unmoving.

"Oh," I continue. "You can't tell me because it's confidential. He's talked to you in an official capacity..."

"Official or not," Roland says, looking far away, "his life isn't mine to talk about."

Mom sighs. "That's neither here nor there. By the time word gets out about the perverted Dean, no one is going to give one flying fu... anything about a gay college guy."

"Not in your world," Dan interjects with surprising honesty. "But here they will."

She arches an offended eyebrow. "Enough to let girls continue to be raped, abused, and forced to have abortions?"

"I didn't say that, Wendy. There has to be a way to take care of everyone."

Mom walks over to the couch and sits on the other side of me. "We're going to fix this."

"There's nothing to *fix*. The damage has already been done. Haven't you been listening?"

"We need to pray about this," Roland states, firm. As if he's not in a room full of skeptics.

I roll my eyes. "Isn't it a bit late for that?"

Roland's eyes fall like I've broken his heart, and my cheeks heat in embarrassment like I may have done just that. "It's *never* too late," he whispers before disappearing into his office in a silent, heavy cloud.

His words and tone remind me of when Asher came to see me at the Buddhist temple in New York.

No one is a foregone conclusion, Kennedy. No one.

"I'm tired," I whisper to my mom and Dan. "I promised my friends you guys wouldn't do anything until after the game tomorrow. Matt and the whole team are really excited about even a few minutes of national airtime, and I don't want to ruin that for them, okay? Can we be kids for a few more hours?" My voice cracks. Mom wraps her arm around my waist and Dan settles his across my shoulders.

"Of course," she whispers, kissing my temple. "A few more hours."

"Thank you."

"Then," she says coldly, "he's *mine*."

"Easy, soldier," I try to say with sarcasm, but it just comes out tired.

I kiss both of them before they turn in to the guest room on the far side of the first floor, opposite the kitchen where I spent my first night in this house so many months ago. Before climbing the stairs, I pad down the hall toward Roland's office.

I rap lightly with my knuckle, a small stream of light passing through the not-quite closed door. There's no answer, so I knock again. He didn't go up to his bedroom, that much I know.

"Dad?" I call softly.

Still no answer, so I push the door open, careful to be quiet.

In the far corner of his office, near a broad window that faces the front of New Life church, Roland is face down on the floor, legs stretched straight out behind him.

"*Dad?!*" I gasp. A small voice, void of breath as my throat closes and I race toward him.

Nearing him, I see with a flood of relief that this position is intentional. His hands are in fists, propped on a small throw pillow and supporting his forehead. He ignores me. Or is so deep in prayer that he doesn't hear me. Maybe both.

"You are good, Lord." His emphatic prayer muffled by the pillow. "Your sovereignty and your righteousness are *good*. Help me. Help me see. Help me help. Protect these girls, Lord. Help Silas. Your will be done with the dean. Give me words to speak, Lord Jesus..."

I've prayed like this before out loud and in front of someone once. Knelt down in front of Asher on a sidewalk not so long ago as he sobbed through the story of how he is who he is today. I've felt the pleas I hear in Roland's voice. I asked God to protect Asher from his pain. I did. I knelt right on the concrete and asked God to take it away. But he didn't. Not even a little bit.

I'm so angry I could spit.

Isn't there some committee I can bring this to? One that deals in justice and fairness over prayer requests? Roland, laying on the floor, stakes his life on these prayers. By all accounts it seems at least some have been answered. He's got me back in his life, an amicable relationship with my mom, a thriving church, and a generally positive public opinion.

Meanwhile, girls are getting raped and otherwise taken advantage of by people meant to guide them.

Where is the balance?

Roland's voice turns to reciting scripture, something I've heard him do in prayer before. As if he's run out of his own requests and is reminding himself of the Word. Eden calls it tattooing scripture on your heart. So that way when crisis or joys hit, you have biblical truths to fall back on.

"Lord, I believe. Help my unbelief!" He keeps on praying, reciting things I recognize from Psalms and Proverbs, but couldn't pull out of a chapter and verse lineup.

I stand there for a second more before retreating to my room, opening a Bible app on my phone and entering the words my dad said. The ones rattling in my brain.

Lord, I believe. Help my unbelief!

Matthew nine fills my screen, and I read again the story of the possessed boy, and the father desperate to save him. This passage keeps coming up for me.

Jesus seems agitated in this passage—something I like about him, that he's human as much as he is divine. He implores the father to believe. That if the father has enough belief, his son will be healed. The father pleads. I can almost see him like, *"Wait, wait. Okay. Okay, stop, wait!"* Instead he tells Jesus he believes, but admits there could be something in him that's less sure. He cried out to Jesus with tears, saying he believes. And, says, *help my unbelief!*

I lie back on my pillow, too tired to undress but I manage to kick off my shoes. The father chased down Jesus to heal his son. He believed. When Jesus challenged him he didn't stand around and try to demonstrate all the ways he believed. He just said *"I do!"* and *"But fix whatever in me doesn't."*

Roland recognizes that there are likely parts of his human heart that don't believe. He wants—needs—his whole being to believe for this battle we're about to face.

Taking a deep breath, I close my eyes and try to recite the line. To tell God that I believe, and ask him to help the parts of me that don't.

But I can't even get the first part out.

At this point, it seems like I don't have enough belief to petition God for more.

"Show me you're real," is all I can manage before falling into a fitful sleep.

CHAPTER TWENTY-SIX
SLOW MOTION

Kennedy.

ASHEVILLE feels the most like New England to me in late October. Family and friends fill the foliage-lined stadium to watch the Carter University Knights play the Guilford College Quakers. It's a non-conference game, as Carter is in the USA South Conference, and Guilford is in the ODAC... Matt explained this all to me. And it matters, somehow, because Guilford is the only school in North Carolina in the ODAC and they're trying to get into the USA South... trust me, if Matt's enthusiasm this morning on the phone is any indication, this matters.

Anyway, according to my fearless, football-playing friend, Carter should have no problem blasting Guilford out of the water. His words, not mine.

"When were you going to tell me about your mom's political assignment?" Roland nudges me playfully as I sit sandwiched between him and my mom on the cold, metal bleachers.

He's doing his best to put on his charismatic face. Cameras are all around, but, thanks be to God, we're not wearing mic's today. There would be too much editing for the sound technicians to sift through, so they just get our faces. But, in another act of so-called grace, all the cameras are focusing on the field, and the intense game that's under way.

I shrug. "Never, probably. I keep secrets, you know. Well, unless someone's life is in danger, I guess."

"Or lots of someones," Mom grumbles under her breath. Dan puts an arm around her shoulder, tapping mine with the tips of his fingers.

"This will be okay, you know," Dan reassures.

I nod.

"Still haven't heard from Silas?" Roland asks quietly.

I shake my head. I texted him last night to make sure he was okay, but was met with silence.

From behind me, Eden leans forward, speaking into my ear. "You're crazy strong, you know that?"

Okay, I *do* keep secrets. Except from my best friend. Anyone who is a woman knows that this is the cardinal rule: The best friend is *always* in the know. I smile, blowing her a kiss and refocusing on the scene unfolding around me.

Jonah returns to the stands with hot chocolate for all of us and, dutifully, my mom slides over—since I don't think Roland would ever slide away from me to let a boy in. Dan wouldn't either, but he has no choice being on the other side of my mom.

"Thanks, you." I blush, inhaling the scent of warm cocoa.

"Thank *you*." He plants a small kiss on my cheek. Right there in front of everyone. My mom giggles, Roland pretends not to notice, and Eden gives us a cooing noise from behind.

"For what?" I whisper as if we have any privacy at all.

"Being you. Being strong and fearless. God pulled out all the stops with you."

Casting a glance to my left, I watch Roland bite his lip and grin before clearing his throat and turning to his left, where

Buck Wells sits. It's really a cozy stadium situation here. And we've got really good seats, too, thanks to all the strings one can pull being on TV. Roland, that is.

I shrug. "I guess."

"Huh?" Jonah tilts his head to the side.

"God hasn't really been showing me his best work the last few weeks, Jonah."

He leans into me, taking a deep breath. "It's when it gets darker that we have to race more ardently toward the light."

I look at him sideways. "Jesus motivational quotes?"

"One of your dad's sermons during Advent last year. When the world gets so dark, then Jesus is born and everything changes."

"For who?" I whisper. "Silas? Courtney and Caitlyn?"

Jonah nods to the field with a hopeful grin. "Look at him out there."

Matt.

The first quarter of the game is underway and Matt is harvesting the fruits of his labors over the last several months. Brawny as the day I met him and even more full of life, he's a far cry from the broken version of himself that sat in the strip club all those months ago.

"But you don't believe it's Jesus' hand at work with him, do you..." Jonah trails off, reading me far better than I care for.

I shrug. "I don't know."

"If I may..." He arches his eyebrow toward me, asking to continue. I nod. "You seem angry that God doesn't fix things, or make them perfect. New. But when we see evidence of true, miraculous healing," he points to the field where Matt stands, "you don't believe it's God. What *is* God to you, Kennedy?"

"The man behind the curtain," I let slide from my lips.

"Oz?"

I nod. "The Great and Powerful. Only, did you know that in the books Oz said he was The Great and Terrible? They changed it for the movie. Less scary."

"But he was a puny old man behind a curtain turning dials and pulling strings," Jonah says, quite distressed. "Is that what you really think of God?"

Perhaps I'm sounding a bit pessimistic, I realize. Cynical, even. "No," I shake my head and plaster on an everything-is-fine smile for my hopelessly hopeful boyfriend. "I'm just... confused. Stressed. Tired."

The truth is, I don't even know what I feel or believe right now, but I do know that the middle of a football game on an otherwise pleasant, if not ominous afternoon with all that we're going to face later is *not* the place to hash out such matters. I want to get through the game in one piece, and hope we all remain as such when the confrontation with the dean is over. Moreover, I'm having a hard time waiting. Just waiting. For the right time. The time the grownups will pull the trigger and all hell will break loose.

The crowd cheers and groans in a matter of seconds. It's a low-scoring game so far. Low meaning we have zero points and Guilford has six—scoring one touchdown but missing the extra point. I think that's how it all went.

Matt's a running back. An aggressive and intense position, which makes his size and athletic ability important. He's on the larger end of the running backs I Googled on the Internet, since I know nothing about football, but he's quick. Not just for his size, either. The boy can move under all that muscle, and this makes him one hell of a player. Roland's words, actually. He said hell.

Apparently, Guilford knows this, because they've been on Matt the entire game. Double, and sometimes triple—teamed. He's bounced up from tackle after tackle, and he seems irritated with a level of testosterone I find laughable. He holds his arms out to the referees every time he gets up, clenching his fists and moving back to the huddle when they ignore his pleas. Some fouls have been called on the more aggressive guy after Matt, but not enough according to CU's fans. I've always viewed Matt as a guy's guy, but it's no more evident than when he's out there on the field.

"Man," Dan half-yells, calling toward Roland and Buck, "They're not going to give him a break. They've studied his moves."

"Yeah," Buck huffs back. "The coach better have another plan if they want to score *any* points this game."

I look to Jonah and shrug, giggling because I know so little about football it's embarrassing that I'm taking up a seat at all.

Jonah lifts his chin to the field. "Looks like they're going to try a different play."

I follow his line of vision then look back to him quizzically. "They look the same as they do every play."

He laughs, and so does Roland, the sneaky eavesdropper. "No, look," Jonah points, "Matt was closer before, and now he's over there. I don't know *what* they're going to do, but it's something."

One new play, but the same ending, Matt is flattened to the field and my stomach goes queasy. I can't believe he keeps getting up. I get up, too, needing a break from the carnage. "I've got to go to the restroom," I say. "Eden?" I turn to her and she dutifully hops up and follows me as we zigzag our way down the few bleachers that separate us from the ground.

"You okay?" Eden asks, shoving her hands in her pockets as I weave us toward the concession stand. "I thought you needed to go to the bathroom?"

I shake my head. "I need cheese. Or more chocolate. Or both. I'm stressed, Eden. So stressed I could throw up right here."

She takes a deep breath and places her arm around my shoulders. "They've got a plan, right?" she asks of the recruited grownups.

"Yeah. I guess. I just... it's all so up in the air and I feel out of control."

"You never had control in this situation to begin with," she says plainly. "It was in motion long before you came into the game."

"You're awfully calm," I remark.

She shrugs. "Because it'll all work out. It has to. God promises good."

"Did he promise that to Courtney, too?"

She lowers her head. "I don't have all the answers either, Kennedy," she says quietly. "I just know that God is good. And I have to cling to that, or none of this matters. But I think we should stop being angry with God for things he didn't cause in the first place. God doesn't rape. Evil does. There are spiritual battles going on all round us, all the time."

"And God lost that one?" I ask, angry.

"Yeah." She sounds as defeated as I feel. "But he'll win the war. Jesus already conquered death. There's healing to be done here. And only God can do that."

"I need a minute," I say. Brisk and cold. "I'll meet you back at the stands, okay?"

She stares at me for a long moment, her deep eyes filling me with hope and despair at the same time. "Okay."

Alone and a few feet away from the smell of nachos, I hear my name. Turning, I find Silas standing before me. Smiling though his eyes are stained red from cried tears.

"Silas!" I leap toward him and fling my arms around his neck, hugging the living daylights out of him. "You scared me," I whisper into his ear.

He holds me at arms length, still smiling. "I'm here. I got your texts but had some things I had to handle with my family last night."

"Like?" My heart races.

He gives me a bashful smile and whispers, so close I can feel his breath, "I told my parents what I'd been struggling with. You know."

"Wow," I whisper back. "Are you okay?"

He nods, almost proud. "I will be now. They're going to help."

I look a round, confused. "Help?"

"We're going to research programs that can help me get back on track and I'll get connected over winter break, up my counseling here, and pray like crazy."

"Programs?" I rub my forehead to check for signs of fever as it's clear I'm losing my grasp on reality.

"God doesn't make mistakes, Kennedy."

"I'm aware..."

"I serve an amazing God who made me perfect. I'm the one who can screw it up. I need help so I can get back to how he made me, for the purposes he made me. To rid myself of my sinful desires and sexual perversions."

My mouth falls open. A common facial position of mine over the last year. "I... I don't know what to say," I admit, breathlessly.

"Thank you," Silas says, giving me a hug. "I needed the push from you to be honest with myself and my family. With what I'm struggling with and to make a game plan to get better."

I shake my head. "I didn't say you needed to get *better*, Silas."

"You're liberal, right?" his tone takes on a harsh edge. Just on the edges, though.

"Yes."

"Open-minded?"

I nod. "Very."

His mouth forms a straight line before he says, "Then *be* open-minded, Kennedy."

"Okay," I force out, slow.

"The women's movement wasn't about pushing women into the workplace, right?"

"No," I admit. "It was about giving the women the choice. Choices."

He puts a hand on my shoulder. "I choose to heal from this, Kennedy."

"You're not sick," I say, still whispering.

He bites his bottom lip, looking a little more like the old Silas. The angry Silas. "Do you presume to dictate what people can be healed from?"

"No," I answer quickly. "I never said that. God, okay, can we talk about this later? I'm really not prepared for this and I don't want to say something that will hurt one or both of us."

He drops his hand. "Fine." He answers, short, and looking hurt.

"Silas. I love you, okay? I truly do. I just don't even know half the words you said to me. I don't come from a place where sexuality is something you can or should be healed from. So I don't even know what you're asking of me.

"Are you going to be my friend through this or not?" His eyes are as wild as they were yesterday.

"I..." I falter, unprepared for this conversation. "I am your friend," I say. "That's why I'm concerned..."

"I'm going to be fine, Kennedy. *Finally*. Don't you want that for me?"

"More than anything," I admit. "I don't want you to hurt."

"So we're okay?" His eyes beg, telling me I have to tell him what he wants to hear.

I nod. "Yeah."

I guess.

He looks relieved. "Good. I should get back to my seat."

"Yeah," I say as he walks away. "Me, too."

Pulling out my cell phone, I tap "healing from homosexuality," into my browser. The sheer number of articles that populate the screen are enough to make me dizzy.

"You're looking well today, Miss Sawyer."

It's him. And now I *am* dizzy.

Turning on my heels with a deep breath, I look into the face of Dean Hershel Baker.

"Why wouldn't I?" I ask, grinning. "It's a beautiful day, I'm here with my family and friends, and it's shaping up to be a good game." I point to the scoreboard, which indicates a touchdown CU must have scored while I was down a weird rabbit hole with Silas.

He eyes me slowly, from top to bottom and back up again. Like a predator sizing up his prey. Something in his face ignites the resolve I thought I'd lost. The one fueled by my initial distrust of the man standing before me.

"You okay?" Jonah says out of nowhere, startling me.

"Yeah. Yes," I say, firm, gesturing to the dean. "Just commenting to Dean Baker that this is quite a game so far." I turn my face from the dean slightly, enough to give Jonah a stern glance. One that, I hope, tells him to shush. Dean Baker told me in no uncertain terms, while stealing my very literal breath, that I was to keep the incident to myself. He has practice with that kind of speech, it seems.

Jonah gives a quick nod. His hand rests against the small of my back. His gloves, a leather coat, and a sweater separating our actual skin, but I'll take it. The pressure from his fingertips tells me he's angry, or nervous. Maybe both. I know I am.

"Jonah," Dean Baker says slowly, looking between us. Of course he knows about our date. The whole *Jesus Freaks*-watching nation does. "How are you?"

I bet he doesn't like it. At all. I wonder, though, if he'll work to try to turn Jonah against me, or cut Jonah loose and throw him to the wolves.

Jonah clears his throat and plasters on a political smile. "Great, sir. How are you? Great game so far, huh? Ready, Kennedy?" Jonah slides his hand across my back and laces his fingers through mine.

Dean Baker's eyes fall to our entwined hands and glance lazily back to me. I offer a bright smile and a wave with my free hand. "See ya," I say as if there wasn't an attempted murder between the two of us a day ago.

Jonah and I turn, Jonah walking a few paces ahead of me as we flee from the insufferable gravity of Dean Baker.

"I headed over because I saw you talking with Silas," Jonah starts. "And by the time I got over here..."

"Yeah. Sorry." Looking over my shoulder, I catch the dean standing in the spot we left him, staring at me with enough force to send a chill down my spine.

I stop. "He told his parents he's gay," I say of Silas. Quietly, aware of my surroundings.

Jonah's eyebrows lift in response.

"Yeah, and they're going to help him get... help?"

Jonah nods as if I told him we're at a football game and I want nachos. Which I don't... anymore.

"Do you... have anything to say?" I hold out my hands, needing someone to remind me which way is up.

He shrugs. "Like? I'm glad he told his family. Secrets are damaging."

"More damaging than trying to heal someone from their sexuality?" My tone is accusatory, because I suddenly feel like this is my first day at Carter again and I'm surrounded by my worst nightmares.

"I don't think we should talk about this here," Jonah says, reaching for my hand. "Or now." His eyes flash over my shoulder, and I'm guessing the dean is still there.

"Ever?" I press. "Because I'm thinking we'll need to."

He gives my hand a gentle squeeze. "Yes. But given all the other things that need our attention today, maybe we could put this on the back burner?"

I want to scream. I want to run to the announcer's booth, hold the microphone hostage, and ask if everyone has lost their minds or have I, in fact, lost mine?

"Yeah," I finally answer. "Back burner."

Tentatively I take his hand and let its warmth embrace me. If he can be so cavalier about what is most certainly a fatal difference in our personal philosophies, why can't I? Why can't I simply enjoy Jonah for who he is? Stunning. Caring. Honest.

Okay, then, the cute boy it is. For now. Until that back burner stares us in the face.

"Kennedy!" A voice beckons from the field. Turning my head, I beam a smile so wide I can feel my face stretch beyond its normal bounds.

It's Matt. Halftime has come and gone while I was in the vortex of Silas and the teams are running back onto the field.

"We'll kill 'em this half!" he promises before his number fifty-seven jersey disappears into a huddle.

"He's optimistic," I comment bleakly as we head back to the stands.

Jonah lets out a sharp laugh, squeezing my hand before we sit. "Someone's gotta be. *They're* the ones getting killed out there. Even if the scoreboard doesn't show it, they're getting *flattened*. Literally."

"They're gonna hurt him if the refs don't do something," Dan says, clenching his teeth. He's seen far too many career-ending injuries to be even a little relaxed during football and hockey games. Other sports have their risks, but these two sports tend to get under his skin the most.

"*Him?*" I question.

"He's the best out there today," Buck answers matter-of-factly. "That ham is playing for the cameras, but he really is this good. He needs to play like this all the time. Guilford is trying to give the audience a show, too."

"Aren't there, like, rules against unnecessary roughness? Isn't that an actual penalty? Unnecessary roughness?"

No one says a word, not even my mother. But, within a few minutes, it's clear that they're right, Matt's their target. One play nearly stops my heart as Matt is again pinned to the ground, but it takes him a long ten seconds to stand up. Clearly upset, he again gestures to the referees, then schleps off the field to the trainer, who fusses over him and checks him out. He's back in a few minutes later, but it hasn't changed anything. It's still brutal out there.

A few minutes later, Carter manages a touchdown *and* an extra point, bringing us in the lead as the third quarter winds down.

The men around me start fidgeting in their seats, and I even catch Roland biting the inside of his cheek. My stomach drops as the atmosphere around me shifts. The whole stadium notices what's going on, too, because the response from the crowd ranges from silence to shouting at the referees to "do something."

"What can they do?" I whisper to Jonah.

"They can take those guys out of the game. It's the same two every time. Every single time. Twenty-two and eighteen. They've been on him nonstop." He shakes his head, his eyes unmoving from the field.

My palms sweat and I press them into the cool aluminum on either side of me, bowing my head to take a deep breath. To pray.

Help me believe. And help them out there.

"I have to move," I say in an effort to keep a panic attack at bay. Jumping from my seat, I weave my way down the bleachers and onto the grass just behind the team. I find Finn, the camera intern guy from NBC who filmed mine and Joy's interaction outside of the dining hall what feels like a million years ago.

"Press only," he says slyly during a long timeout.

"I bet I've seen more airtime than you," I answer nervously.

"Sarcasm. Nice." He runs a hand over his brown curls before adjusting the lens on his camera.

"This is... intense, huh?"

He nods. "About as intense as all the prayer in the locker room."

"Seriously?"

"Seriously. I've filmed a few interviews for college teams around New York, and I've never seen locker rooms so quiet at half time. Just a few new plays and the captains leading prayer."

This does little to comfort me. If I were allowed in the locker room, despite my nothing-knowledge of football, I'd, I don't know, maybe go over plays nonstop to prevent the carnage.

"It's been a great game, though," Finn continues. "Your guy there is going to be a star after this game."

Folding my arms across my chest, I roll my eyes. "*My* guy?"

He shrugs. "Whatever. You know what I mean. He's more your guy than he is mine."

I laugh, which drains some of the tension from my throat. For a moment I forget about Silas, Jonah, Dean Baker, my weird, blended family in the stands... all of it. I'm just at a football game. In college.

Casting a quick glance over my shoulder, I see the outline of the family that's come to the game with me. The family that's circled their wagons and has vowed to address this Dean Baker "issue."

Then, it hits me.

I promised my friends *I'd* help them with Dean Baker. However I could. I promised my friends, my dad, and almost anyone who asked that *I'd* fight for them on camera, for this *Jesus Freaks* show. That I'd be side-by-side with them, making sure the best I could that there was fair coverage. Fair play.

I've done none of that, because I'm scared.

When did I become so scared?

Isn't that what this whole journey has been about so far? Digging for the truth? About my roots, my dad, Christianity, and "those people." Am I *seriously* going to let one bad, *bad* man change the person I am?

No, I can't.

I'm not some meek, shy-minded girl who needs handholding when she's been trained her whole life to know the difference between right and wrong and where to go when things go wrong. And, I'm *right next* to a cameraman for a major network for crying out loud.

Say something! Speak up! Rally!

I look toward the end zone, where I bumped into Dean Baker and see him still standing there, hobnobbing with God knows who, a smile on his face that would rival the most charismatic villain. Cunning. Enticing. Inviting you in so he can destroy you.

I *promised* I'd do things my way, to show that God's love surrounds all of us. To show that you can cuss a little but still fall at the feet of Jesus. Because we're all fallen. All falling.

"Finn," I say, making direct, intentional eye contact with him. "I have something really important I need to tell you. Not just *you*, but your producer, the camera, and everyone on the other end of that lens."

He looks startled for a moment, his eyes shifting from side to side as if checking to see if he's missed something. Then, his ears perk up as his mouth stretches into a charming grin.

"Finally," he says, assured.

"Finally?" I panic, wondering if he knows anything, which would be too much.

"We were told to leave you alone, to let you come to us. And I'm the lucky bastard that happens to be at the edge of the woods when the doe emerges." He's nearly bouncing with excitement.

I take a deep breath. "Easy, killer, or I'll find one of your buddies to make famous. But I trust you. I don't know why, but don't blow it. It's about to get real around here."

"Can it wait until the end of the game?" He sounds like he hates to be asking.

I nod. "But right after, okay? I run the risk of chickening out if I wait too long," I lie. I just want to get to the media before anyone else does. Before my dad, before my mom and whatever high-powered attorney she's undoubtedly got waiting in the wings. Before Dean Baker, even, because I don't take him and his ability to preemptively strike for granted.

A few seconds later, both teams are back out on the field and the stadium is nearly silent. Just a small hum of energy rippling through the crowd as the third quarter clock ticks away second by second.

It looks like Carter is going to try the play they did a little while ago, where Matt starts on the far side of the field and weaves his way closer. I have no idea what the purpose of his position is in a normal game, but he's been all over the field through most of this one.

"Here we go..." Finn says as the ball is tossed and action starts.

This play has lasted longer than most through the game and Matt is giving it his all. Everyone is. The energy is almost suffocating. Slowly, cheers and hollers rise from the stands as Matt draws the play farther down field and he makes his way toward the side I'm standing on.

But, it doesn't last long.

A hard, loud collision sucks the wind from the crowd and straight from my lungs. Matt is hit from the front and back. Hard, by two players as big as he is. His body goes limp in an impossible instant and he falls at an angle that doesn't look real. The rest of the teams dump on them in a massive pile, unaware, it seems, of just how unlikely it is that this is a normal play.

"God," Finn whispers, looking up from his camera and straight at me.

"What?" I ask, panicked, looking between him and the field. I want him to tell me I didn't see what I just saw.

Before he answers, slow motion kicks in, and everything falls apart.

CHAPTER TWENTY-SEVEN
THE FOOTBALL PLAYER

Kennedy.

BUCK. *Flash.* Roland. *Flash.*

My mind takes in the information in slow shutter speed. Clicks on a camera. It's not until I catch the sight of Dan racing by me, in step with Roland and Buck, and my mother, Eden, and Jonah circling Finn and me that I can fully process what's going on.

Player by player the tackle breaks apart. And almost everyone stands up. Carter players lunge after Guilford players and a small brawl breaks out. But it stops quickly. Because only *almost* everyone has stood up.

We're just close enough that I can read the number on the jersey lying in the grass, and my legs immediately go weak. Number fifty-seven. Matt is on the ground, face-up and unmoving.

Silence chokes the crowd and not a single sound can be heard over a CU player, number eighteen, screaming for help.

"He's out! He's out!"

"No," I whisper once before it turns into a moan. "No!" I lunge forward, but am pulled back by my mom and Jonah.

"You can't go out there," Mom says. "You know that. Just wait. And breathe."

I can't do either of those things. I shake myself free of their holds, not even hearing what Jonah's saying, and I race to the rope that separates spectators from the field. The trainer who's tended to Matt for most of the game is on the ground next to him, *checking for a pulse.*

"Do something!" I hit Dan's arm and gesture to the field as if he's engaging in the most egregious form of malpractice.

He puts his hands up, gentle, addressing me while assessing the field. "They're doing what they can right now, Kennedy."

"But you're a *doctor*," I plead.

"You are?" Buck asks, anxious but trying to hide it in his tense jaw. "Come."

"I don't think we can go out there," Roland tries.

Buck eyes him, gesturing to Dan. "With him we can. And, that's my son, I'll do what I damn well please. I know to stay out of the way."

The three of them walk to the assistant coach, who mouths something into his headset that gets the attention of the head coach, who is on the field next to the trainer. The coach waves them onto the field, and in an instant, Dan is kneeling next to Matt, engaged in a serious conversation with the trainer.

Get up. Wake up. Get up.

Both teams kneel at center field. A common practice in football that I recognize from high school when any player gets injured. Looking behind me, however, I see most of the spectators with heads bowed, and some on their knees, too. Including Eden, who's with a small huddle of students about ten feet from me.

"You're filming this?" I hiss at Finn.

He shrugs. "Camera's rolling." But he's chewing on the inside of his lower lip.

Roland picks up his cell phone, talks into it briefly, then jogs back to where I'm standing. Mom and Jonah come to either side of me.

"What is it?" Mom asks, sounding uncharacteristically shaken which does little to help my nausea.

Roland's jaw flexes before he talks—terrible news is on its way. "I've called the ambulance. They're on their way. He's unconscious but breathing, which is good."

"It's *good*?" I snap.

"Head injuries happen all the time in football. We won't know anything else until he's X-rayed and wakes up."

Anything else.

I turn to Jonah, gripping his hand like it's my lifeline. "He's going to be okay though, right? Tell me he's going to be okay."

"He's going to be fine," Jonah says, pulling me into a hug.

Which I would have believed if he hadn't taken a second look to the field before answering me.

After about a year and a half, the ambulance comes and Dan stands, having what looks to be a thorough discussion with the EMT's. A backboard is lowered to the ground and it seems like ten people surround Matt. The trainer, Dan, three EMT's... and just... all these *people*.

To my horror, the EMT's administer some sort of IV to Matt once he's on the stretcher. *This can't be good.* And I push forward, my body demanding access to the field and, ultimately, him.

"Ma'am," a police officer says as if my best friend isn't in a heap, "you have to stay back."

I go hysterical in an instant, calling after him until my voice grows hoarse. As if I have the ability to wake him. "Matt!" I scream, and again, "Matt! Matt! Matt..."

In the private waiting room the hospital was gracious enough to provide, I pace. Back and forth in front of Roland, Dan, and my mom while Buck does some pacing of his own between the emergency room and where we are.

Roland had the solemn duty of calling Buck's wife, Matt's mom, to fill her in since Buck wasn't sure he could make it through the call. There's barely any information anyway, which is the worst of it all. Word is she's on the next flight out which will have her arriving here by morning.

Eden and Jonah asked me to join them in the chapel and I told them I would, but I lied. I'm not going anywhere.

"What was with that IV they started on the field?" I ask of the bag hanging over Matt before they loaded him into the ambulance.

"Steroids," Dan answers. "When there's risk of spinal injury—"

"*What?*" I half-shout.

Dan swallows. "He hit the ground *really* hard, Kennedy, and was knocked unconscious. Spinal injuries are common in football, but are worse if the cord swells or other things swell to press on the cord. When that starts to happen, a situation can become more critical by the second. Permanent nerve damage to the spinal cord is not something you want to deal with. The steroids help reduce and prevent swelling."

I nod, slow. A knock on the door turns me around to find Caitlyn staring shyly into the room. "Kennedy?" she asks soft, "can I talk to you for a second?"

Surprised to see her, I nod and exit the room into a much louder hallway. "What's up?"

"I came to the chapel," she starts, nervously. "Some people said they saw you and Jonah and Eden take off and figured you'd be here. They're in the chapel with some of the team-mates and the coach..."

"Okay..."

"Sorry," she flushes and takes a deep breath. "I was going to find you after the game, but..."

I nod. "Yeah. But."

"Any news? On Matt?"

"No." I shake my head. "But why did you want to find me after the game?"

"Courtney's ready to tell," she blurts out. "I called and filled her in on everything, but not Asher, though... I still don't know what to do with that." She looks to her hands.

Startled by the news, I still offer her comfort. "Yeah, me either. Is she sure?"

Caitlyn nods. "Yeah. She doesn't feel alone."

I sigh, relieved. "I was going to talk to Finn after the game, but... I just... I don't know what I'm going to do right now." I gesture to our new, ominous surroundings.

"I thought your parents were going to—"

Holding up my hand, I cut her off. "We've got to do it," I say of *The Resistance*. "It's the only way it'll work, don't you think?"

She shrugs. "Not the *only* way, but certainly the most fun way." She offers a small grin.

"Is the main waiting room a madhouse?"

Caitlyn nods. "You bet. Even though they asked people to either return to their dorms or stay at the stadium for a prayer vigil, people are still here. Some to support Matt, and some jockeying for camera time."

My nose crinkles. "Seriously? Ew. Anyway, I'll let you know once we kind of figure out what the... heck we're going to do, okay? I can't even think about it right this second, but it'll be done. Soon." I feel like I'm splitting in two. I don't want this life right now.

Caitlyn gently rubs my arm. "It just *seems* really bad right now," is all she says before walking away.

Seems.

I return to the small room seconds ahead of Buck, who tells us Matt's been moved to a private room, still unconscious.

"The good news is his brain scans are showing a mild concussion."

"That's the good news?" I ask.

Buck sinks into a chair next to Roland and cradles his head in his hands for a second before rubbing his face and facing us with what I suppose will be the bad news.

"Right now it looks like he's got a pretty good compression fracture to at least one of his lumbar vertebrae, and a herniated disk, maybe a blown one, that'll likely needs surgery but they can't figure out yet what nerve damage, if any, he has. Dan," he addresses my stepdad, "would you come with me to talk more to the doctor? I could use another set of ears."

Dan rises. "Of course."

"Can I come?" I beg, wearily.

"I don't know if there's anything to do," Mom says. "Except to wait."

"Maybe I can wait in Matt's room?" I ask with renewed hope.

Roland and Mom protest, but Buck holds up his hand. "I'll see what I can do. Maybe it'll do him some good to have a friend in there. Who knows?"

My chest warms at the thought of just seeing him. So much so that I nearly sprint all the way to where he is, quiet in a dark room surrounded by machines and beeps. I enter the room before given clearance, behaving bold in my G-List fame. I trust

Dan and Buck will take care of it, and I don't intend to touch him or anything.

Well, maybe just his hand.

"Oh, Matty," I whisper, sinking into the chair next to the bed and reaching for his fingers. Finally, I cry. Good and hard like I'm alone in the room, I rest my head on his hand and sob over the sound of the beeps. "I'm scared, Matt. I'm scared that you're really hurt. But you can't be, right?" I continue as if he can hear me. "You worked too hard to get here, and have so much going for you. That game was great," I ramble. "You were the star."

There's a light knock on the doorframe, and I find Dan waving and motioning for me to join him in the hallway. Reluctantly, I go, not taking my eyes away from Matt until the very last second.

In the hall, I'm greeted by Buck, Dan, Mom, Roland, Matt's coach, and the captain of the team.

"They're hoping he wakes up soon," Roland says to the coach. "So we can assess what surgery needs to be done."

"Can you do the surgery?" I ask Dan.

He chuckles, but soon realizes I'm serious. "No," he answers plainly.

"And why not?" I ask incredulously.

"For one thing, he's not my patient and this isn't my hospital. For another, it's been years since I've performed surgery. And most importantly, if there's something wrong where we're seeing damage, that's going to be a neurologist's call—the spine is outside my area of expertise. This isn't a blown kneecap or torn Achilles heel, Kennedy. This is someone's ability to walk altogether."

I mean to answer Dan, to apologize for my rudeness and to ask more about Matt's potential injury, but a large, dark shadow encases us.

"*Get out,*" I spit toward Dean Baker. A horrified look spreads across my mother's face. Tension and confusion fill the rest of the faces.

"I beg your pardon?" he asks. He has the *gall* to ask.

"*Now,*" I sneer. "This is no place for you."

In an instant my mom grabs my hand and yanks me away down a side hallway. "Get your act together, young lady."

"No!" I squeak out in a tiny wail. "He's awful. Matt's hurt and he's sniffing around. He needs to go away."

She takes a deep breath. "Yes. He does. But you can't cause a scene. Not here and not like this. I'm going to get coffee. Do you want to come with me, or can I trust that you'll keep it together until things have calmed down."

I roll my eyes. "Keep it together," I answer like a scolded child.

Mom seems to have recruited everyone to go with her, because the hall soon goes silent. Footsteps rounding the corner startle me, until I realize it's just Finn.

"Hey," I say, my voice hoarse from all the crying I've done in the last few hours.

"What was that about?" he asks, leaning against the wall, facing me.

"What?"

"I was rounding the corner earlier when I saw you snap at the dean. Does this have anything to do with what you wanted to tell me earlier?"

I sigh and start to deflect his question. Only start to. Then I recall my earlier chat with Caitlyn, my promise to my friends and myself, and I think of my helpless best friend lying at the mercy of modern medicine.

Something has to give.

"It does," I finally say. "Come with me." I give his shirt a quick tug before wandering down the hallways of the hospital.

"Just out of curiosity, where are we going?"

"To find a police officer."

It's well after ten p.m., and visiting hours have long since ended, but that doesn't stop me from sitting next to Matt, holding his hand. Mom and Roland left an hour ago, and Dan has promised to stay as long as it takes to get answers and translate them for me. Buck basically added me to the family list, so I've been here in my own private vigil for a while.

Jonah and Eden talked to me before they left, and have each texted me since. Jonah's clearly giving me space, and I appreciate it. If he's insecure about this situation in any way, he's not showing it. And, I'm not sure it would do him any good if he did.

None of them know that I talked to Finn, and to a state police officer we found patrolling the waiting room. I had a hunch I needed a state cop over a local one—I don't know how far Dean Baker's tentacles stretch. She told me she'd be contacting me in the morning, and to expect to have to come to the station for questioning.

That's all secondary, really, to the beeps and the still body of my best friend.

"Hey," I call to Matt in a whisper now that we're alone for a few minutes. "You wanna wake up?"

Nothing.

The TV in the corner of the room catches my attention. It's a preview for the eleven o'clock news, and it's flashing pictures of Carter University and Dean Baker.

Can it be?

Immediately my phone rings and chimes with calls and text messages. Mom. Roland. Eden. Jonah.

I turn up the volume and am glad to hear my name isn't mentioned at all. Not yet, anyway. The preview team promises breaking news and legal action at one of the nations "most sacred universities."

And so it's done.

The cat's out of the bag and the skeletons are all free to dance.

I sit for ten minutes, ignoring phone calls and texts. Even one from Stephanie, the NBC exec. I just sit in the silence that is sure to end quickly and not come back for a long time. I don't feel as scared as I thought I would.

I answer my mom's tenth call, quiet so as not to disturb an unresponsive Matt.

"Hello?"

"What'd you do?" she asks plainly.

"Stood up for myself and at least one rape victim," I answer just as plain.

She pauses. "Fair enough. Are you ready for this?"

"I have to be."

A disturbance at the nurses station catches my attention.

"Mom, I have to go, I'll call you back in a few minutes."

I tiptoe to the door and look straight into a nightmare when I see Dan face-to-face with Dean Baker.

"What has she done?" the dean asks. "And where is she?"

Quickly I turn against the wall, facing Matt, hiding like a cat burglar.

"I don't know what you're talking about," Dan answers. "And she's home with her mother right now while we wait for a very hurt kid to wake up. I suggest you take your anger elsewhere."

He's flawless and unflinching in his response.

"Then why do I have police calling me, telling me to report to the station at eight a.m. tomorrow for questioning?"

"I don't know why you're asking me about your personal affairs, sir. I don't even believe we've ever met."

Before the conversation can continue, a police officer breaks it up and instructs the dean to leave. There's more scuffle, more angry conversation.

"This *isn't* the last of this," the dean says. Meaning it by the venom in his voice.

No, it's not the last of it for you, that's for sure.

But a small movement out of the corner of my eye draws my attention away from the nurse's station.

"Matt?" I ask, watching his hand move again. I race to the bed. "Matt?"

I know I should press the button they always press on TV when things like this happen, or at the very least go tell Buck his son is waking up, but I'm so frozen in place that I can barely breath.

His eyes flutter once, twice, and three times before they open and he's staring at the ceiling. He turns to me, looking tired but quite like himself with an impish grin.

"K. Sawyer," he says. "How long have I been out for?"

I choke back tears and check the time again. "Like seven hours," I answer.

He nods, as if in approval. "That must have been some hit." He gives my hand a squeeze and I squeeze back.

"You remember it?" I ask, taking this as a good sign without any medical knowledge.

Before he can answer, Matt's eyes widen and he looks panicked, which causes me to press the call button and shout toward the door for someone.

"Matt?" I ask above the thrash of his hands against the sheets. He looks like he's having a psychotic episode. "Matt, what are you doing? Are you okay?"

Before he can answer me, two nurses, Buck, Dan, and a doctor race into the room and one of them asks the same thing.

"Matt? Matt what's going on?"

He ignores them, turning his head to capture me in his wild stare. "My legs," he croaks out. "I can't feel my legs!"

If you enjoyed this book, please share it with a friend, write a review online, or send feedback to the author!

www.andrearandall.com